THE PERISHING

ALSO BY NATASHIA DEÓN

Grace

THE PERISHING

A NOVEL

Natashia Deón

COUNTERPOINT

Berkeley, California

The Perishing

Copyright © 2021 by Natashia Deón
First hardcover edition: 2021

Library of Congress Cataloging-in-Publication Data
Names: Deón, Natashia, author.
Title: The perishing : a novel / Natashia Deón.
Description: First hardcover edition. | Berkeley, California : Counterpoint, 2021.
Identifiers: LCCN 2021012290 | ISBN 9781640093027 (hardcover) | ISBN
    9781640093034 (ebook)
Subjects: LCSH: Women, Black—Fiction. | GSAFD: Fantasy fiction.
Classification: LCC PS3604.E643 P47 2021 | DDC 813/.6—dc23
LC record available at https://lccn.loc.gov/2021012290

Jacket design by Dana Li
Book design by Jordan Koluch

COUNTERPOINT
2560 Ninth Street, Suite 318
Berkeley, CA 94710
www.counterpointpress.com

Printed in the United States of America

10 9 8 7 6 5 4 3 2 1

For you
I did it for me.

they say malcolm knew his journey was ending
martin knew he wasn't long for this world
no i don't think myself a martyr
i am merely a black woman
which means the same thing

bridgette bianca, be/trouble

People like us who believe in physics know that
the distinction between past, present, and future
is only a stubbornly persistent illusion.

ALBERT EINSTEIN

at best
we will lose each other
at something we have been taught to call the end.

CHIWAN CHOI, my name is wolf

THE PERISHING

ZERO

SARAH

My name is Sarah Shipley and I've slept with five women. Since I married a man, no one asks the kind of persons I choose anymore. I've been married six times, all of them men, all of them taken from me, by God or by man, death in all cases. My first husband is who I remember most.

First Husband was once born in 1948 and was murdered just like my third, but I wasn't surprised. Devastated, but not surprised. We're all on the verge of somebody else's violence.

It used to scare people when I'd let down my guard and confess that my husbands were murdered. They would call me cursed, not unlucky. In fact, the word *unlucky* would only be used by those who thought I had something to do with it. "'Cause no one's that unlucky." So now when people ask how my husbands died, I say they stopped breathing. And for my own sake, I don't remember the faces of those who took their breath anymore.

I was forty years old when First Husband died the first time. And in every life, forty is the age when I start losing things—memories, my glasses, my friends—the frequency of their deaths make dying pedestrian.

But not always.

Sometimes, it is life altering. Hurts me to watch the anguish of others who don't understand it's not always over. Not for everybody.

First Husband was devastated when he lost his mother, Florence "Mary" Clay. She had nine kids. In 1956, when he was eight years old, Mary walked off the cotton fields to work cleaning classrooms, 7:00 a.m. to 7:00 p.m., two-dollars-a-week slave labor, but "We all thought we were rich," First Husband said.

Mary was the first woman janitor at his school in Mississippi—preschool through high school—one school for all the Negroes and she kept the whole school clean by herself. At lunch she worked in the lunchroom making sandwiches for all us children, he said, serving warm plates and apples. Never missed a day, so folks respected my momma.

On Sundays, he and his brothers would walk up Columbus Street, their skin dark as wet soil and their new haircuts lined and shaped into something like a helmet full of black flowers.

They'd wear Sunday suits then, each pressed paper-hard and without crinkle or sound, hand-folded around their bodies like wearing origami.

Folks would point and say, "Those're Mary Clay's kids," and they'd make room for them. That's how I knew about people, he said. Not by the way they treated me but how they treated my momma. Respected her. That's how I decided who I liked and who I didn't. The other children at school would straighten their chairs and pick up trash before the school day ended because they knew my momma was coming.

First Husband was eighteen years old when his momma died. Sixty-one years of age. So at her funeral, he started counting down his own life because he was convinced he wouldn't outlive her. He counted forty-three more years to make something of himself. First thing he did was call off the wedding.

You see, his girlfriend Olive was pregnant, and marriage was the Christian thing to do, but since his momma was gone, they had no reason to pretend they were religious. So he moved to California and Olive said she'd stay with her family in Mississippi to have the baby, and that was that.

By the time I met First Husband, he was thirty-two years old and had already stopped chasing the son he'd abandoned. He decided the best thing to do was to wait and let his son find him when his son was ready. And every birthday that edged him closer to sixty-one, he reminded me that he didn't have much time. "I know I'll die by sixty," he'd tell me, "because I'm not worth more than what Momma had."

I'd argue.

I'd tell him no one could know when his time was to die, but he said he did know and then he proved it. First Husband died at sixty years old and I don't disagree with him anymore.

AUGUST 1887

NOGALES, ARIZONA

CHARLIE

His cheeks and neck were shaved close to the skin, wet from a razor's nick that left three red streams running down his jugular—a cat's scratch. Above it was a patch of coarse black hair, trimmed into an island of mustache and beard that smelled of gin and pine. I would bury my face in it. I was seven.

This landscape of hair was meant to give the illusion of normal because First Granddaddy's face was uncommonly long and scarred, though I wouldn't call it freakish, out of respect. And anyway, he was aware of his condition.

His wiry bristles would tangle across his thin lips as if to tie them down and keep him silent, and on the rare occasions he spoke, the hairs would pull apart like fingers slowly unclasping to release the safest two words a Negro could speak: "How do?" or "Yes, ma'am."

The last night I saw him, he sat at the edge of his bed dressed in his war uniform, staring at his own mirrored reflection across the room; his eyelids drooped at the edges like fifty-year-old drapes on the wall of his face—he was fifty, he told me, maybe, since he was born a slave.

In Georgia, his owner, and that of his momma, had documented his arrival with the usual effort, so his birth record was sparse and unreliable. He had no full name except Benjamin, son of Thomas and Pauline, but the census I'd found in his mattress listed him as forty-eight and adopted.

But that ain't him.

Not around here.

If it was, I'd have the most to surrender—my name for one because I'm his namesake. Charlie, for short.

He was careful not to look at me that night, and I didn't regard it at the time because his eyes only ever seemed to open two ways, vacant or with one expression—tired, but letting light in.

He touched his coat at the chest where his nipple would be and fiddled with the star of his Civil War medal, said he'd leave it for me. "Boys need to learn to be brave, and you can start with this," he said.

First Granddaddy became a soldier while he was still a slave, then after the war he became a refugee because his side won, and to him this wasn't an irony. He couldn't go home to Kentucky where he said he'd been mustered so he enlisted again. He wanted to serve honorably, he said, for equality under God, he said, and also that he was no hero. He considered himself *just* a veteran of the most recent unpleasantness and warned me that life is meant to be one calamity after the next for us. "So, what you gon' do about it, son?"

My mother was twenty-three years old then, and after that night she never met a man she didn't try to destroy. She said she didn't do it. Whatever happened to First Granddaddy he did to himself, she said. "And, anyway, he's missing, not dead."

But I saw her outside in the moonlight with him. Saw her standing behind him on the hill talking. Saw him fall but not on his own. She could've pushed him. He could have collapsed but if so she gave him no mind because she didn't move to help. She just stood there. And stood. I don't know how long I kept my eyes on her from my window before I fell asleep. But by morning his body was buried because I couldn't find it, he never came home, and I know he'd never leave me.

JULY 2102

LOS ANGELES, CALIFORNIA

SARAH

When First Husband was thirteen years old, he had a best friend named Sammy. At thirteen, Sammy told him, "I'll be dead in a week," and was.

My husband and Sammy were in the Mississippi Youth Gospel Choir together and they'd been invited to sing at a church in Alabama. The pay was food and shelter and rumors that Mahalia Jackson would be there. Mahalia was Sammy's savior, after Christ himself. A goddess. And she was the reason Sammy's momma never broke his legs.

His momma had heard that Mahalia had the same condition as Sammy, legs bowed like a wishbone from his hips to his feet, yawned open at his knees and hardened like roof pitches curved outward.

Mahalia was the only Black person alive, she thought, with legs like his, so Sammy's momma did what Mahalia's momma did. Instead of having the doctor break and reset his legs straight as prescribed, she rubbed her boy's legs down with grease and bathed him in boiled dishwater. The heat was tolerable. It would relax the bones, she thought, like chicken bones tumbled in hot broth, softened and flexible, and would dry stiff and straight in the sheets she'd wrap around his legs at night, and come morning his ankles and toes were blue from the tight bandages. It would take time, of course. The hope of this cure is why Sammy's legs never got broken. They never got healed either.

Each of the kids, if they were going to go on the trip and sing, had to pay their own bus fare, so the whole choir got good at chopping cotton for nickels a week. Sammy and my husband, who was then just Billy Clay, put in hours every day, from first light to nightfall, singing songs that Sammy had made up and written in ink on his arm with the ballpoint pen he found under the bus station bench.

Sammy's falsetto became like the sweet sound of a cooing woman, so good that he earned himself the lead spot in the choir. But five days before they were supposed to leave on the bus, Sammy's momma told Sammy that she'd used his travel money. She said, "You need it to pay for school clothes and not some trip to Alabama."

Sammy was so disappointed when he found out about his money that he fell on the ground, crying, right in front of everybody. And after he begged his momma one more time, unsuccessfully, with dirt and straw tumbling down from his cheek, he made a new wish. A few days later, he started telling his friends, "You're not going to see me anymore."

"But, Sammy," my Billy said, "you'll see me, right? We're best friends."

"No, not even you, Billy."

The day before the choir left for Birmingham, Sammy asked Mary Clay if she'd make him his favorite dump cake and she did. So before the bus left, before Sammy's week was up, Sammy and Billy snuck into the church building, sat in the pews, and ate a mess of pineapple and peach and butter and nuts with some mint, all dumped and baked into cake batter. The end result was the distinctive flavor of strawberries. Proof that dump cake is life. No matter what you put in it, no matter what you try, how you're received is not always up to you. And when they finished, Sammy sang what my husband described as "Sammy's last bit of sweet-lovely, his notes high and soft like a fairy."

It was the Wednesday of the ride back home from Alabama when everybody heard the news. Missus Johnson had phoned ahead to the school to let them know our failure—runners-up out of twenty-five—and that we were on our way. When she got back to the singing hall to meet us, no one noticed her changed expression before she told us, flatly, "Get on the bus." It made sense to all the children because we had come to win, after all.

It had been hot that day, my husband said, and the night hadn't cured it, so the starless 11:00 p.m. sky was like a boiled rag thrown over Birmingham, our bus an oven, its windows bleeding with moisture.

First Husband said that about halfway through the ride Missus Johnson stood up and gripped her seat's back cushion, full-fingered, making frown lines in the plastic, then she told everybody what happened. That earlier that day during summer school, some big kid in the lunchroom lifted Sammy up by his collar, then pushed him into the wall in such a peculiar way that it broke Sammy's neck. Thirteen years old and he died instantly. My husband's momma was the one who had to clean his urine off the floor.

So you see, we know, my husband told me. Sammy is proof that there's no point in trying to outlive the date you've been given. Folks like us, we just need to leave something good behind. But you. Not you, he told me. "You've got forever," he said.

He said it because I'd told him everything.

Because I promised to try to find him again.

Because I can't be sure I can.

Because some people are bonded over lifetimes. Not a "soul mate"—a wasted term—but a kindred spirit. No, not *spirit*. The inarticulable part of ourselves.

Everybody I love dies and no matter. Most people won't survive everyone who loves them. Our lives are meant to mimic a passing breeze that won't return.

Not me.

I have to live with my losses forever. Life after life in new bodies, new cities, and new countries where I've always been Black, not always a woman.

But people who are meant to be in our lives will find us. No matter how far we wander. Even if when we find each other we're lost. Together.

So sometimes I'll find my pair—like First Husband—even though I won't search for him. Even though I promised. Because, for a while, I'll forget our *before this* and finding him will be like a rediscovery, a shock of holy hallelujah.

We're supposed to forget ourselves and each other after this. But I remember because I'm broken now. He won't remember, because he's not.

This is my undoing.

AUGUST 1907

NOGALES, ARIZONA

CHARLIE

The night when First Granddaddy disappeared, I had a dream. It was the first dream I remember having so maybe that makes it a memory. It's been twenty years since I was seven years old.

I remember being embarrassed in this dream to be a girl, and worse, desiring the comforts of a man because I, too, was a man when I was awake, a preacher's boy and the son of an intolerable mother, so I was relieved to be asleep so no one could harm me for my attractions.

I was also aware it was an ancient time in this dream, this I knew from my clothes, my hair, and the tent. I figured I'd conjured the place from my own imagination, biblical inspiration from that day in Sunday school, or a little intestinal disruption from Aunt Minnie's collard greens that must have had me passing gas in my sleep.

The tent was handmade of pulled ties and a geometric patchwork, tinged yellow from firelight, its shadow quivering on the canvas like a tear ready to fall.

Outside, stars fell but they were out before they hit the ground and the moon had melted into the running river of the Samchuna, leaving its path gleaming for miles like an unclasped silver necklace.

A girl was reading to me—not my sister—and I don't recognize the name she called me or why she used the loving tone she did—like we'd known each other. But I only remembered the place. It was north of the Dead Sea and this was home for the night to all the girls. We weren't the only ones. There were other tents.

When the flame licked the last of its oil, our tent was brought to complete darkness and the girl couldn't see so she began tracing my face with the tips of her slim fingers, following my features the way the blind read clay tablets—flattening my nose, poking my lips, a finger slid into my mouth. I pushed her hand away. "I'll get the oil," I said.

When I set it alight again, her face was close to mine and she touched me where she shouldn't, and I told her we couldn't touch that way. I thought she should know.

We were awake only because we were preparing for a rite that would take place the next morning at sea. We needed to practice. We sat on the floor, face to face. The tiny mole on her cheekbone was a scar. Like a searing hot twinkle fell out of her eye and charred a dot there.

We sat with our legs crossed and I held the edge of her white dress while we chanted some prayer of protection in Greek. She and I spoke three of the same languages. Greek was one. She had four. I spoke more. The Greek alphabet has twenty-four letters from alpha to omega. Phoenicians have twenty-two. My native language had forty-seven, including the rolling *n* and *r* and short *o*, so I could pronounce any new language correctly the first time. But language is not just a people's words. Language is their way of thinking. It controls what we think, limits *how* we think. There are some words I don't say in some languages because they carry a lot of weight, like *friend*, a word of mutual respect and vulnerability, and phrases we live without in languages, like *I love you* spoken from a parent to a child. A child can go a lifetime without hearing it.

And there is no pleasant word in my language for people who desire physical intimacy with their same sex because that's how we feel about 'em.

I was sorry for her.

DECEMBER 2102

PEOPLE OF CALIFORNIA

V. SARAH SHIPLEY

SARAH

The skin on my mother's hands was unusually soft and smooth, but the bones underneath were long and felt brittle. When I'd hold her hand as a child, it was like holding gathered bones, wrapped in wax paper, small as fried chicken wings, her knuckles like knots of gristle.

I can't remember my mother's face now. Or if it ever fit in mine—maybe this reckless mouth. I remember her intentions toward men, so I have to be careful with mine. I haven't always chosen rightly.

I've forgotten much of my birth mother now, but I imagine she was a person who stood for herself all the time. I'm not her, so I won't take the court's stand.

The judge says, "Calling case number A5520, Matter Number 5 on the court's calendar: *The People versus Sarah Shipley*. Good morning, everyone."

"Good morning, Your Honor," our courtroom says in song.

My mother's not the only reason I won't take the stand. I can't blame everything on her, especially in court where any time a woman testifies, she's every woman on trial. Without tears, clear displays of emotions, or a "respectable" man vouching for her, she's a guilty bitch.

The judge says, "We have twenty-five cases to get through before midday, so let's get started. Please come forward, ma'am. Thank you. Counselors, please state your appearances for the record."

"Attorney Sarah Shipley, Your Honor. I'm present and representing myself."

I'm not the first woman who's had to defend her life. Or the first woman who's lived more than one. To have found her new identity in the same place where she'd once been someone else—in her kitchen, her car, her doctor's office, her marriage. A person can simply find her true self and get reborn in it, announce, "I'm a new person now!" and be met with laughter or cruelty— from those who don't matter.

"That's Sarah, spelled with an *h*, Your Honor. I'm out of custody and representing myself."

"John Goodwin, attorney, representing the People of the State of California."

"Good morning to you both."

"Good morning, Your Honor."

Being born or reborn is like walking onto the stage of a play already in progress. There are already characters developed and on stage and people seated in the audience—whether you've invited them or not. Your arrival is forcing everybody else to change who they thought they were to each other and to you.

The judge says, "On April 23, 2102, this matter was last here, and the defendant, Ms. Shipley, made a request. One, to represent herself, and two, to continue this arraignment to today. The court granted her second request for more time. Again, Ms. Shipley, I'd encourage you to obtain other counsel beside yourself. If you can't afford an attorney, the public defender is available to you. I understand it's been some time since you've last worked a criminal matter."

"Thank you for stating so, Your Honor."

"In any case, an attorney from the public defender's office is there, sitting behind you, here on standby, in case you change your mind. I don't have to tell you that representing yourself is—"

"I know the dangers, Your Honor."

"Like having a fool for a client. For instance, you could've used the court's virtual services today and avoided being here physically, saved the risk of being arrested again on the spot."

"Thank you, Your Honor."

"What I'm telling you is you're already messing up, Counselor. Part of my job is to make sure you're competent to represent yourself and I'm already witnessing poor judgment. You're facing serious charges. You're facing life in prison. Did somebody bully you into thinking you could do this yourself?"

"No one forces me to do anything."

"You've been accused of—"

"I've been accused of a lot of things. Been around a long time."

"How do you plead, Counselor?"

"Self-defense."

"So you're pleading guilty?"

"He got what he deserved."

"You're saying you fought back?"

"I didn't always."

"I just need your answer, Counselor. You know this process better than most. This is your arraignment, and here is where you can plead guilty, not guilty, or no contest, and no contest has the same effect as guilty. Do you understand?"

"I understand."

"So what do you plead?"

When I'm reborn, I *am* a new person—not always a woman, but always Black.

"You asking me if I did it, Your Honor? You should be asking me how."

"So you're pleading—"

"Not guilty," the public defender says in my stead.

I don't need anyone to speak for me.

I can defend all my lives. How many could say the same? And anyway, no woman kills unless in self-defense. If not in defense of a current wrong, for all the wrongs that came before without justice. Men are accused, sure. Men die; that's never pleasant. I've been men and I've been women, and many women have to fight for their bodies, trade their bodies, build new life in their bodies because someone else wants to take more from her than they ever gave. I only want what's fair and to not be forced into surrender. This isn't the first blood on my hands, but I beg God that this was my last.

SARAH

The thirties were the decade I learned to fight back. To unlearn helplessness. It was the decade I'd come to believe in First Granddaddy, became convinced that he existed, and that Charlie did too. And that the man who'd become First Husband lived somewhere other than my dreams. I still need that kind of imagined-love-made-real.

First Husband was the first to ever *become* for me. First to fight another person for me and to do it with vigor. To be enveloped by such a rage of protection that he seemed to depart his own body for me. Left his eyeballs on the table of his face for me, upright above his nose with all their whites showing, the colored parts like smooth river rocks dropped in milk.

For me.

But in 1930, I woke as another woman—and was unaware of all these things.

That night, the orange sun was setting inches above the cloud-lined hills where those puffs of white turned dark as smoke, the hills blackened with shadow. Together, they were like a campfire going out.

My naked body was slumped against a city building, a broken figure in the alley where inky shadows crawled along bricks then dipped and colored me there.

I was surrounded by monstrous brick dominoes, buildings reaching halfway to heaven with no regrets since earthquakes could and would take them down. This was Los Angeles. Spring Street near Third and it was December. Christmas tree lights were flickering green and red throughout the warm city because Southern California Christmas is often a summer night.

The late of evening had left downtown empty and absent of the black suits that dressed business by day. Someone was working late on the fourth or fifth floor above me, maybe an accountant or lawyer, a cleaning crew whose workspace had an uncovered bulb that cast light down on my hand as if asking me to grasp my own ideas. It was this moment that I became aware something had happened to me. Something deadly important, but I was disoriented, like I'd walked away from a car accident unharmed, but my mind was trying to sort through the hazy facts, trying to recall the other car's color or who or how or what went wrong. It was jumbled and unclear and fading fast. My legs didn't work.

I pushed up to sitting using only my arms until I was straight backed against the wall and breathing heavy. I rubbed my legs with both hands until I could feel sensation. Just dead legs, I thought. Give it a second. Was still in those moments. It was how I came to realize I had no memory. I didn't know when or where, in time, I was. Had I known, I might've decided I was like thousands of children in foster care who once belonged to families now fleeing the Great Depression and were unsaddling themselves of burdens, including the children who couldn't pay for themselves.

I felt a weight on my shoulder. Musk of hot trash rose in a humid cloud from the woman whose head slid down onto me. Her matted mess of gray hair leaked the shine of oily sweat and what smelled like excrement onto my shoulder. Was something else moving there? Her loose gray strands tickled my bottom lip.

I pushed her away and stood, spitting her hairs as I rose, leaving her propped and abandoned like an oversized stuffed doll won at a carnival, floppy and not right.

Her body tipped over and stuttered down the wall, slowed by the bricks, till finally she lay on the alley floor. Not a thud, just a soft finish.

I wiped the sweat she'd left on my shoulder and for the first time felt myself naked. Saw myself naked. Another surprise: I am a woman. A young woman. A couple of years the far side of puberty. The hairs at my pelvis were not new but not too coarse either. Fifteen or sixteen, maybe. This seemed strange to me—my female body—for reasons I couldn't understand. I thought I was secure in some other understanding.

I needed the woman's clothes.

A large woven bag was next to her. It was wrapped so tightly around her leg that I couldn't take it before she woke. She yelled, "Thief!" and we both tugged on the bag. Her drunkenness made her a victim. And I was sorry when I took it, sifted through it.

Inside were clothes, soiled but folded, and batteries, keys, the bottom of one shoe, a candy bar, another candy bar—almost everything inside I threw to the ground. There had to be another shoe. I needed the other shoe.

The sound of knuckles ramming flesh from down the alleyway caught my attention. Blurry figures swam in my eyes like floaters or ghosts. Could've been cats down there. No, breaths were being expelled with force, and all at once. Young men were fighting. I could see a skinny white boy was winning, besting three other boys his age—my age too. A new window opened above me, and I stepped back against the wall, but its light found my side—my leg, my hip, my left breast. The alley woman groaned and searched for me with half-closed eyes. I stayed still, breathed slowly. Made myself a brick.

The three boys down the alley looked rougher than the winner, seemed poorer, dirty, with the facial features of new immigrants, unmixed with the locals. "I'll take you one at a time," the winner said, winding his fists around the air, his feet positioned one slightly ahead of the other. One of the straps of his overalls slid from his shoulder.

When the second boy stepped closer with his hands up, the winner dropped him with a left hook to his chin. That's when he eyed me, crouched now and naked, with my hands in the woman's bag, staring at him.

I pressed back deeper into the shadows, hoping he couldn't make out my shame and the crime I was committing. I was a dark-skinned brown girl and imagined I could be just another shadow in the night to him or invisible from where he was. But he kept looking my way, redrawing my erasure, pausing too long to actively be in a fight. Then he was hit. A cheap shot.

Air escaped him with each new punch. He was thrown to the ground and soon overtaken by all three surrounding him, kicking and punching. I took the opportunity to search the groggy woman for the other shoe. Where's the shoe?

Under her leg was another bag. I reached for it and paused. A dark eye was staring me down—the barrel of a gun, unblinking and pointed at my face. The alley woman's hand trembled behind it. "Get back!" she said.

I didn't move.

"Get back!" The commotion behind her, down the alley, spooked her into turning ever so slightly to the right, and she toppled over with little effort. I grabbed the gun—foolish, not foolish—and bent her fingers back from its handle. A cap gun. "Help!" the woman yelled. "Help me!"

In the window above us, a head, a white face, bobbed over the window ledge, looking up and down the alley, then rested on the sight of the fighters instead. I grabbed the woman's bag and ran, pulled on clothes as I did. Her drab gray dress was mine. There was another shoe. I had a pair.

The young man on the ground was yelling far behind me. I turned around to look just as one of the three men yanked the necklace from him and emptied his pockets. Winner was Loser now and he called toward me. "Help!" he said, and shouted words I couldn't understand.

I kept up the alley in the opposite direction, away from the woman and the fight, raked the bottom of her bag with my fingers, searched for whatever else I might use, shoved two fistfuls of cap-gun caps into my dress pocket, turned the bag inside out. Dropped it in the alley and stumbled from the narrow mouth of the alley into an ocean of space.

I was devastated.

Before me was a manmade terrain of wide streets and block after block of buildings that were too high and standing up on end, all of them touching and side by side, like a giant's fingers pointing to the moon. My eyes darted wildly.

I headed south up a street marked Third toward a building with the words LYCEUM THEATRE. Just behind it, at the top of another building, was a perpendicular lit sign that read TALKING, and I didn't know how I could read.

Twenty feet ahead of me, a police officer was popping his gums, talking to some short, fat shadow of a man, and I stopped, tried to turn back, watching him at the same time.

He carried on, strolling up the street. He passed the window of a building called Douglas Building, where red and green lights streaked his face and were absorbed into the black cloth of his uniform. He didn't see me.

For a second, I wanted to tell him about the injured man in the alleyway, but I didn't. I kept the other way. Needed to cross the street, staggered off the sidewalk.

A black Ford honked its horn and swerved, missing me by inches. A white man leaned out of its window. "Watch where you're going!"

Another car sped from the other direction, offered, "What are you doing on this side of town!"

Another voice, closer to me, said, "You'll get yourself hurt, is what." He grabbed my forearm. It was the officer. LAPD on the badge of his shirt. "You shouldn't be here," he said. "Certainly not after dark."

I felt faint.

"Are you drunk?" the officer said. "Where are your parents? What's your name?"

And then I realized.

I didn't know my name.

PART ONE

ONE

SARAH, 2102

Los Angeles has always been brown.

And unlike all the other great American cities—New York, Chicago, Philadelphia, Boston—there is no sensible reason for Los Angeles to exist.

Los Angeles was born with no natural port, no good river connections, no suitable harbor sites, and no critical location advantage. And precisely for these reasons—because being born with very little and having no safe place are the fuels for the greatest imaginations—Los Angeles would rise. Imagination and enthusiasm are the currency of world builders.

I was a teenager and had imagination when I arrived in Los Angeles that December night. 1930. It was what Mrs. Prince said. That I was a dealer in fictions. A liar for telling her "I don't know how old I am." I was so confused as I sat in her office that she could've asked me if I was a talking tuba and I'd have had to look at myself, at the curves of my own body, the harmony of my own voice, and then tell her the truth: "I'm not sure."

That night in her office, Mrs. Prince stood across from me for thirty minutes, her manila folder opened in her hand like a prayer book, her pen hovering over the blank pages inside. I was scared to look at her.

I sat with my head bowed, ankles crossed, fingers intertwined—tighter when she moved. Ceiling lights buzzed above our silence like a fly caught in the bathroom.

And when Mrs. Prince turned the corner at the edge of her desk to finally sit down, I looked up instinctively and waited for her to start her questions again. She gave it a couple of minutes, closed her file, opened and closed a drawer, replaced her pen with a pencil, then a pen again, pretended for a moment that I wasn't there, then continued.

It didn't matter.

I still didn't know my name.

Soon, someone would name my teenage self *Lou*.

"Are you a liar?" Mrs. Prince says, tapping the tip of her pen on her notepad, its thuds hollow.

"No, ma'am," I say.

"How about 'Yes, ma'am.' That's the right answer."

"Yes, ma'am," I say.

Mrs. Prince is a social worker. It's her job, she said, to check on my well-being and that's why she's asking me questions. "So how is it that you just appeared in an alley with no name?"

"I don't know, ma'am."

"D'you hit your head?"

I touch my head.

She rolls her eyes.

I told her three times already that I don't remember a home before the accident or before I stole clothes from the woman who pulled a toy gun on me, and I don't remember my name.

"Nothing at all before the accident," I say.

"Tell me about the accident?" she says.

"I don't remember any accident."

"But you just said 'before the accident.'" She throws her file across her desk. "What *do* you know?"

I pull my knees into my seat and hide my face on my lap, and her soft orange skirt fans past me on her way to the door. It smells good. She must've been dressed for some other occasion tonight, somewhere that called for red lipstick and hairpins to keep her dark hair off her neck.

Her perfume is stronger than my own stench. She smells of dandelions. Of wet soil and weak pollen, a bright flower growing here in low light, a long tube of a room, white and thin.

She stands at the open door now, lingering. I can feel her looking at me.

I flinch when the door recloses and she's still here, sucked back in like liquid medicine at the tip of a dropper, the rubber bulb released prematurely. "You know what polio is?" she says in the nicest tone. It calls me to look at her. "It's a horrible disease. One you could've caught out there on the street." My eyes widen. "Could've spread. You even care about my health? The others here?"

"I'm sick?"

"You know what polio does? It first heats the body. And while you're still piping hot with fever, it'll eat your calf muscles and back shanks."

I grab my back.

"What's left are withered legs and spines. A disease like a medieval torture device. Screws people to wheelchairs. Pins 'em to walkers. That's what happened to Roosevelt."

I rub my legs.

"You don't look well," she says.

"I'm sick?"

"Franklin Roosevelt delivered his speech on two crutches at the presidential convention, d'you see that? Got a standing ovation and he wasn't even a candidate. Most people wouldn't have known him if they didn't pity the man for being a cripple."

"You think I got it? Is that why I can't remember?"

She only looks at me.

"People's pity will only get you so far. You've got two choices. You can help me find your family or you can help me find you a new place by letting me know I'm not bringing a plague into someone's God-fearing home."

I bury my face in my lap and she comes back in the room. I feel her skirt brush by me again. She bends into her seat and scribbles in her file folder. I listen to the sound of her pen strokes. She's spelling out words in English. This is English. We're speaking English, I remind myself.

"Let's start again," she says. "You found yourself in an alley?"

"Yes, ma'am."

"And before then, where were you from?"

"New Mexico," I say, and she writes my answer.

"What part?"

I lift my shoulders. *I don't know.*

"What part?"

I point to the book on her shelf that reads NEW MEXICO. FEELS LIKE HOME. Azure skies and balmy breezes.

"You a smart aleck?"

That doesn't feel like my name.

Fumes seem to rise from the top of her head like the stench of my skin through this prison jumper after my whole body was naked-washed at intake with bleach. A soap bar was tied to the end of a stick and dipped in a pail of water. Everything is still unrinsed. My pits itch.

She leans forward and, as if in the slowest movement of time, she repeats her same questions from before, her voice deeper and slower. Then another question comes out without her waiting for my last answer, her words straining themselves out from behind her teeth then given an extra push by her tongue. I choose not to hear her anymore.

Before she first came in, I was lying on this cot and could see the heads of chess pieces poking up from the game board next to her desk, paused and waiting for somebody's next move. It occurred to me that I remembered the game. How did I know this game? It's like a well-executed revolution.

Mrs. Prince is quiet now and writing something else in her notebook about me again. I close my eyes and listen to the hollow sounds of her hand-writing and see if I can trace her in my mind like a memory. If I can trace her, I might remember other things the polio stole from before the accident.

Her desk was made by inmate 2312. Could have been a man, woman, or child here because this place houses police headquarters and separate departments for male, female, and juvenile inmates—the place that washed me naked—but I imagine 2312 was a woman. Her metal ID tag is still on its leg along with the words LAPD CENTRAL NUMBER ONE.

The door next to me snaps open, unlatched by the pressure built up inside here. Police officers are walking past her door, barely ajar, and headed many ways through the station. A brown man in cuffs is being pushed up the hall. I stare up and down the hallway and then at Mrs. Prince. That's when I realize it. There are no brown people here except the inmates, the workers, and me. I wonder if Mrs. Prince notices.

Chattering down the halls blends together a symphony of men's tones; one has a lisp so his voice is like whispers. Fat fingers are hammering out reports on typewriters, slipping off the cliffs between keys. Hard-sole shoes click along the floor in rapid succession, a metronome keeping time for the orchestra of noise.

"Take your hands off of your face," she says. "Put your feet down."

She finishes with a scribble, then punches her pen on the paper as if to dot an *i* too hard. She takes a breath. "We've got three places that might take you in . . ."

Her door opens completely. A square-headed man wearing a brown suit and bowtie fills the space. "Hey, dollface," he says, leaning into her office, his shoulder pinned at the doorframe. His tweed cap is in his hand, his hair disheveled from having worn the hat past supper then finger combing it straight. It's thinning at the front; his hair is peach fuzz above his temples, like cowlicks of empty space. She smiles for the first time I've seen. "Merry Christmas," he says, bringing forward a small gift box from behind his back.

"Well," she says, a relief and a welcome. "Where have you been?"

An unassembled newspaper is under his arm, a half-completed cross-word puzzle asking for guesses. He steps into her office but stops when he sees me. He backs up directly. "She got the crippler?" he says.

I don't know if he's talking to her or to me.

"Polio would do her a favor," she says. "She's not sick. Hit her head, maybe. Can't remember who she is, where she's from. But I'd guess a field. A wheat with no training."

He hands me a wrapped sweet from his pocket. "You should have her outside if she's sick. Sunshine's cheaper than disinfectant. Air's cheaper than medicine."

"Feet down," she tells me.

He pulls the corner chair over to where the chessboard is and sets down his hat, puzzle, newspaper. She says, "You don't always have to be Santa Claus to everybody. It's your move."

She walks back to her desk and starts flipping through her notebook, searching for something. She says, "I don't know if I have a Black family available, so it'll be a long night."

"Why Black?" I say.

She treats my question like I did hers and ignores it completely.

"Check," he says.

She comes back to the board and nods over the game like giving it a blessing.

A woman screams from the hallway. "That's her!" I turn round into the pointed finger of the woman from the alley. "That's my thief from the al-ley!" She wrestles with the officers holding her and they drag her along, still screaming. I melt back behind the doorway.

They're staring at me. Without words, Mrs. Prince and the officer seem to be asking me the same question.

I shake my head.

I don't know her.

TWO

SARAH, 2102

Of course I knew I was Black the night I arrived in Los Angeles that time. It wasn't the first time I'd become acutely aware that the shade of my skin meant something. But Black throughout time meant power or nothing or fear to others—certainly in 1930s America—and usually nothing in between. But every time I arrive, the body I came into always wanted to reset itself at simple humanity.

My bodies have always first recognized that people are made up of different shapes and sizes and shades, except the face. The face is a limited pallet, only nine distinct shapes and about twenty combinations of where the eyes, nose, and face are placed, repeating in every culture. So how I appeared, skin color and all, was merely a fact to me, not the basis for what should be expected of my character. I would learn of America's (and the world's) darkness soon enough, though I don't compensate for the wicked understanding of others.

Not anymore.

I don't make myself small or silent. Not because of my skin or gender or class or neighborhood, religion, or how I'm expected to behave or speak or wear my hair or vote.

I am in love with my body. Its systems. This glorious machine. I've read that the human body, like yours, has a natural sleep cycle. On a typical night, it'll cycle four or five times, accelerating tasks like healing and growing and moving short-term memory to long term. And this cycle of sleeping is the body's way of bringing home bags of groceries, then sorting them on the counter. Some things you'll put in the refrigerator, others in the freezer, some on a dry shelf. When you finish unpacking, you're free to begin whatever's next in the day.

When your body completes the tasks of a sleep cycle, it'll filter out chemicals that kept you asleep—melatonin is one—then let adrenaline rush in. You wake naturally, different than using an alarm.

An alarm will wake you without regard to what's been put away—a gallon of ice cream can be left melting in the sink—but you wake anyway, disoriented and sluggish, interrupted from some activity you can't remember doing in the first place. So nothing is missed. Not really. Just the lingering feeling.

Our body craves sleep much like it hungers for food. Our desire builds throughout the day, and when tiredness reaches an apex, it'll make us sleep whether we want to or not. The major difference between it and hunger is that your body can't force you to eat when you're hungry, but when you're tired it can put you to sleep behind the wheel of a car.

Death is deep sleeping. A craving our bodies will also satisfy. Another human cycle that shuttles our short life into some distant memory, then recycles some perpetual remnant of ourselves to be born again soon—a next time—some inevitable alarm. One that sends us crying, groggy, and confused into another "virgin" life, and most of us won't remember our dreams anyway.

I first remembered Lou's.

LOU, 1930

It's my third day seeing Mrs. Prince because I had to sleep at the station for as many days, and now she says I'm going to a home.

Her surname, Prince, she said, is from her ex-husband, a poker player who lost their house in a game of cards. The loss, she said, was irregular since his winnings usually paid their bills. "But this is L.A.," she said. "Fortunes change with age."

The nurse came up this morning and gave me a bag with things that belong to the homeless woman. I didn't tell her they weren't mine. Inside the bag are her Mary Jane shoes and no stockings, her dress, and five small wheels of tightly rolled paper—her cap gun and caps, each with little pressed-on dot-pods of gunpowder like aphids on the underside of a leaf. I wave bye to the man on the poster running for U.S. senator and his second name, "Keep California White."

Mrs. Prince's car smells like her coat, tobacco smoke with a shrug of perfume to cover. I ask her if she likes this car even though it's ugly and she says she does and thinks it's ugly too. "Thank you for your honesty," she says.

I ask Mrs. Prince if she used to like poker with her husband? Before he left her? Or does she hate it because it's what he enjoyed?

"I didn't like the scam," she says. "How we made money off of our friends." She says, "To play the game, my husband had to first be invited to somebody's table. To be invited, I had to charm a wife, and that's how he got to their game, with their friends, and then he'd clean 'em out. Do you have a sweater?" she says.

"Yes, ma'am."

She turns onto Central Avenue and grips the steering wheel tighter. "This is South Central, Los Angeles," she says. "Does it ring a bell?"

The foreign sun is setting through my window at the right of me, where brown hills are a dinner table set with orange orchards. None of it is mine.

Closer to our car, along our road, the trees are mature and stabbed into the ground like darts thrown from heaven. Their tips glow with embers of sunlight and stutter over my seated body as we roll along the street.

"That's Wrigley Field," Mrs. Prince says, pointing to a fence. "Home to the Los Angeles Angels and Hollywood Stars. Same name as the one in Chicago, scaled down but still grand."

All I see is dirt except for a few white lines that form a diamond center. The grass is only in the outfield, graying now under the shadow of clouds.

"This ballpark," she says, "and the one in Chicago were named after 'Bubblegum King' William Wrigley Jr. It sees 850,000 fans a season.

"Here," she says, reaching into her purse—a wall of black leather set between us. My thigh rolls into its skin when the car bounces. She hands me a short square tube, peeled open. Four flat sticks covered in paper wrappers are inside. "Don't chew it in school," she says. "It'll get you expelled. And it's no time to be changing homes or schools, you understand?"

"Yes, ma'am. Thank you, ma'am. Eight hundred and fifty thousand people? That's a lot of people."

Out on the field, rows of bleachers are a moat wrapping around the inside of the ballpark, but it only stretches three-quarters of the way, leaving the back open like a sleazy dress.

"The Dunbar Hotel is there," she says.

I stare at its painted taupe bricks and the brown woman walking to its front doors with a dress over her shoulder. Redheeled shoes are in her hand. "Whorish" is what officers called shoes like hers at the station. Must be common here.

"My husband loved Black jazz," she says. "Count Basie, Lena Horne, Louis Armstrong, Duke Ellington, Cab Calloway. They've all played the Dunbar."

"And what's white jazz?" I say.

We slow behind the red taillights of the car in front of us, second in line at a four-way stop. Mrs. Prince's hands tremble. The glowing red tip of her cigarette too. She's nervous driving.

It's almost five now and streetlights are buzzing themselves to life, casting light into the car in front of us, tracing the head and shoulders of the brown man driving, his hair cut short, both hands on the steering wheel, placed at ten and two o'clock. He lifts his hand to let the driver on the right know he can go first.

We turn right at the corner. Mrs. Prince's thin lips are pursed and her hand-drawn eyebrows raised. I can recognize the difference between her and me now. She's very white and I'm very brown.

"Help me look for it," she says, turning right again along a new street and slowing. Brown children are still in the streets playing baseball—catch, but not hitting balls for the sake of neighbor's windows. Other teams are running over lawns playing football. A long pass takes a runner into the street in front of us. With quickness, Mrs. Prince rams her toe knuckles into her brakes. I fly into the dashboard. The boy is washed in the spotlight of our car's bright beams. His hands hover out in front of him toward our car like he caught us in air. But he's startled too. Green stains are on the knees of his trousers and split brown grass is stuck by sweat to his forehead and hair. Two more boys walk out behind him, their shirts ripped from rough tackles.

They call a time-out and stand out of the way along the side of the road. We pass slowly now, and they look inside our car and stare at us . . . see her, very white, too, and me in her passenger seat, browner than they are. I don't feel different anymore. Not on this block. Most everyone I've met has been the color of Mrs. Prince, and it seems to me that people have expectations around skin tone and curly hair. The boys smile at me as we pass, then their expressions relax when they look at Mrs. Prince.

"Green house," she says with a quiver in her voice. "Ten houses down on the left."

I am amazed by these houses. "Craftsman," she calls them. Like brown wood gift boxes, better than the station, better than the alley, better than the blocks leading to here. She stops in front of the tenth house and hesitates to open her door. I don't think she wants to get out of the car.

She takes a deep breath, closes her eyes, and her lids light up red. When Mrs. Prince finishes her exhale it's like she's a new person, chipper now.

We walk over the driveway, up the three concrete steps. I wait behind her as she knocks.

A Black woman opens the door and covers the doorway. A Black man follows, looking over Mrs. Prince's shoulder toward me. I look down at my stockings. Someone gave them to me at the police station—Salvation Army—and I've got a rash under them that I won't scratch. Mrs. Prince told me not to in public.

Mrs. Prince turns her body, inviting me closer. She puts her arm around me and smiles like we're old friends. A warm smell of pinecones and cinnamon wafts out of the front door. Farther in, a vine of red yarn is wrapped around a tree and silver and red balls hang like earrings. A large silver cross is shoved in the center, haphazard, like the oversized washboard that's on the floor, tilted against the wall like they forgot to put it away.

The Black woman says, "Welcome to our home."

I think she's pretty. She's asked me to call her Mrs. Miriam and her husband Mr. Lawrence. They have three children, she says, five, eight, and eleven. The oldest is a girl like me. "You two'll get on," she says. "She's at her mother's," triggering Mrs. Prince to clear her throat. "I'm his second wife," she says, unashamed.

The front door closes softly with me inside the living area now, and it feels like a coffin with no bell to ring if I ain't dead. I imagine Mrs. Prince ran to her car directly, leaving me stranded.

Mr. Lawrence and Mrs. Miriam stand behind me. "Let me show you where you'll sleep," Mrs. Miriam says.

The brown boy, the youngest, takes my hand to hold and I shake it loose. "Boy!" Mr. Lawrence says. "Get over here with your brother."

I don't want nobody touching me.

The boys sit in the armchair next to Mr. Lawrence, like cameras hidden behind one wonky branch of the Christmas tree that's bent, maybe broken. The camera lenses of their stares follow me across the room. I take a photograph of my own then: them, in front of the fireplace.

I'm behind the wall of the hallway now.

I press my bag of stolen things against my chest, cross my arms over them like they're my most valuable possessions.

The walls around the door are papered with a floral print where Mrs. Miriam stands, about to push it open. "You'll be sharing a room with Pauline when the time comes," she says. "She doesn't snore."

She walks to the window and struggles to lift it from its paint-glued frame, so I put my things on the bed and help her pull up. I'd guess it'd never been open before. "It's the chitt'lins," she says. "That smell is the chitt'lins on the burner. It certainly accumulates in this room." But I don't mind the smell.

The window opens. White paint peels from the bottom ledge in strips and hangs like long, fat, flimsy fingernails. I count six.

She crosses her arms and says, "Mrs. Prince let us know that you don't have a name."

"I have a name," I say. She waits for me to give it. "I just don't remember what it is."

"Very well," she says. "Then, politeness would be to call you something other than 'the girl.' I was fond of a girl named Louise in school. Just until you remember?"

I try it out. "Louise," I say. "Yes, thank you, ma'am. Lou will be just fine."

She walks past me to the bed that smells of mothballs. "You'll make your bed," she says. "Bathe at night. At least three times a week. But on your monthly cycle, daily. Do you have napkins?"

"No, ma'am," I say.

"Then I'll get you some."

"There's one toilet and Mr. Lawrence toilets in the morning at 5:00 a.m. so stay out of his way. Then Mitchum, then Pauline when she's home, then Douglas, the baby. Then you'll go in and wash your teeth and face, then join us for breakfast."

"And you?" I say. "When do you toilet?"

She flinches and is quiet now for an embarrassingly long time.

"I'll give you time to settle. If you need anything, call out. We're just in there."

"Pencil and paper," I say. "Please, may I have pencil and paper?"

"Alright," she says, then lingers at the door, considering me. "Pauline may not be back," she says. "Daughters belong with their mothers." She pauses, as if inhaling her whole person. She says, "I imagine this can't be easy for you. Without your mother. Both Mr. Lawrence and I were fosters. We married after his wife had . . . restarted her life. So we understand what it's like be left and to live and share differently."

"I wasn't left," I say. I pick up my stolen belongings from the bed and press them to my chest again. "I just can't remember, is all. The polio."

"I toilet after Mr. Lawrence goes to work," she says, "and after you all go to school."

I nod.

"Do you need anything else besides a pencil and paper?"

"No, ma'am."

I don't sit when she leaves me. I want to stand here at the open window and watch the breeze flutter the weak nails on the windowsill. Take in a new aroma—trampled tomato vines, their fragrance strong enough to resurrect some faint memory and a curiosity for how tomatoes have had the audacity to grow in December.

THREE

SARAH, 2102

Petit mort is French for little death. It means breathing like you're dying. The sound pleasure makes. An intoxicated rapture. And this *petit mort* finds me in every lifetime but not like it does for others.

For me, the call of death is high-pitched like a dog whistle—no, a siren, wailing for me—but can't offer me release.

Instead, when I come to meet it, others are already there, some I know or am supposed to know or love. And as I wait with them in their final moments, it's like watching them masturbate—their last solo boast—and I don't want to be there. I have no agency with death. No device. I can only witness, maybe assist while listening for the tune I used to regard as sadness but now I'd call the arrogance of mortality.

On the night I arrived in Los Angeles, back in 1930, Betty Ann Mulley's body washed ashore. The call of her death reached me there in the alley till it was cradled in my lap. It was what woke me that night, but I didn't know it yet.

Had the world's nations not been paused between two world wars and been in the throes of the Great Depression, others might have heard her body splash down into the Pacific, too, or seen the man carrying a large burlap bag with someone wrestling for her life inside it. But as it was, there was nothing to report on the poor dying woman until it was too late.

Poor was common then after the stock market crashed the year before—October 29, 1929. Almost every country and every class, especially those dependent on heavy industry, disintegrated. Banks went bankrupt, unemployment rates were sky-high, as were suicides. Bread lines were long but tempers were short. So was Betty Ann's life.

Her husband, who later confessed to her murder, said she'd stopped living as a proper wife and had put on too much weight. She was dead long before he killed her, so she wasn't a victim, he said. He was. Or if she was a victim, he was too. And City prosecutors would say, in part, that he was right. There was a double homicide.

Betty Ann was twenty-six years old and seven months pregnant when she died, her white breasts and thighs by then were like plump pillows half-stuffed into cases, resting on the frame of her small bones. Her husband called her fat. He said it in a way that made the word *fat* seem disgusting and ugly, and when he spoke the word, his bottom lip would tuck back under his front teeth and he'd spit out the word with a chunk of his lip and a shower of spit. But she was a masterpiece. If you've never stood in the glow of a fat woman, you've missed a sunrise.

Betty Ann had been reading more than usual before she died. Was seeing the world through the eyes of Selina in *So Big*, a novel about a woman who married a Dutch farmer and together had a large-size baby and when the woman was asked "How big is the baby?" she'd respond, "So-o-o-o big." Thus the book's title. It was a wonderful story, Betty Ann wrote her mother in a letter sent home to Topeka. "Rumor has it, the studios want to make the book into a talkie." This prospect delighted Betty Ann. That the writer, Edna Ferber, a woman like she is, wrote a story that others, including men, would want to retell. Betty Ann wondered what it would be like to be its main character. To live a life teaching or farming or raising the son she might be carrying. She'd love a daughter just the same, she thought.

After a while, she noticed her weight gain. From the baby. From her choices. All normal and healthy, her doctor assured her.

In her third month of pregnancy, she hung a wood sign on the wall next to the front door to remind herself not to be afraid of what was happening to her body and was amazed by all the things it could do, how it could transform with or without her involvement. No, she told herself. There was nothing to be afraid of.

She placed the wood sign near the front door because her husband never came or went through the front. He'd never see it. He'd sometimes kiss her cheek on the back porch when he was on the way to the dock for work but only if he felt she'd deserved it.

The wood sign was reliable.

It had a front and back. On the front were the carved words IN CASE OF EMERGENCY, TURN THIS OVER.

When she'd flip it to the back, it read NOT NOW, STUPID! IN CASE OF AN EMERGENCY!

This made Betty Ann laugh. Every morning, it helped cool her anxiety about her pregnant body and the recent whereabouts of her husband, who had been staying out all night, overnight. For one night, then two. She only asked him where he'd been the first time he did it. He didn't like being questioned, he said, and his tone scared her so she didn't ask again. And anyway, he rarely had anything to say to her. Or so she thought.

Her mistake was believing his absence wasn't his statement. He *was* communicating with her. And unfortunately for her, he was communicating his insecurity. She didn't hug him or react to his sad faces or his body showing the burden of his struggles at work. And insecure people want to see that they've impacted you, mattered to you, especially when they're doing their worst.

But Betty Ann was distracted. She had already fallen in love with books. Books were among her first free choices. Besides food. But she should've been bracing for impact.

Her body was tossed into the Pacific Ocean from the dock where her husband worked, and she and her baby drowned. Their dying is what called me there. The coroner's report would clarify that Betty Ann was still alive when her husband did it. There was water in her lungs. So to cure my own sadness, I tell myself the water entered her mouth from smiling freedom.

LOU, 1930

Tonight, I've spent the last fifteen minutes at the table listening to Mr. Lawrence spank Mitchum in the bedroom while Mrs. Miriam waits with her head bowed, though it's not a protest. "Spare the rod, spoil the child," Mr. Lawrence explained to me. This was "love" in their faith tradition, but it seemed to me the rod was an instrument to inflict immediate violence. And, based on the twenty-third Psalm, written and framed on their wall, a rod should be a comfort, a prepared defense against violence, but I don't much know these people.

Mitchum's the oldest boy and the splat sound is of an open hand on a flabby naked butt cheek and the boy hollers between the stop and go. It makes me flinch each time, but I abide.

Before Mrs. Prince left me here, she told me to "abide" by the household rules and I do because I don't want to be like Mitchum and, secondly, because I enjoyed yesterday's music lesson.

I like the accordion.

When Mr. Lawrence asked me to sit down on his chair and laid it on my lap, it felt like being given a new baby to hold but was surprisingly heavy in my arms, even forced me to lean back for balance. I sat there with my skinny brown limbs belted around it, pushed it up with one knee and shimmied the straps back over my shoulders.

I studied the smudged buttons on one side of the box and the small piano on the other side; was readjusting my arms when I knocked into the tiny metal latch that held the accordion together. It bubbled open as if its folds were made of expanding marshmallow. I tried forcing the sides back together but the air hardened in the middle, the box turned, and my feet shuffled. The straps slid down my arms.

I was wrestling it steady when Mr. Lawrence reached over, smashed the sides together, and with no trouble at all made it vacuum shut. A stale, metallic odor rose from its center, like walking into the old washroom in the basement of the police station. This turned my stomach for the accordion.

"Try it again," Mr. Lawrence said as I sat balancing it on my thighs. I smiled and shook my head, shy I'd mess up my next try. I didn't want to play anymore.

"Like this," he said, making movements in the air, harsher than they needed to be, jerking his arms in and out.

Mr. Lawrence reached for the box, opened it up, and said, "Give it some air. Push the buttons. Let me hear it." He seemed agitated.

I tried tugging it open, but it was stuck closed. I hated myself for being weak. "I don't know how," I said.

"Open up the damn thing and play!" he said. *I was wasting his time.* He had papers to grade. Only Black teacher at the school. I got it opened and closed, banged on the keys and it bellowed silence.

I heard her before I saw her. Mrs. Miriam was stern with Mr. Lawrence, said it was enough for today, and he seemed gripped by his own actions. Wanted to apologize. He said he just wanted the best for his children.

And now, at dinner, we aren't allowed to eat till Mitchum and Mr.

Lawrence get back to the table: beef roast and peas and white rice covered in melted butter.

The boy is hobbling back to the table now, wiping his tears. He's having a hard time sitting. They all bow their heads when Mr. Lawrence sits. I don't. I only stare at the darker skin mask around his eyes. I hope he's satisfied with what he's done tonight to Mitchum.

"If I don't do it," he says to me and reaches for Mrs. Miriam's hand, "the police will. Do you understand?" Mrs. Miriam keeps her eyes low. I join her as he blesses the food.

FOUR

It's been nineteen days and I haven't started school yet on account of Christmas and the New Year and not having time to enroll.

I've been to work two days with Mr. Lawrence where he teaches at the middle school and a week with Mrs. Miriam to clean theaters—all seats ten cents before 6:00 p.m. except Friday. Closed Sunday. "People still want to go to the theater," Mrs. Miriam said, even though the world crashed with the stock market. "Get their minds off. Keep their world usual. And we need to be here to help give folks such a place."

She and I cleaned between the weekend shows and stood at the back, in the dark, before closing credits and watched the last fifteen minutes of a silent picture that ended with kisses and a muted car ride into the fading horizon. Then the lights came up and soda pop fell.

I'll be joining Jefferson High in the morning, a Tuesday, not a beginning. "An integrated school," Mr. Lawrence said. "All races together," he said, "Just keep your grades up. Join a sports team, doesn't matter which.

Girls are good as boys on the field," but I'm not athletic. So when Mrs. Prince knocked at our door before breakfast this morning I was hoping she'd have some good news, like: I'm too late for tryouts. Instead she just said, "Come with me," and now I don't know where we're going.

We bump over a bridge into a part of Los Angeles I've never seen. She says, "Do you want to stay with Mr. Lawrence and Mrs. Miriam?"

"No," I say, because *no* is easier than asking for them to choose me, to admit I've enjoyed some of my time with them, and *no* because I wasn't giving up on my real family. I have a family.

"Try to be grateful," she says. "Stability is good for you."

We're on a main street, BROOKLYN AVENUE the sign says, and this is the kind of neighborhood that makes Mrs. Prince's cigarettes tremble. Black kids are walking and running down the street. So are Mexican and Chinese—a brother and sister, maybe. About ten years old.

"It's Boyle Heights," she says. "L.A.'s first neighborhood. East of Downtown, between the city boundary and L.A.'s disabled river."

The river is disabled, she says, because its legs are feeble and unable to meet the special needs of our thriving city. "We need more water here."

Nurses stand outside a hospital on Fickett Street. "For Japanese," she says, and the B. Charney Vladeck Center on St. Louis is for the Jews. It advertises a banquet hall. I feel like we're driving in circles.

"This is a bizarre place," Mrs. Prince says. "Not Christian. Not really. All sorts of religions—Catholics and Buddhists." I thought Catholics were Christian but her tone tells me she believes all of these people are of a lesser god. "Do you recognize anything?" she says.

"Freedom," I say.

She only looks over her shoulder at me, disapproving.

She points to houses along the road. "The Wilson family's there," she says. "The Tsukamotos, the Nakayas, the Stumps, Arciniegas. That one's the Goldmans. Across there is the Marcovitchs, Kazarians, and McCradys. See that one with the flag on the porch? That's the Calhouns. Good people."

"You know everybody," I say.

"It's my job to." She waves hello to a woman outside of the Arcienega house. The woman seems to see her but doesn't wave back.

On the sidewalk a chain of five-year-old students walk hand in hand like a living rosary, crisscrossing along the sidewalk. She says, "Japanese, Chinese, Irish, Turkish, Black, and Mexican," but I only see children. She says they're from First Street School.

They shimmy around a food cart, the fish man's cart. "This fish man comes twice a week," she says. "Fresh fish, tofu, produce, and all kinds of Japanese food for sale."

We slow as we pass a green space of grass. A dark blue lake is at its center. "Hollenbeck Park," she says. "On weekends, people hang around from dawn to dusk, playing ball or posing around the lake for *quinceañera* photos, all fancy-dressed like a colorful wedding starring children. But there's proper weddings too." And she sounds rude to me: *proper*.

We turn down a street of brick houses and she slows in front of one, two, and now a third house. I tell her the truth when she asks me, "Does this place ring a bell?"

No was the truth but only half the truth because I was answering the question I thought she was mostly asking. "Did you live here?" The answer is no. But if she were asking whether I recognized this third house, my answer would be different.

We don't pull into the driveway. Instead we pull up along the sidewalk. It's a brick house that's so clearly abandoned in this neighborhood already peppered with families and life that it's like a gray front tooth in a mouth of white.

She reaches over my lap and winds down my window and takes in the view of the house from over the top of her glasses. She reaches in her purse for a sheet of paper and reads the address. But there's no address on this house to match.

"You think this is it?" she says.

The house is crying from its front two windows, like actresses' mascara running down its brick face and drying there. Fire damage.

"Does it ring a bell?" she says, and it's the third time she's used that phrase, so I wonder if her question means our memories are supposed to make bell noises or if our bodies are supposed to quiver or even break like the bell Mr. Lawrence teaches his students about in history. The Liberty Bell.

"I don't know it," I say, but that's a half lie too.

I did quiver a week ago and hear a sound. But it was in a dream. A house that looked exactly like this one was in my dream.

"A family was discovered dead here," Mrs. Prince says plainly. Then says they might have been mine.

She waits for my emotions to rise from her words, but they don't. These unfortunate people burned up, but they weren't my family. I'm sure.

"Problems with the electrics started the fire," she said. But that's a lie.

Electrics didn't do it. Not in my dream.

She leans back into her own seat and pulls a small tube of lipstick from her small purse. She pops its lid and slides color across her bottom lip, rubs both together. "Officer Adams'll be along any minute with one of the lieutenants from the fire department. He'll let us in, and they'll ask you if you remember anything."

"I have polio," I say. "Memory loss."

"You don't have polio."

"I used to have it."

"You wouldn't be walking now if you did."

"I didn't have polio?"

Officer Adams pulls up behind us in his plain black car. We watch him in our rearview mirror preparing himself and gathering his things. She rolls down her window and reaches an arm out and waves. "Let's wait for him to come and get us."

I saw this family die in my dream. That's what I remember. Saw them sleeping and then not sleeping anymore. Just lying in the same posture but gone.

Mrs. Prince says, "It's sad, is what. They were squatters. The house was empty, folks thought. No one found them until after the fire, two days after it happened and the children had been missing school. All dead at the back of the house, burned up."

It had been unusually cold that night, Mrs. Prince said. "Forty degrees Fahrenheit," and it was the week or so before I came on that hot night. "But December is a wildcard in L.A.," Mrs. Prince said, "its weather as rowdy and unpredictable as a Sagittarius."

"Girl's clothes were found near one of the bodies," she says, "but among the bodies were only sons, so the LAPD reckon those clothes belonged to you. It's why you're here," she says.

A Black man, another officer, gets out of the passenger side of Officer Adams's car. Seeing his brown face makes me proud. "He's not an officer," she says, "but a fire lieutenant from Engine Company 4, the Black fire department." He had to be Black because this was a Black family that died. Death is racial.

"What're you waiting for?" Mrs. Prince says, opening her door.

No one talks to each other except to nod until the front door opens—a somber moment now. A silent vigil for the lost.

We walk in and are smothered in a funk like burned barbecue ribs and yams stuck to the bottom of a metal pot. Mrs. Prince asks me to sit at the kitchen table, in the chair untouched by fire. She asks to let it jog my memory since most family life happens while eating.

The lieutenant opens all the windows, and Officer Adams and Mrs. Prince have bumped hands three times while walking around the living room once. They say they're searching for signs of the old me.

Mrs. Prince joins me at the table, and I sit up straight. Officer Adams comes up next to her; their knuckles dust each other's again.

"Do you remember this house?" he says.

"No."

"Nothing?"

"Uh uh."

Mrs. Prince whispers something to him and he walks away, eyeing the walls.

"Look," she says. "If you say you do remember, this'll be the end of it and you stay with Mr. Lawrence and Mrs. Miriam."

"And my family?"

The Black lieutenant joins us at the table and ungloves himself. "Where's she staying now?" he says.

"The Willards'," Mrs. Prince says. "Lawrence and Miriam."

"Good people," he says. "They'd know something about abandonment and abuse. Weren't they . . ."

"I'm not abused."

Mrs. Prince says, "We went to all the Black churches on Sunday. No one recognized her."

He says, "How about the Foursquare Church at Angelus Temple? Five thousand people. Somebody oughta. Or . . ." His breath catches. "Have you considered that her family's done what they meant to do?"

"A family'll come forward soon," she says, as if she's hopeful. No. Not as if she's hopeful. It's what she thinks I want to hear.

She waves her hands. "It's all unusual," she says. "Her memory. Her situation."

"Has anyone reported her missing?" the lieutenant says.

"No one," Mrs. Prince says.

I say, "Families can report the missing?"

She looks at me strangely but doesn't answer.

"They're not looking for me?"

Neither does he.

I can't breathe.

FIVE

SARAH, 2102

Good decisions can't be made in grief. Not really. Because emotions are an incomplete guide.

Especially love.

My kind of grief is continual because grief is the form love takes when someone dies. The emotion a confirmation of our humanity. Sometimes bubbling up, unexpected.

We grieve the end and the future we'd imagined at the same time, even the conversation we'd hoped to have one day with the person, now lost.

In grief, our weak phrases will fail us—the right words lost in some ancient tongue, prehistoric. *I can't find the words. Not even to comfort you.*

Grief isn't reserved for death. Most everybody is grieving the loss of something: a job, a contest, a relationship. Hope. We cope with stories we tell ourselves about the lost thing and those involved, and these stories include lies like "I never wanted it anyway."

We lie about what we really wanted because we don't want to feel rejected—a form of abandonment. Makes us feel abandoned. But not asking for what we want is worse. Self-abandonment. And when we agree to relationships and situations we don't want because we can't bear to be alone or don't have the courage to ask, we become a victim of that not-asked-for thing, grieving for ourselves. But the truth is, you abandoned yourself way back there.

You can choose differently.

In Lou's life, I would.

LOU, 1931

It had been quiet and still on campus—my first day—but when the school bell rang this morning, the campus stirred to life as if from the bottom of a stew pot, all colors, shapes, and textures unveiled at once.

Mr. Lawrence got me to school an hour early, said early would give me time to get acquainted, find my place. "Jefferson High School's a big cow." And it was. The school bell turned its stomachs with flipped trashed cans, regurgitated combative students who were shoving and screaming. It's too late for me to chase down Mr. Lawrence's car and climb in the trunk.

"Three minutes to tardy!" an older student shouts in the hall behind me. "Young lady, why aren't you headed to class?" He leads me to homeroom, and I take a seat.

Castor oil wafts from every student's lips and mine, served by the spoon-ful to those whose fathers had gone to war. It's vitamins, the newspaper reads. The *Los Angeles Times* is the only one Mr. Lawrence trusts.

In class we sit in rows facing the chalkboard, except for the two of us asleep with heads on desks. "Us" because we're Americans, the teacher said after our flag salute: "With liberty and justice for all."

The school counselor made me a senior. This means I have another half year of school before I graduate.

Mr. Lawrence told me to take the calculus test, said girls are as good as boys in mathematics, too, and Jefferson High is one of the few high schools that prepare students for the U.S. military service academies—West Point and Annapolis—so I'll need calculus. He said West Point hasn't seen a Negro cadet graduate in forty years, not since his cousin Charles Young. And never a woman, so I should take advantage of the opportunity.

I said I would try.

I tested high on my calculus exam, though my counselor suspects I cheated but can't prove it, said I didn't solve the problems the way I'm supposed to, so she put me in basic math. Now I can learn to reach conclusions the same way everybody else does.

But she let me stay in Senior English. Said my vocabulary was wanting from lack of exposure but my grammar was excellent. If she had asked, I'd tell her (or is it: I would have told her) that it's all language to me. Language is easier than making friends. At lunchtime and during the morning breaks, I go to the empty baseball field and watch students and teachers from under the bleachers. I can mind my own business there and they can mind theirs.

I sketch with the pencil and paper Mrs. Miriam gave me and draw towns and a man without a body because I can't draw legs and I'm not good at hands. I like to draw eyes. Sometimes my sketches are of only his eyes. But not this one.

I see him in my dreams. I finished his face today and his neck and shoulders and arms. I'm trying hands now. I have him holding the metal bars that make up the frame of the bleachers around me but his hands look like a bunch of bananas. A bulb of knuckles around the seating scaffold.

I quit and fold it.

Put it in my pocket next to Mrs. Prince's pack of gum I'm not allowed to chew in school, and I run a roll of dots along the broken concrete under the bleachers. I remember the hands of the old woman in the alley and how easy it was to take the toy gun.

Two dots pop, the others duds.

A smell like sulfur rises from the paper before it releases a thin line of smoke. I try it again and it burns the tip of my finger. I suck the spot and taste the bitter. I put my last line of paper back in my pocket.

Through the slit of the bleacher steps, on the other side of the metal frame across the field, there's a girl hurrying this way. She's the one other students call yellow. She's dressed in her costume, pink with pale flowers on her sleeves. Around her waist is a purple sash. Oriental clothes, my theater teacher calls it, but I don't understand the phrase.

An older white boy, a senior from class with weak posture, is following behind her, across the baseball diamond now, pulling and holding one of her braided ponytails. She yanks it away.

Other students are walking on the grassy hill above us, taking the short cut to class. It's the hill that younger kids from the elementary school cross over. They get out of school an hour before us.

The girl is in our school's musical, *The Mikado*. Everybody knows who she is because she's pretty and her voice is an angel's. She's playing the part of Yum-Yum, an engaged and beautiful Japanese girl who's being pursued in love by another man.

She's shuffling away from the boy faster now. Not running, fast walking, and has opened a distance between them. At her feet is a plume of white and orange dust. The white is from the powdered lines drawn between first and second base.

He catches her and slaps at her ponytails. She stops completely, her fists balled to stones. Boulders. Better than I could draw.

Both of her shoulders are rising up and down from her breathing hard. This might get good.

She turns to face the boy.

Another boy student, who's breaking school rules with a stain of facial hair on his chin, is up the grassy hill looking down on them, yelling at them, "That your girlfriend?"

He's laughing and has got his hands in the dress pocket of a girl he's pulling close to him and kissing roughly. They've both got what Mrs. Prince calls a "white trash face": weak bone structure with thin lips and crooked teeth. The girl is squinting 'cause she needs glasses.

The boy on the field stops chasing. "She's not my girlfriend," he says, and pretends to not be interested in her now.

"I think it *is* your girlfriend," the unkempt boy says, making a thrusting motion with his hips.

The girl in costume is running now, coming this way, past the field's dugout, next to my wooden bleachers.

"Gon' chase her," the hairy boy says.

"Back to China!" the girlfriend says, and makes strange noises like she's speaking another language, and it's a jumbled mess of idiocy. The couple explodes into laughter because of it, and I'll admit it hurts me. It hurts me for this stranger, this girl who's running and is different like me, like a foreign object out of place, in a time when the thoughts of other strangers begin with how to get rid of us.

I stay out of sight. The couple disappears behind the hill but the boy who was chasing has started toward her again, toward me, hiding. I do believe his persistence is wrapped in his fondness for her.

He grabs her braid and forces her to stop, to turn around to him. He draws in his chapped lips, about to use the words that girl on the mound said, "Go back to . . ."

With the quickest hands I've ever seen, the girl strikes him twice with one fist—once in his nose and then his cheek—quick jabs made of straight knuckles, palm side down.

His nose is bleeding, his cheekbone swells. He covers his face with both hands, and in perfect American English, she says, "This city's my home, asshole!" She straightens her dress. "Even my parents were born here."

The lunch bell rings, sending the cherry-faced boy back to homeroom with tears and probably some excuse about a door or falling down.

The girl watches him go but doesn't move from her fight stance. He disappears into the buildings.

I love her dress.

We're gon' be late for class.

She bends over to tie her sneaker not far from my face, behind the facade of the bleacher steps in front of me, and I hold my breath.

She looks toward me. *Did she see me?* I smile in case she did. Nothing.

She finishes her loop above the tongue of her shoe and stands.

She heads toward the school building behind me. I turn around to cross my legs, to reach in my pocket for the last of the gunpowder, and there she is, swinging from the highest rails under the bleachers, her silky dress a cascade.

"This your castle?" she says, and hops down from the rail. "A watchman up in her tower, smoking?"

"I don't smoke."

"I definitely smell smoke," she says. "Isn't that why you come out here every day?"

"From my cap gun," I say. How long has she been watching me?

"You like guns?" she says.

"Not a gun," I say. "It's only a tiny dot of powder." I show her my last roll, then press a dot on the concrete and strike it like striking a match. It pops and the paper catches alight, burns my fingers, but I don't drop the roll, I put it in my other hand, see my fingertips singed black and yellow, then rub them together. The blackening wipes away. "Just powder," I say.

"Gunpowder is no good," she says. "Unpredictable," she says. "Like Black Death."

"Why black?" I say. "Why not yello—white death?" I say. "And don't call me Black, if that's your next thought."

"Then what do I call you?"

"We'll see," I say.

She reaches into her dress pocket and pulls out a small pack of thin paper and tobacco. The fingers of her jabbing hand stay gathered like they were glued that way after the punch she gave the boy's face. She holds those now-swollen fingers with her other hand and they seem limp. "Can you roll?" she says.

"Can I touch your dress?" I say.

"What?"

"Are the flowers painted on?" I say. "But it looks smooth."

"You're wacky. It's just a costume. Go ahead and touch it."

I do, taking my time to feel the lining. When I finish, I roll her paper and tobacco. It's easy. Like I've done it before. Many times before. I roll a second one for her for later and it surprises me how good I am. She throws me her matchbook and I light her cigarette, take it from her lips and drag it started. The smoke feels good in me. I give it to her. Her head rests back, enjoying the burn off. She says, "You think I was too hard on him? The boy?"

"He got what he had coming."

She nods and exhales her smoke. "Esther," she says, officially introducing herself.

"Louise," I say. "But I prefer you call me Lou."

SIX

—◀○▶—

LOU, 1931

It's been two months and no family has come for me.

I wake up some mornings before school with a stream of tears dried down both sides of my face. This morning Mrs. Miriam said, "Chil', you look like somebody's rain-stained windshield. You alright? Because it's fine not to be alright."

I nodded that all was well but after breakfast, when I'd just finished cleaning my teeth, she caught me at the bathroom door and asked me to stay behind for a minute. "Let the children walk to the bus," she said. "Lawrence'll drive you to school."

So now I have my hands folded in front of me at their dinner table like I did at that dead family's house—the family who didn't belong to me, either—while Mr. Lawrence and Mrs. Miriam sit across from me, silent, like they don't know where to start.

Am I in trouble?

Morning light hits the left side of their faces and turns their black

hair gold. Mr. Lawrence starts by telling me he's sorry. Sorry for doubt-
ing my memory loss—I didn't realize he had—sorry for not being more
welcoming—but he was. Says he and Miriam were adopted by different
families when they were young and were fortunate to be surrounded by a
family full of love, the kind he hopes he and Miriam can provide for me. He
wants me to know that I'll probably go through some sadness because "As
much as we want to be like your parents, there's no replacing your true family," he says, and "We're not your saviors—that would imply you were someone in need of rescuing and, true or not, that's a lousy burden for a child."

"So we're just here to support you," Mrs. Miriam says. "For as long as
you need. We'd like to adopt you before you turn eighteen or you'll be left
with no support should something happen to me or Lawrence."

"Something like what?" I say.

"We won't abandon you," Mr. Lawrence said.

"Lawrence served in the war and I served," she says. "We got death ben-
efits for college for our children. Survivor's maintenance. As our daughter,
you'd be entitled." They've given up on my family too. "If that's what you'd
want, of course."

I want the sunlight to turn me gold and wash me out.

"Well, you think about it," Mrs. Miriam says. "Mrs. Prince will be by
tomorrow to discuss it in detail."

They're all in on it.

I ride with Mr. Lawrence to his school in silence, staring out of the window from the back seat where blurs come into focus as we slow at the top
of a hill. Mr. Lawrence says he needs to make a stop before school and by
"need" he means Greenblatt's Deli in Hollywood for a bowl of homemade
matzo ball soup that he'll take away in the container Mrs. Miriam gave him.
They'll wrap his hot pastrami Reuben and a thick slice of double chocolate
fudge cake separately.

Adams Boulevard is a main drag of the city. We make a turn down another and our nicely preened, paint-coordinated neighborhood gives way to

block after block of concrete buildings and businesses. A random house will be built between an ironmonger and a car repair shop. No careful neighborhood planning like the suburbs the City's building.

I tighten my thigh muscles to keep from bouncing on the back seat. He turns up his radio and sings along, "Sitting on Top of the World" by his favorite fiddle band, the Mississippi Sheiks, a group from Mississippi, not Arabs. Mr. Lawrence says their name is why he likes 'em most. Because *sheik* is a name inherited from your father, a name given to royal males at birth, and the father of the lead singers was a slave, a musicianer, but they still call themselves royalty and that's somethin'.

He cranks the handle on his door till his window is rolled all the way down, then hangs his arm outside, lets it fall along the door, where he taps the metal to the beat. He follows the tune mumbling inaudible words, then belts out lyrics with a slow country drawl, a musical twang that I've never heard from him before: "Just when she left me. She's gone to stay. But now she's gone and I don't worry. I'm sitting on top of the world."

I scoot over to the middle back seat so I can peer out through the windshield and into the world he sees. The HOLLYWOODLAND sign is up on the hill, a distance away. Thirteen big block letters, each fifty feet high, all white and not alight because it's not night. "Sittin'-on-top-of the-world," he sings.

Mr. Lawrence leans into his windshield and swipes his finger across it like he's writing in some condensation there but he's pointing to the mountain. He says, "When the letters were first raised the whole of them were studded with four thousand light bulbs. Flashed in segments, lit up one by one and then together: HOLLY. WOOD. And LAND. Advertisement for a local real estate developer. Segregated, of course. Laborers Black, of course. 'Cause they want brown labor but not brown neighbors."

"I think you and Mrs. Miriam are good neighbors," I say. Mr. Lawrence smiles at me. Maybe for the first time ever. And from this close, I can't help but notice his teeth are bigger than I thought they would be. Large and out of sorts, like the eyes on Betty Boop, and pretty too. I won't tell him that because Mr. Lawrence says Boop is immoral. "A shame grown men would look at a children's cartoon that way."

Down the hill, along the street, trimmed lawns and airy shops are already open; women are pushing small children in prams. I rest back and let the words of the tunes of the sheiks run through me. "But now she's gone," they sing, "and I don't worry." We slow at the red light. Restart on green and get a good pace again.

Mr. Lawrence yanks the wheel left and it throws my body across my seat to the right and I don't know how long it should take for my mind to catch up with my body. He swerves right and slams on his brake.

I hit the side door, yanked sideways by invisible hands, thrown forward over the seats, my chest hammering brown skin and tendon and bone, his outstretched forearm, belting me on impact, saving my life from the teeth of the windshield, my body an almost-sacrifice.

"I'm sorry," I say, immediately, pushing away from him, dusting my knees and climbing back onto my seat cushion.

"I told you to sit behind me," he yells. "Behind my seat!"

"Yes, sir," I say. "I forgot."

"Next time you could be dead. Forgot."

"Yes, sir," I say, crying now. But there was no reason for it. I'm alive because of him.

He pulls to the side of the road and frees a deep breath, rubs his chest, his heart, grunts, closes his eyes, resting there. "You scared me, is all," he says. "I didn't mean to yell at you."

I nod. Wipe my eyes.

"How about I get you a good slice of that chocolate cake too? For later?"

I nod to Mr. Lawrence. Wipe my face. Wait with him as he gathers his focus.

I was yelled at last night too. It was during a dream so real that when I woke from it, I couldn't open my eyes or move, like a person was holding me down on my bed. So I just slid off my mattress with my eyes closed and ran blind into the wall. Like Mr. Lawrence's clothesline.

In this dream, I was in England. I knew it was 1620 because the vicar announced it as "the year of our Lord" in a prayer service.

I had a friend in this dream. She taught me our ways. We are *via media*, she says. Not Lutherans, as I came to believe, or Calvinist as she did, but somewhere in the middle.

We are nineteen, and in this dream I desire to be near her. I tell myself it is my fondness of her teaching, not her face. Her cheeks and chin are blushed a dark crimson from a birth condition, she'd told me. Not wine or spirits, though visitors to our church have accused her of both.

The splotches on her cheeks reach high and wide like sheer scarlet fabric hung from her forehead, avoiding her nose. The vicar calls this condition the roses. I say they're drapes of roses for me. I tell her that her smile spreads curtains, but she is committed to her god. Except in our prayers. Except in the scriptures we recite aloud in the chapel, when our breath finds each other, while the stone floor bruises our knees. We'll read the book of Jeremiah aloud: "I have loved you with an everlasting love," she'll say, and I'll respond, "I am my beloved's," and in this way, I tell her I love her through scripture.

In my dreams, my prayers are a conversation. Ones I'll never have in public or with her. My best prayers are made in silence on the mornings I worked alongside the cobbler. Our shoes are made to fit either foot—left or right—its sole attached to a strip of leather, and it doesn't make sense to me that one straight shoe should or could fit both feet without regard to the difference, but Mr. Smith tells me to mind my work. I tan the leather and pray in silence as I do, hand-holding my sinful thoughts and desires, trembling, because everything we want is disguised as danger.

Before the dream ended this morning, before I was paralyzed awake, the last thing I remember was crying behind the gray stones of our simple church, its steeple and cross condemning me. It was the afternoon, I was lying in the mud, and it was raining. Always raining. And she squatted beside me—cheeks red as ever—and she was disappointed in me. Disappointed because I asked her, "How much harder do I have to love you?"

Then she took my face in her hands and said, "Don't look to people to give you what only God can give you."

Then I woke with my tears in paralysis, wanting her to touch me again and tell me something else I needed to hear.

"We're here," Mr. Lawrence said as we rolled to a stop next to the sidewalk near the deli, our tires crunching over soda cans and the browning wet newspaper there, popping glass bottles. "I won't be but a minute," he said, and opened his door. The sweet stench of beer-urine and something like tanned leather wafted in.

SEVEN

LOU, 1931

"Smell my finger," Wally said, soon as he walked in our class, and I wish Mr. Hill would move his seat from next to mine.

"I won't," I said, and swung round on the piano stool—a gift from the theater department, they had nowhere else to store it—and went to my desk. Class would start in fifteen minutes.

When Mr. Hill walked in one minute late, the whole class had already arrived, and it was like he ignored us, went straight to his chair, put his hand in his tote, wrestled inside it till he lifted his text, and splayed it on his desk. "Take out your books," he says. "Turn to page forty-two." We're reading about a writer from Gibraltar. "There's more in the world than just Los Angeles and I'll teach whatever pleases me in my class."

Mr. Hill is my twelfth-grade English teacher and he's retiring this year. Said our school paper would be the last good thing he does before he leaves, and he wants to leave on a good note.

He wanted to teach us about Los Angeles, he said. About Hollywood.

And said Hollywood lives here but Los Angeles will not entertain you. He said the City wants a real relationship with us, and if not, she'll treat you like a floozy, or worse, a tourist, no matter how many years you've lived with her or how much money you've spent in her. A casual encounter. The boys giggled.

"Her beaches, her mountains, her deserts and quiet streams," he said, "are spread for us." Wally snorted, and it began another round of the boys' laughter. "You'll have to give to get and even if you do, your relationship with her is still casual. You'll need a car," he said. "Who you don't want to be is one of these fly-byers who go home neglected saying, 'I didn't see anything in L.A.' If they're honest, they'll also add, 'because the city is as empty as I am.'

"The point is," Mr. Hill said, "we have to engage in our world or the world will only show you who *you* are. Or what you expected."

Before me and Wally, the school paper was just Mr. Hill. Mr. Hill said he didn't want to teach the meatheads in sports or the future dropouts in welding, not because he hated welders but because they didn't need school to make money.

My friend Esther told me, "Why in the world would you join the school paper? Journalism is *really* white. Do theater instead, where people have some imagination about the world."

She's probably right. I mean, I understand I am Black, and that Black means something more than aesthetics and hair type, but I like to write because of Mr. Hill.

Before his class, writing prompts seemed silly. Every week on Monday my homeroom teacher gives us a different one. The prompts are sometimes fun but mostly a waste of time. But not Mr. Hill's. He wrote on the board once, "*If you could go to the moon and start a colony, what is the first thing you would do for your colony after providing basic human needs like oxygen, food, shelter, and water?*"

"Make posters," I said.

He asked me to stand so the class could hear me. I could feel cool air across the hairs on my calf muscles as they tensed. "Make some posters," I said again.

"Propaganda?" he said.

"Just pictures," I said, "of good living that'll help people see what's possible. Give hope. Then write a song. Make everybody learn that song. Get a flag. And we'll need heroes."

"More than one?" Mr. Hill said.

"At least a couple."

That's when he asked me to be on the paper. Said good journalists ask good questions and understand one question gives birth to others.

Wally got on the paper, too, because of me. Because he won't let me stop helping him. Because he's needy on account of his headgear and leg braces.

His helmet has rubber straps that come down along the sides of his face and around his neck and lead to the metal wires in his mouth. "For my teeth," he said. "They'll realign my jaw," he said, and the polio braces on his legs will help him recover. He looks like a robot or Tin Man from the *Wonderful Wizard of Oz* and all of this makes him a target at school.

I was the first to call him "Metal Wally." Was the first to tell people to leave him alone when he came back to school as an appliance. Wally Stone was teased and pushed down and spit on, and I had my first shoving contest on his behalf. And anyway, he's only little.

Even though he's a not-nice white boy, we're friends. He's got a condition people can see too—his is temporary and I'm Black. He traded with me for his eraser. I gave him a stick of gum for it. But after he took my gum, he told Mr. Hill that I stole his eraser. I called Metal Wally a liar and said I traded for it fair and square; that's when Mr. Hill asked me to prove it. Asked me what I gave Wally for it and I couldn't say gum or else I'd lose more than my eraser.

"I'm just kidding," I said. "I was just hiding his eraser."

"Then give it back to Wally," he said.

Wally whispered to me, "Fair and square." I rolled my eyes. "We can still be friends?"

I nodded.

"Los Angeles is growing fast," Mr. Hill said. "History is dying all around us."

"But aren't we always living in history?" I said.

"We are," he said. "But we usually don't acknowledge it acutely. Not until we start losing things rapidly and suddenly."

L.A.'s population doubled in size the last decade, he told the class. "In just the last eighty years, since Spanish-owned California joined the Union, Los Angeles went from an isolated agricultural village of 1,610 mostly Natives and Spaniards, some Negro Spaniards, into a city of 1.2 million and a metropolitan district of 2.3 million people. Fourth in population in the U.S., second in territory, and ninth in manufacturing. Ours is the most extraordinary expansion in American history," he said. "Railroads bring people by the fistfuls from the east. City boosters promise relief from the hard labor of cold winters and the sweltering summers on the prairies."

I raise my hand.

"Lou?" he says.

"Were there 1,610 people before or after the massacre?"

"Massacre?"

"The native tribes who were here before? The disease and relocation." Mr. Lawrence taught me about it.

Mr. Hill's face wrenches at my question like he smells something bad and the class laughs in one song. I had been on a roll with good questions and now it's over. I'm not teacher's pet.

Mr. Hill turns back to the class. "'There's perfect weather in L.A.,'" he says. "That's what the boosters would tell their prospects. 'A fertile countryside, and above all, relief from asthma and other cold and hot weather sickness. No happier paradise for a farmer can be found than Los Angeles,' they're told. So we have to capture Los Angeles before she goes." He looks at me. "Like the others who went before us."

Mr. Hill promised me and Metal Wally that he'd show us the real Los Angeles. Not only Los Angeles, but the world, and he told us not to confuse his bringing us on for being nice, because he needed at least one student to join the paper with him since it was supposed to be student run and he wanted to stay in his office. So me and Metal Wally and Mr. Hill have become *Jefferson High Worldwide News*. "The paper," Mr. Hill said. We're going to write about water.

Metal Wally wants to write about mind control because he says, "We're all slaves to the government. They're controlling us in the radio," but Mr. Hill convinced him to let go of his radio theory by planting a seed about our water, that maybe the government is putting something in there, and that piqued Wally's interest.

Water is holy here. Los Angeles doesn't actually have any. Mostly. We tap into the water supply of our Northern Californian sisters, so they call us thieves. San Francisco among 'em.

"Domestic water is as necessary here as streets and railways and transportation and jobs," Mr. Hill said. Politicians have been fighting the California water wars for years now to keep our water rights to the Owens Valley, for the city's residents to keep green lawns and to brush our teeth too long. And yes, to drink and bathe. Even farmers have to make a case for their fair share, asking, "Is it a waste of water to grow food?"

Metal Wally got assigned a special story.

The story is about soldiers who came home from the war. France. And he's supposed to go and talk to men who never went to the war. It's Mr. Hill's idea. He said, "Men who aren't allowed to fight suffer too."

Mr. Hill made a rule that we're not allowed to write about Hollywood because "Hollywood writes about itself," he said, "and it ain't journalism. Journalism isn't about being likable. It's about telling the truth, and the truth, like a right decision, will still hurt somebody. Or make 'em hate you. So you have to decide what part of the truth is worth revealing."

"What about the whole truth?" I said.

"No such thing," he said, "because no one person could possibly know it."

Mr. Hill brought us to the archives of the L.A. Times Building. The archive librarian is helping me and Wally find the information we need for our stories. "I'm constantly learning," she beams, excited to show us around, her skin as smooth as her ironed red hair; her thin wispy fingers brush along spines of leather-bound newspapers, volumes stacked on bookshelves, thick as double encyclopedias.

"I want to work here too," I told her, and she didn't lose her smile. She only deferred to Mr. Hill, and he said there are many jobs in the building. So I clarified, "As a journalist."

"Then you'll need to work harder on your writing skills," he said.

"And not be Negro," Metal Wally said.

Mr. Hill took us to the coroner's office next. He said these were our most important field trips because a person's death can reveal a lot about how they lived and who we are as a country and a city. How the poor die of preventable diseases and hunger is a reflection of us. It's the gauge of our national health and civility—how we take care of the least of us.

We have to tell the stories of folks who have no stages and no film to capture them, Mr. Hill told us. The voiceless. "Hollywood tells their own stories in moving pictures. Not like the east. The East Coast creates fleeting memories. New York has stages and eager audiences. Broadway. And if you missed it in person, you missed it fully. What Hollywood captures on film lasts forever."

I want mine to last forever.

Even if I'm Negro.

EIGHT

SARAH, 2102

I've learned you can't wait for other people's permission to accept your own blessed life. Your life *is* magical in whatever way it is. Accept it and be glad in it, despite other people. It'll be over soon. For most of you.

Others will call your joy a fiction or call you a liar or immoral or dangerous for your happiness, but their conclusions are only a reflection of their limited imaginations, their own abilities, their being stuck in their lives. It's not a rewrite of yours.

At worse, their wrong conclusions and attacks are because you threw your pearls to pigs. Throw them anyway.

Throw them if they can help somebody else who's losing hope and being slain, boxed, and labeled by the Limited. Because when you live a life filled with experiences that are true for you and *are* you or are you *now* but are beyond other people's experiences, beyond their boundaries, morals, or courage, even if you're poor, even *when* you're poor, you'll be first feared. Maybe always. And for this, the Limited can become vicious.

Not just to you but to those like you who are trying to thrive in this life they're called to.

So fling your pearls high and wild so they can come down hard and stay for another who needs to hear from you, who needs to survive too. Then brace yourself. You'll be impacted. The backlash won't feel good, but the process that opens the door to another person's freedom rarely ends in orgasm. It's just the right thing to do.

NINE

—◄◯►—

LOU, 1931

We hurry to the theater building with our school bags rattling between our shoulder blades because Esther's the only one who signed up to make show costumes. She calls it a production of garments cause it involves patternmaking, laying, marking, dying, washing, cutting, stitching, checking, finishing, pressing, and steaming.

I help her sew on buttons.

I fix splits, too, even though I'm not enrolled in the class, I do it because she's my friend. Mrs. Miriam and Mr. Lawrence said I should make some Black friends, too, and I will.

We run through the side door and through gray dresses hanging on the washing line threaded across the whole backstage. Dozens of pieces are waiting for us. The director, Randy, throws Esther another dress. She catches it one-handed and collapses cross-legged next to her sewing station. I take her backpack off and set it next to mine on the floor and sit down in the far dark corner in front of another sewing machine. I pick up my first vest. Its seam is split open into a *V* so I dot the thread across it mechanically to bring the letter together like closing its lips into a capital *I*.

Other costumes are bagged and tagged around this room and in the rafters, an excess of colors and greed because hundreds of these will only be worn six times while most students have one set of clothes for school, one for church, and one for playing. All the girls got dresses and one set of anklet socks and none can come to school wearing shorts and pants; those you can only get away with at home.

Esther has already started her ironing, so I got to start mine too. I grab a pile, leave all but one piece on a raggedy chair somebody donated, and press the hem of white trousers. These are for the dance number in *The Ace*. Even though Esther doesn't have speaking lines, she's committed. Opening night's in two weeks.

My iron is lukewarm. I run it over the trousers a few times, feel the place where it was. Not hot enough. I mess with the cord. Wait for it. Hold it in my hand.

"Lou!" Esther says, rushing over to me. "Your hand!"

I drop the iron. "It wasn't hot," I say. She scared me, is all. Esther picks it up, sears her fingertips.

"Let me see your hand," she says, and reaches for me.

"It's not burned," I say.

She pulls my hand toward herself.

"See?" I say. "Not burned. It was scarcely warm when I held it. Did it surge?"

I don't want her to suspect I'm different, the way I suspect I am. It's not the first time something strange has happened to me. I sliced my finger open while cutting collards with Mrs. Miriam, wrapped the spot with a dishtowel, and rinsed the blood from my greens, but when I unwrapped the red rag, no place on my hand was torn. Whatever I'd cut was missing without a trace. I don't want Esther to stay away from me the way folks do Metal Wally.

"Well, don't do a fool thing like hold the face of an iron again," she says. "It's a puzzle how you score so high on an English test and your same brain will let you hold a piece of orange coal."

Not a puzzle, I think. I've never been good at homemaking. Language, like English, is different. Same as tests. Tests are just mirroring the language your teachers spoke to you.

This is not even my only accent.

In the last three months, my accent has changed from Mrs. Miriam's to Mr. Hill's and at least four more. And it's not just how I speak that differs. It's also how my hands and body move and that depends on who I'm talking to, since body language is language, too. I didn't even know Japanese till last Saturday.

After spending the morning with Mrs. Miriam's Japanese neighbor Mr. Ito, I understood his language. Me and my brothers painted his fence, and I could watch him talk to his wife through his open door.

Not only could I hear him, but I could mimic his posture and the way he moved as he spoke. By the time the day ended, I wished him *sayonara*, and he thanked Mr. Lawrence for the use of his children—his helpers— then told Mr. Lawrence my body language was Japanese.

Most people don't like to change. But I don't mind, especially changing language. A person could move from the Virgin Islands to Chicago and keep their "Yah-man." Could be their rebellion. Their pride. Maybe they can't hear themselves speak. But I'm a mirror. My accent changes immediately upon arrival. The one you're hearing now is the one I hear in my head.

Whose is it? I don't know.

"You speak so eloquently," Officer Adams said.

I had been in the waiting area of the police station, practicing other people's body language. But now I'm only speaking like him and it's not eloquent. It's midwestern-poor-pretending-to-be-learned but I think he's smart and wise anyway. It's why I asked him to be my first interview for the paper.

I didn't expect that Mr. Hill would say yes to my interview because it's common knowledge that he doesn't like adults. Or maybe it's just other teachers he doesn't like. "Students are different," he said, and since Officer Adams is the law, "It'll be good for the both of you on account of the poor relations between Negroes and the Los Angeles Police Department," he said. "You never know when you might need an officer's help." But Mr. Lawrence said the police are special helpers who, unlike the fire department, might kill you.

So maybe Mr. Hill was right to say yes to this.

Officer Adams brought me origami. He did both times he visited me at Mr. Lawrence and Mrs. Miriam's. Said children like me who are placed in homes by the government—foster care—go missing all the time.

Today he brought me a crane. Said *tsurus* have lifespans of a thousand years. Longevity, he said, is what they represent. That and wisdom, happiness, and peace. He asked me to take a look while I wait outside his office in the hall so he could finish his meeting.

I sit on the bench in the hallway under plain walls. Policemen are walking past, some with their guns showing, like penises, exceptionally large ones, so I look for Goldie. Goldie's a brown egg of a woman, and if I was crafting in art class, I'd glue a red felt dress on her shell, the kind of red dress she always wears with different shrugs and coats. Her face is mannish but pretty.

I met Goldie at Mr. Lawrence's church, the pastor's daughter. She sometimes does work for the police—I don't know what—but she was off duty and patrolling round the church last Sunday, yelling at two boys, "Keep it in your pants, sinnah!"

I volunteer at the church in the blue nursery room caring for babies and watching other people's children under eight years old during service because no one else wants to do it. Not even the parents. Since I've been attending, I haven't heard a single message from the pastor, but people ask me if I'm a believer. I lie and say yes because I must believe in something.

Goldie brings me candy before she goes into service to take her seat at the organ. She almost always starts with "Amazing Grace," and I can feel her deep notes pluck the walls of the nursery like they were lined with bass guitar strings. The babies and I vibrate inside.

I should be reading Bible stories to the children but I don't understand them, so instead I read the paper and let the children play. I don't have a problem with Jesus. So far, my problem is with his followers.

The weekend *L.A. Times* said the LAPD is attempting to soften its image after the last few years of Chief Davis. Among his accomplishments, it said, were that he hired a fifty-man gun squad in his fight against alcohol dealers and announced that "the gun-toting element and rum smugglers are going to learn that murder and gun toting are not in their best interest," and he would "hold court on gunmen in Los Angeles streets. I want them brought in dead, not alive," he said, "and I will reprimand any officer who shows the least mercy to a criminal."

Officer Adams got a promotion since I last saw him. He didn't tell me. I read that in the paper, too, next to the headline about police cracking down on vice. Mrs. Miriam said it should read, Police Violence Escalates Against Our Communities Again.

Officer Adams is the second in line under one of the deputy chiefs now, and he's already made a new rule that there will be "No propaganda"—no political and campaign posters at the station. And although he himself is a political appointee, he said, "The blue line should not be divided or broken by politics." And I think he's right.

Maniacal Mondays, they call Mondays like these at the station because of the men being released into the arms of wives, mothers, rarely fathers, after their drunken weekends. DO THE CRIME, DO THE TIME reads a poster nailed to the wall. Alcohol is illegal, but cheap bathtub gin is plentiful. Made with socks, water, and decaying fruit. But not all the crimes are public drunkenness.

Some are domestic.

There was a baseball game last night, the Los Angeles Angels, and as usual, as if by cause and effect, women were beaten more cause of game night. Mr. Hill told me not to write the story about beaten women, said it's too personal an interview and it could get me hurt, or worse, and the women can't escape, so there's no help for them in your words.

On the wall across from me, there's a line of framed photos—the last six police chiefs. Every image shows a white man with a straight line for a mouth.

"Ready, kid?" Officer Adams says, walking past me in the hall toward the door. I jump up and follow.

He's got a chessboard under his arm and a velvet pouch dangles from his fingers. There's a brown paper lunch bag in the other hand. "The sooner we get out of here," he says, "the better. Too many greaseballs."

I trail behind him along the sidewalk to the Hall of Records a few doors down, where he lays out his chessboard and takes game pieces from his velvet pouch. People watch us as they pass by.

"If you make yourself less timid-looking," he says, smiling, "it won't seem like I'm questioning you."

A Black trolley driver sees us and slows in the street; he nods his head. I smile. Other people walk up the steps to the Records building and along the sidewalk. A white man with a camera kneels down and snaps our picture.

"I think that man took our picture," I say.

"See," Officer Adams says, ignoring that and showing me a chess piece. "This is the bishop. The spiritual advisor." He sets the bishop next to the king and queen. "Sitting next to the bishop is the muscle—the knights— and next to the knight is—"

"The castle," I say.

"Not a castle," he says, setting the castle down on the board. "People make that mistake all the time. It's called a rook. A rook is a war chariot—heavily armored, with a driver and weapons bearer hidden inside. It's next in power to the queen."

A kit of pigeons swoops down from concrete eaves above us and the wind from them knock the castle off the board. I catch it. "Flying rats," I say.

"Misunderstood doves," he says, and smiles. I give him the castle . . . the rook.

"Doves," I repeat.

"When you play this game," he says, "you have to have a strategy before you start. If you're developing one when you're in the game, it's too late. If the other person gets your king, the game is finished."

"Why not the queen?"

"It's a man's world, doll." He puts his king on the board. "I'll teach you. You'll need to at least know what the other person's move will likely be so you're not putting your pieces in danger if you don't intend to."

"You can put your pieces in danger on purpose?"

"For the greater good," he says.

"Is that what my parents did to me?"

He only looks at me.

He reaches for his bishop and pinches the top of it, preparing to move. "Are you in danger, doll?"

I lift my shoulders. I don't know.

"If you were, you'd tell me, wouldn't you?"

I nod my head, yes, then lift my shoulders.

"This bishop can move as many spaces as he wants diagonally," he says, "but he has to stay on his own color. Anything that gets in his way he can take. Your goal is to take away the most powerful pieces—the ones that can move the farthest. So you keep them corralled. If you want to kill anything, limit its movement and exposure. Even its mind."

"Why can't I remember? If there's something wrong with me, just say it."

"There's nothing wrong with you."

"Then, why did you stop looking for my parents?"

He lets go of his bishop. Takes hold of his knight and moves it up and over—three down and one across, an *L* shape. "Lou," he says like a sigh. "Parents who leave their children don't often double back. That's for the children to spend their life doing. Looking and waiting for word, often that their parents have died."

"They're dead?"

"Don't know, doll."

I move my bishop. He laughs. "You already know how to play this game?"

"I'm just trying not to look like your suspect," I say, and warm up to smile.

After a few moves, he says, "Check."

I move and he says, "Check."

I start to move again, and he says, "You can't move there because you'll be in check again but with another piece." He points to it. "You can only move out of check, or else you might as well forfeit because the next move you're out."

I rest back. I don't want to play anymore. For no reason, tears drown my eyes.

"You're not trying to give up, are you? You really only have two choices here, Lou. Learn to do to others what's been done to you. Or learn from it."

I don't want to play anymore.

"The past doesn't matter," he says. "The past is the past whether it was good or not. Because if it was good, then you know it can be good again. If it was bad, you can change who you are and show people that it doesn't always have to be bad. That's all the past is good for."

"Even for Black people?"

"Sure," he says. "We can be who we want in this world."

I can be anybody I want.

He taps his temple. "Just put your mind to it."

He reaches into his lunch bag and pulls out his sandwich wrapped in wax paper, gives me half. I take a bite. It's beef but not good roast beef like Mr. Lawrence's. A pigeon hops toward us and stares.

"So what's this interview for the school about?" he says.

"Ohio," I say. "My teacher thinks it's good to show that the world is bigger than L.A. And Mrs. Prince said you're a hero from Ohio. Is she your girlfriend?"

"You're a pill."

"I'm sorry," I say. Sorry for being in his privacy.

"I'm married," he says. "Happily," he says.

"Can we talk about the prison fire?"

He winces.

I take out my pencil and paper and ready my hand to take notes. I ask my first question without thinking. "People died in the Ohio prison fire?" I say. "You were there?"

He doesn't answer.

I look up from my notepad. "Is it alright to talk about this part of your past?"

He doesn't answer.

I say, "If you don't remember, that's alright. We can talk about—"

"People died," he says.

"Thank you," I say, and write *people died*. "But you saved some?"

"I brought people out," he says. He reaches into his paper bag again and unwraps a slice of pickle and bites it. His right cheekbone flexes, shifting the light on the side of his face.

"Men were hollering and screaming for help and some of them were praying and some were cussing and praying. I felt too slow," he says. "There weren't enough of us, enough guards. Eight hundred prisoners, all of whom were behind doors that needed to be opened one by one."

He stops talking.

"When did the firemen come?"

"A passerby kept going back in the building over and over again and saved as many as he could. His last trip cost him his life. He's the hero."

"Then help came?"

"Some prisoners had to wrestle guards who refused to open cell doors. Took keys and ran back into the fire to save other inmates."

"Then you went in?"

He folds the wax paper back over his sandwich, unfinished, then squints from the brightness of the sun. Takes another bite of his pickle.

"He was in solitary. Two guards were needed for Daniel Ford Diaz. To open his cell, we needed two.

"He was half-native from his mother. High cheekbones. Green eyes. Golden-brown braids." I imagine gathered feathers. "And he was homosexual," he says.

I cough.

"Daniel was just two months into eighteen. Was caught with a boy a year younger. Statutory rape by an adult of a minor. Got twenty years. Child molestation."

I know what child molestation means.

"The arresting officers were up in the mountains that night looking for bootleggers. Had planned to give it just an hour and be home to their wives by dinner. Decided to split up; one went east and one west.

"Officer Boyd was the one to first approach the boy's car, gun drawn and alone, and he didn't rap on the window. Instead, he shined his torch-light in quickly, then ducked. Nothing. Then again. That time, there was movement inside. And that second time, he stayed and watched. The boys were unaware.

"And Boyd had mistaken Daniel's long hair and thin frame for a woman and signaled his partner with a flash of his torchlight to come see.

"Months later, his partner distanced himself from Boyd, as did every officer at his station. His partner would testify on the stand at trial that he was called over by the boyish glow of Officer Boyd. The incident would cost

Daniel Ford Diaz his freedom and Boyd his career, his manhood, as he saw it. Got reassigned to the jails.

"It was Boyd who stood at the closed door of Daniel Ford Diaz's cell with me. And through the slit of that door we both saw Daniel's green eyes, his face still swollen from beatings, and Boyd had a choice. To turn the key with me or not.

"He let him burn."

I look at the chessboard and pretend I'm thinking about something else now. My next move.

"April 21, 1930, was the worst prison fire in United States history. Three hundred and twenty-two prisoners died. Your move," he says, and I reconsider the board. It's just a blur.

"You won't tell that story, will you? Good," he says without my answer.

TEN

<del>◀O▶</del>

LOU, 1931

The city of Boyle Heights is not a church but has a congregation of believers who've responded to its altar call. It's the most racially and religiously mixed neighborhood in Los Angeles, and what they believe in is the promise of the American Dream, an idea not limited to race, religion, tribe, or culture, we're told. Esther's father built his boxing gym here.

Below us on his canvas floor is heavy breathing and coordinated fists punching through the air; the sound bounces off walls like the patter of bird wings.

Bodies of the fighters are sweat-shiny and chiseled, the hairs on their head shaped into crew cuts. Some boxers are in t-shirts, some with the shirt-sleeves ripped off. Guys are hitting the bag. Other guys are inside the ring. Coaches are hanging over the ropes.

They're not training. Mr. Lee is the only trainer here. "Most trainers," Esther said, "are veteran fighters who got out of ring just in time, so my dad still has all his faculties."

Right now, he's preparing Jones for a sparring session because sparring partners get trainers too. Three rounds.

It rained most of January and February, landslides and flooding, because even our land doesn't know what to do when water falls from the sky. And nobody knows how to dress for it either. We're mostly drenched runners, awkwardly moving from door to door—bus doors to school doors, car doors to house doors. But now it's March and sunny and hot, and me and Esther got her umbrella, which I call her sun-brella because she didn't put it up to get it wet. "It's for the sun," she said, and it's summer temperatures, head-in-an-oven hot outside.

We're the only girls allowed in the gym. We sit under the red L in the painted letters in MR. LEE'S BOXING GYM, doing homework, and this is how we finish our school days together.

The big fans in here are only blowing the sweat-wetness around—a stew of body runoff and leather that'll stay on me till I get home. I'll smell it again when I start the shower.

We don't eat the same food anymore. She's been eating grass. What I call grass. She's vegetarian now.

Mr. Lee wants Esther to give up acting for college. But she's talented and she's got a chance. She's won costarring roles in every school production since last year, one with her wearing whiteface and a blonde wig. Got a standing ovation, I heard, and her performance kept people laughing. If I would've been there, I'd have been the loudest because she's my best friend, my sister, and nobody is better than she is. Especially on the stage.

Mr. Lee's in the ring wearing his beanie and jacket even though it's hot. He's yelling instructions to Jones: good points, bad points. "You're moving good," he yells, "but don't stay in the pocket too long. Move out of the pocket! You're staying too close all the time. Use your jab and set him up! Everything comes off the jab. Your whole fight comes off your jab!"

Sometimes I practice their moves. After hours and late at night when they've all gone and the lights are low, I'll make an opponent of the speed bags that hang from the ceiling. I'm not fast and my wrists are weak.

Once Mr. Lee found me that way, practicing. He didn't see me before turning up the lights, and when he did, he didn't say a word. He simply walked over, shifted my stance by knocking his foot into mine till my feet inched over, then he lifted my hands and went on.

I was better for it.

Esther untwists the cap from her thermos.

She's been sipping from it since she disappeared to the bathroom before we started our homework. I thought it was melting ice, but the heat has brought out an aroma of sweet wine. When she comes back, I'm already laughing. "Are you drinking?" I say, and look over my shoulder to see if anybody heard.

"Sometimes," she says, "your dad is gifted an expensive bottle of wine that he keeps in his office. It's from a castle in Italy."

She's drunk.

"And you think to yourself," she says, "your dad won't drink this. Won't know it's gone. There are others. So this bottle must be for you, and now is the time to enjoy this bottle. But only one cup. But this is your fourth."

"Will you stop talking in second person, like *you* is not you?"

"And because the wine is so perfect," she continues, "and tastes so much like a real plum, a fruit fly comes out of nowhere and dives in. You cross your eyes to see him in your cup, and you can't drink anymore." She eyes the contents of her cup. "You watch him backstroke through your pool of golden sweet liquid, dossing around. You call him a drunk bastard . . ."

"Maybe he's not the only one," I say, laughing through the next bell.

Down on the floor I can tell who's training for what. If it's a real sparring session, I can see it from how they're hitting the bag, how they're moving around. I can tell the hangers-on too, people just coming to look like fighters, and I can tell the real old-time professionals too—journeymen. They're so-so fighters used to bring a prospect up. A prospect is a fighter who's done well, maybe as an Olympian, and is talented and could cross over and get the big money, but for now, the journeyman's job is to make a prospect look good.

A prospect's record is twenty wins, no losses. But a journeyman is thirty wins, twenty losses. He'll have a lot of skill and experience, so you want a prospect coming up to face a journeyman. As time goes on, you put the prospect up against stronger competition. Journeymen will fight him good but not hurt him. Mr. Lee doesn't want to hurt his prospect. He has a new one. He's talking to him now—Wilkerson—about the big fight that's coming. His journeyman steps into the ring and Mr. Lee says, "Let's go, baby. Put him through the paces."

The fighters use sixteen-ounce gloves for sparring. They're bigger gloves than the ones in a match. Can punch hard with sixteen ounces and won't anybody get hurt. Bruised but not hurt. Some trainers put resin in the gloves because heavier gloves make the hands quicker. Not Mr. Lee.

In a real match, the gloves are twelve ounces. Matches go fifteen rounds. And when it's over, fighters usually have major cuts under their eyes, bruised lips, closed eyes, cuts around the front of their face where the skin spread and tore. Men fight through concussion. Concussion in the ring means you can see the fighter is off just a little in his step. He doesn't want to be off.

Some fighters had cartilage surgically removed from their nose before the fight, so they can get hit in the face without getting their noses broken. A trainer will throw in the towel and stop the fight if his fighter is bleeding too badly. Might be from a twelve-ounce-covered fist or the constant butting of heads.

In sparring, a trainer doesn't want a real injury. Certainly not a knockout. And in practice, the trainer is the one who dictates the day, what the fighter is going to do. But the fighters already have an idea of what's coming. What he's willing to give of himself that day. One has a mantra: "Suffer now and live the rest of your life as a champion."

A trainer with the best fighter can keep him fighting. So fighters have to stay in shape. Might get only a day's notice of a fight. And sometimes, Mr. Lee will send his fighters to one of the major fighting camps in the outskirts of the city—Ventura, Oxnard, San Bernardino. Vigorous training. Run, breakfast, nap, bag work, sparring, training, dinner. A spartan life, Mr. Lee calls it, because sometimes you have to leave the city to see what you're made of.

Women and wives aren't allowed here. Neither is alcohol or cigarettes. It's potatoes and eggs to keep the weight on, and steak for protein, to stay strong. And no matter their condition, the fighters have to have heart. And if I could choose the kind of heart they'd have, I'd choose one like Henry Armstrong. He's a fighter who's been beaten from St. Louis to L.A. but keeps coming back. Didn't make the Olympic team but went pro anyway, defying naysayers who taunted him about his losing streak. But Armstrong knew the only way he'd truly lose was to believe them, to allow them to keep him caged and incapable of breaking out of who he needed to be for them—a loser. But he wasn't a loser. And now on the occasions he wins, people will respond not with applause but "I remember the time so-and-so kicked his ass."

Fighters are a commodity. Boxing is big money. And the American Legion or the Olympic Auditorium is where the big fights happen here. Celebrities from the studios, like Clark Gable, invest in fighters and make money. The mob, their prostitutes, and those "connected" are into the fights too. Sometimes those connected come to the gym to watch the sparring before they bet on the matches.

Wilkerson is out of the ring now and Mr. Lee's assistant, Aaron, has hold of his hands, taking his gloves off for him, wiping him down. Aaron is new, a white boy who gets in the ring and goes through the paces with fighters and comes out without a single mark on him. They go too easy on him, so now he's too confident and thinks he can train fighters here. He's listening to Mr. Lee now, taking it all in while Mr. Lee greases his next fighter's face, puts on his gloves, and gives him instructions about what to do in the ring. The day might come when Aaron'll become a main trainer. That's what assistants hope for: that at the right time, he'll have his own stable of fighters. But for now he's a gopher who never interrupts, who wraps hands, makes sure there's water.

Aaron's on the canvas warming up a journeyman. He's slow and unco-ordinated, just walked into somebody's perfect punch, and me and Esther cringe, draw up our shoulders, and cover our mouths. It nearly floors him. On his knees, Aaron reminds me of someone I know. Maybe one of my brothers. A trick of lights.

Mr. Lee is shouting at Aaron now. He's staying out the ring, but af-ter the fighters spar, his job is to massage them promptly, their arms, their hands, and his job is to know which of the fighters hit the heavy bag first and which now need to go to the speed bag or jump rope. No matter the order of the wind-down, they all end up with his rub-down after the bell dings three times. The bell is the timer. At the end of the timer, both fight-ers go back to their respective corners, and today it's clear that both fighters gave it their all. All heart and determination and smarts. And above all, a strong jab.

"Your jab comes off of your lead hand," Mr. Lee said, and showed me and Esther four times before Esther started drinking today. I imagine it reminded her of her sister. The way he'd trained her. But Esther said she's always been slower to learn than her sister.

"The lead hand is the hand out front," Mr. Lee said. "The one closest to your opponent. The one he can see. But your power hand is the one in the back position. When you use it, when you generate your power, use your hips." To show us how to move our hips, he put both his hands on mine and then Esther's. The whole gym seemed to stop and look. I was embarrassed. Esther was beet red. "When you get in close," he said, putting his body near Esther, "generate your power! Use your right hand," and he shifted his own hips to show us. He swiveled left, then right, then put his hands on our hips again. "See, swivel, left. Right!" We both did. "Power," he said.

ELEVEN

●──◆──●

SARAH, 2102

Power is neither good nor bad. It's how you use it. Power can be misused, especially by leaders who want compliance, not commitment. Commitment requires shared dreams, connections, mutual respect, earned relationships, valued input, and allowing unique participation. Compliance is "do what I say do"—a dictator.

I've seen power throughout my lives. When I see it now, a chill rises up my back from my hips and then rests on my shoulders like a shrug made of ice. I have a reaction. I'm not the only one.

Our old lives reveal themselves through quirks. I've still got some of Lou's. They can come like noticeable ticks and anxieties, sicknesses and fears. My ailments almost always have to do with my wrists, passed down like genetic memory. Except it *is* my memory.

Once I was institutionalized—insane—wrists chained to my bed till they bled. Once as a prisoner. Once, a slave. This time as an inmate being transported to maximum security.

Once, my wrists were impacted by cancer; the shooting pains began at my elbow.

Once, a lover braided a bracelet of blue beads for me. I wore it even after I married someone else.

I'd tell you my wrists are weak and my injuries are engraved inside of me, but my doctor has said I have carpal tunnel syndrome. He says it's from holding my hand at the wrong angle for too long, sometimes falling asleep that way. "Stop doing that," he said, but he doesn't know better. He doesn't know how our bodies, our blood, and our veiled memories keep the score. My healing, now, is a matter of reminding my soul to put old postures and symptoms in the past where they belong.

"Everything you can do illegally in the United States, you can do legally," Mr. Lawrence said as he drove me to the bank. When he's done, he'll drop me off at school, then drive a block to the middle school where he teaches.

He keeps his money at Freedman Savings Bank. "A bank," he said, "that once helped freed slaves transition into capitalism, from *being* capital to becoming capitalists. But American capitalism will always require slaves of some kind. Don't chose to be one," he said. The bank lends to coloreds now with two years' proof of employment and a house to lien. Mr. Lawrence has both, but he said he grew up poorer than poor in Texas. "My life choices were simple. Make money legally or not legal," he said. "Want to sell drugs? Become a pharmacist. You want to rob a place? Work for a lender."

"So you could rob people?" I said.

"Naw," he said. "So the government and corporations can rob me less. And I'll teach you about money so you won't be afraid of it. So you'll learn to give your money permission to take care of you. But also, you need to learn to think critically."

"Read?" I said.

He looked at me, proud, then repeated, "Yes, read," and I pretended to be proud, too, a good girl. Told him I was excited to go to Bible study tonight, and Goldie, the preacher's daughter, was going to pick me up.

Instead, she snuck me and Esther into the Dunbar's live show an hour ago.

Jazz notes scatter across the floor and through the dark here, some float, and me and Esther are pretending this is our usual. Our under-aged eyes are traced in dark liner, mirroring what we thought other women did in here, but most only wear lipstick that makes 'em look like they're wearing a plump vagina on their faces.

We walk awkwardly, heels and all, like newborn calves, the same way I move when I'm around Metal Wally. My lower back and legs will feel weak when he's near, and Esther will tell me I'm rude, tell me to stop teasing or else one day I'll have children exactly like him. But I'm not teasing and I'm not having children. I don't want to be a mother.

That Esther isn't Black isn't a problem for Goldie. Or for anybody here, because Goldie's the kind of woman who wakes up in the morning waiting to be offended.

She wants somebody to say something off-putting so she can let 'em have it. And if Goldie didn't like you, you could be on the verge of a small disaster. That's what happened to a bar patron who called Esther a bad name. Nobody saw what Goldie did or how she did it—we only heard the thud and turned around to see the man out cold next to the bar stool. And there was Goldie, our chaperone, her large body swaying above his, gloating. "Give me a minute," she said, smiling. "You gotta lick your teeth when you finish eating."

Goldie protects us. She's a decade older than we are—twenty-seven—and since Mr. Lawrence and Mrs. Miriam have misplaced their trust in her as the pastor's daughter, they've given her charge over me, to lead me in the ways of the Lord, and apparently the Lord knows how to party. "My daddy grew up on a potato farm, made potato vodka for the whole family and neighbors and their babies, preaches his Sunday sermons after a fifth. Shit, in my family, you've got to be an egg in a really big pickling jar to have a problem with alcohol."

But alcohol is illegal.

She still always manages to have it, same as the Dunbar. The mob pays good money for police to look the other way, even for Negroes.

Goldie's tooth is where her name came from, a gold cap on her front one. When it fell off the other day, that tooth was gray. She raised the money to get it refitted by digging ditches and she said, this way, her money is always where her mouth is.

"Can you taste that tooth?" I asked her.

"And my tongue," she said.

"You can taste your tongue!"

Me and Esther got matching heart tattoos for Esther's seventeenth birthday ten nights ago, illustrated under the haze of dim tunnel lights and lit yellow candles that danced below Chinatown. Tunnels run for miles under our city, where pushers run rum and drinking dens.

We were there for Esther's first tea-leaf reading. The idea behind it was to drink the tea; while you did, your movements or spirit or some such affected how the leaves swirled, so when they settled, the shapes would be unique to the drinker. That said, I didn't want to go in.

I walked with her up to the mouth of the maze of underground L.A. and Esther took my hand and pulled me in. I made it easy cause it was her birthday, and now I'm not sure if it was my hands balled into fists or the loud bang behind me that made me duck and swing at nobody, or my outburst, "Get back!" that made her want to comfort me. "We have to be careful of hidden dangers," I said. "Nobody would find our bodies in here."

She looked me in the eye and slowly pulled my fists down like a lever, said, "We're alright. Take a deep breath. You're alright. Lady Barren Shirin is just up this way."

"I don't trust her," I said.

"You haven't met her."

She was haggard and dangerous looking, as I expected, and when we sat down in front of her cross-legged in the tunnel, she raised her middle-aged, long-time-smoker hands above her head and moved them in a sort of performance—dance hands. Her sleeves and dress were like a series of stitched headscarves, red and gold. A pile of tarot cards was beside her on an upturned bucket. I watched her closely as she packed our cups with herbs. "The leaves are a divination tool," Esther whispered.

Soon Lady Barren Shirin was considering Esther's leaves, told her she'd be famous, work in Hollywood, be a star. It was everything Esther wanted.

I didn't drink from my cup. There's nothing I needed to know.

"It's my birthday, Lou, just play along. Don't you want to know something? At least your past? Your family?"

It was her birthday.

After Lady looked into my cup and saw my constellation of tea leaves disappear before her eyes, all of our eyes, she seemed more curious. "Is that supposed to happen?" Esther said.

Lady tipped down the corner of my cup to hold it in the light, then shoved her fingers to the bottom of it, twisted her wrists, and wiped the porcelain to a shine. When she pulled her fingers out, she examined them, rubbed her thumb slowly across all her fingerprints. Nothing. Our time was finished. Without a word she started packing her black box of leaves.

"What's wrong?" Esther said.

"The leaves are no good with her," she said.

"Then tell her future with your cards," Esther said.

She tossed her pile of tarot cards into her bag.

"Then do that," I said, pointing to the paper sign affixed to the wall behind her that read TALK TO YOUR LOVED ONES. THEY'RE NEVER FAR.

"You have no past," she said, throwing her arms up, her scarves rising like shed feathers.

"Doesn't everybody have a past?" I said as she stood, and laid a hundred dollars on the table, my whole savings.

Her feathers settled back on her body.

She struck a match, touched it to the tip of a candlewick at the center of her table. She waved me and Esther closer.

"Tell me about your father," she said.

"I don't know my father."

"There's a man here," she says. "He says he's your father."

I shake my head.

"Well, he says he's your father. You want my help or not?"

"Yes," I said. "I want to know my blood family."

She closed her eyes. Moments later the air seemed to tug at her expressions as if tiny strings with tiny balloons were attached to her cheeks and lips and eyes and forehead, then a violent wind blew them all away from her face.

She began speaking words that weren't English or, strangely, any language I'd ever heard. She called out to my past in English as if all of it would come sprinting down the tunnel to bowl me over.

When she stopped, she opened her eyes and, her hand shaking, she slid my hundred into her blouse. "I'm sorry I can't help you," she said.

I grabbed her arm. Not for a refund. I wanted to know what she saw in her mind's eye. But she only said, "I'm sorry for you, *mija*. Death is better. And also irreversible."

Esther pulled me away. We went to the next cavern, where a man took his painful needle and shot ink under our skin between our thumbs and index fingers. Esther dared me but I would have volunteered. I needed to feel that pain too.

I'm hiding my tattooed hand from her. Keeping it under my long sleeve in case anybody sees it. Specifically Esther, because my tattoo's missing.

The morning after, it smeared away with spit and my thumb. My skin bore no mark of the needle. Just like it didn't with the hot iron at school or the knife in the kitchen with the collard greens. I didn't have the heart to tell Esther she's the only one with a tattoo. So ever since, I've taken a black fountain pen and drawn it back so our love sign can be permanent.

Goldie's friend Sylvia is meeting us tonight. Sylvia hadn't been expected to live. Not after she lost the baby. Another one. Not after a grief like hers. Her electroconvulsive treatments meant passing currents through her brain to reshuffle her deck of cards, to give her new luck and a fresh hand, but Goldie asked me and Esther not to mention it. So I don't tell Sylvia what I'm really thinking when she arrives—that I think it's aces she got lightning to her face and survived.

Goldie's friend Barbara is how we got into the club tonight. Minimum age here is eighteen on account of the minimum age for tobacco and just walking in these doors brings lungs full of smoke. I like it. It relaxes me.

The doormen and hosts didn't pay attention to our age anyway because Barbara is pretty. Barbara's like Esther: more slender in the butt than most Black men prefer. Still, Barbara got the most beautiful, plump, green-eyed Black man in L.A. to marry her. He's also cheap. It's why we're snaking through this crowd and now along the back wall where people are waiting to be seated. We paid the cover charge for the live band that's playing, but Barbara's husband, Darnell, is coming in free.

Barbara opens the side door and lets him in. He is cleanly dressed, running his fingers along the lapel of his shiny suit coat, pulling it down and pressing his hand along it. His skin and hair are moisturized, only outdone by the shine in his shoes.

The notes from the jazz band pour into the audience from the dimly lit stage. I notice for the first time that I'm the shortest of our group and have to look up at everybody. Esther's a foot taller—taller than most average-sized girls in our high school. She elbows me in the shoulder. "You see Vera over there?" she says.

"Where?"

"At the bar. Next to the slap head."

"Slap head?"

Esther looks over her shoulder toward the shiny brown globe of a bald man having a drink at the bar. "Don't you just want to slap it?"

I laugh a little, shake my head so I don't encourage her. Remind myself to be cool since we're breaking the law like Vera at the bar. She's a grade younger than us. Her back is out and her dress is hanging just below where a bra strap should be. Her spine is shooting a column of dashes down her back.

Esther elbows me and points to Vera, gives Vera a once-over, not with condescension but like she's going shopping over Vera's body, commenting on Vera's nice belt, her dress, her earrings. Esther will have found every piece by week's end and on Saturday will wear 'em to her next party.

"We need a booth," Darnell says over the music. He signals to the host like he is a VIP and a girl comes over and sits us in a preferred spot near the stage because he and Barbara are good-looking. Youth and pretty are currency in Hollywood, and being next to it is just the same. Everybody wants to look good.

The hostess leaves glasses of water on the table and when I pick mine up, condensation wets my "tattoo," and my heart smears to an oblong circle. I switch hands, hide the other in my lap.

Darnell and Barbara sit across the table from me and Esther, and they're already necking and sucking face. Goldie bumps them over, sliding onto their side of the table with a scotch in her hand. "You know how I hate sitting with the door at my back," she says.

I feel smaller now. At the table Esther looks older. She could always act her way into any age or maturity on stage and now here, taking out a cigarette from a silver case like she's an old spinster, like she don't give a damn what anybody thinks.

"Y'all are going to kill yourselves with all that smoke," Goldie says. "I need me some different liquor. Waitress!" she yells, searching the room.

"You gon' get us arrested," Darnell says, "and this place shut down, ordering liquor the way you would a pork chop."

"They know me in here," Goldie says. "Waitress!"

Esther rolls her shoulders with her eyes closed, seat dancing, swimming in jazz notes.

Goldie eyes a man standing too far away to hear her over the music. "Well, hello, hello, hello, Mr. Good-Looking," she says, then asks me, "You think he's packing?"

"You're asking me?" I say.

"I need to get laid," she says, not waiting for my answer. "And he looks ... friendly."

"You have to look at his feet to know," Esther says like it was nothing, like she's still in her old woman character. "Be a doll," she continues, "and hand me that napkin, will you?"

"That thing about small hands and feet," Barbara says, "is a lie because my Darnell ... "

"You're nasty," Goldie says. "Nobody wants to know about Darnell."

"Look how he's walking," Esther says. "If something's small, it's his shoes. They don't fit him. His toe knuckles are bulging like his feet are stuffed in there."

"Ain't that nothing, horse hooves," Goldie laughs. "Prancing around the club like he's a big shot."

"So the answer to your question is yes," Esther says. "He's packing something. Just not the way you thought."

"Hello, Mr. Mare," Goldie shouts across the room.

They're all laughing now. Both these women. The whole table. But Darnell won't 'cause he's a man.

"Where's your brother?" Barbara asks Goldie, changing the subject.

"Work," she says. "Always that."

"But I've heard the fire station's restricting time," Barbara says. "Layoffs and things. There's a new captain and—"

"He was headed to the fire up on Larch when I left," Goldie says.

"Must be bad if they sending Negro firemen into the white neighborhoods..."

"Why don't you drink my scotch," Goldie says, and slides it to her.

"I don't drink scotch," Barbara says.

"It wasn't for you," Goldie says. "It's for us. To buy us some silence."

"You don't have to be rude, Goldie," Barbara says. "See, you're why I don't have female friends."

"You shouldn't be proud of that," Goldie says.

"What?"

"To have no female friends. If women aren't choosing you, which they aren't, it means they don't trust you and you're probably controlling in your relationships. They see who you are. I believe women."

A scramble of jazz notes spit on us from the stage, drawing our attention. It's Black giving to Black, myself being reflected back to me.

PART TWO

TWELVE

SARAH, 2102

I've decided to accept the court's help of a public defender because I lost.
Not my trial but my bail hearing, where the prosecutor surprised me (and
the court) with a copy of an old travel itinerary with my name on it.

"I planned the trip before!" I said, then stopped myself.

"Before what, Counselor? Remember," the judge said, "anything you
say can and will be used against you." So I didn't say anything else. Didn't
say what I was planning or describe all the places I've been and will go
again; couldn't disagree with the judge when he called me a flight risk, then
remanded me to prison custody to make sure I wouldn't flee the country—
as if he could stop what happens to me—and now I'm on suicide watch. I
thought I'd try something new.

Prison guards had to cut me down in the nick of time, they thought,
minor rope burns around my neck. I don't recommend it. There are other
escape hatches in life that aren't suicide. If you're going to be a flight risk, let
the destination be the place where you get better. *You will get better.*

And anyway, you don't have to be suicidal to be suicidal. There is also *I wouldn't take my own life but I don't mind not being here.* It's called passive suicidality and there's nothing wrong with you unless you're ready to stop gambling with your life and can't. Cause what you're doing is self-aggression: *I won't wear my seatbelt while in a speeding vehicle. I'll have unprotected sex with strangers. I don't care if I get that disease. Don't care if I die from that chemical high, that jump, that combat. Not really.* Various extremes, and if yours is not listed there, fill in the _____. We all have at least one way we cope poorly.

"Have you wished you could go to sleep and never wake up?" the prison doctor asks me. She says this is my assessment.

"No." *Truth.* Sleeping for me is fighting fever dreams.

"Have you had thoughts of ending your life?"

"What I did wasn't accidental."

"How often have you had these thoughts?"

"More than a hundred years."

"I think you mean days? It's best we're straight with each other."

"Alright."

"Have you thought about how you'd do it? If you'd try again."

"What are my other options?"

"To live," she says. "You could choose to live. You don't have to be hopeless."

What does she know about my kind of hopeless? Or living? And contrary to popular belief, suicide requires so much hope. It's faith in the goodness of an unknown *after.* Or that there's nothing at all. But I'd say it is faith equal to a religious conviction. A belief that death will end suffering and that death won't put you back into a miserable new life, handing it back to you differently. Because the universe recycles *everything,* leaving me stranded in the longest single day of my life, extended over centuries, every deed and every experience repeating itself in a number of familiar ways.

In 1989, I'd lived in the same house for almost ten years with First Husband and there is where my passive suicidality began.

That night, I had just opened my front door and was, in my usual fashion, going to take out the trash for Monday morning collection and there it was, at the edge of my front lawn—a spotlight from *beyond* ready to abduct me. I was amazed at that bright light. It was everything the dying had described.

Without hesitation, I dropped the trash bags from both hands and ran toward my ever-after light, tripped and fell somewhere between the front gate and the middle of the lawn, and then slid the last part of the way toward the sidewalk, into its glorious beam, and with tears in my eyes and a mouth full of turf, I cried, "I'm ready! Aliens, take me! Correction. Kind, nonprobing, and loving God, take me!"

And that's when I heard First Husband behind me at the gate. "Honey?" he said. Our second baby, just nine months old, was saddled on his hip, bouncing to the music video playing on the big screen inside, Def Leppard's "Pour Some Sugar on Me."

An empty tin of baked beans rolled into the side of my husband's slipper. With concern in his voice, he said, "Are you alright?"

At first, I wasn't certain how I could hear First Husband calling out to me since he was, to my understanding at that moment, very much alive and I was gone into the light where hair band music should've also been.

"Honey?" he said again. "Do you need help?"

I sighed when I reached the only possible conclusion—I was neither dead nor asleep.

"Oh, look," he said, as I stood to my feet, unaided. "After all these years, the city finally got our streetlamp working."

LOU, 1931

We didn't throw our hats in the air at our graduation ceremony. Once Esther found out that her sister wouldn't be back from China in time to see her leave high school, she said the hell with it. I'd been saying that all along.

We stood tenth row back on the grassy football field with three hundred other graduates who had to find jobs, find a wife or a husband, join the army as their fathers and brothers had; if another war comes, some should expect not to return. Esther and I, we're unemployed.

"We're born into adulthood," our school principal said in his speech. So we were expected to be law-abiding citizens, capable and whole. All of us graduated with a similar understanding of the world—whites like cream, at the top, the rest of us somewhere below. Most of us had four years to be taught the same history, the same science, the same American worldview. Girls in home economics, boys in wood shop. This is what's expected of us.

When our class of 1931 was announced, Esther and I put our hands on our heads, pressed our graduation berets flat as we could make them, slid them under our black gowns, and walked off the field. We got wasted at the park, alcohol "borrowed" from Esther's dad's collection, a homemade gift from the wife of one of his fighters. Two months later and me and Esther are trying to keep unemployment from becoming a habit. Watching the fighters from morning till noon is one we want to keep, though.

Every day before we look through the paper for *real* work—hers not-an-audition and mine not-writing—we meet at the gym at 10:00 a.m. The fighters are on their third round by then. It's not even noon and already the summer-hot August is making our bodies sweat, drenching our clothes in this ninety-degree 10:00 a.m.

Down below on the canvas, Mr. Lee is training a fighter. He's on the side of the ring and his head is bobbing as he talks. "Look, son," he says, "you've gotta thread that needle." *Thread* means to hit straight through the body of the other fighter. "Thread him like you can come out the other side."

His fighter's body is a moving statue, bendable only at the joints. He's listening, taking in Mr. Lee's instruction. "When you go to his body, his head will follow," Mr. Lee says. "Go to his body, his head will . . ." *Follow* means his head will lean to the side that was hit. "Then hit him in the body!" Mr. Lee says. "His ribs and kidneys. Give him those rib shots. Break his ribs off!"

Rib shots force a man to bend at the waist and cover his body, bend his arms at the elbows, move side to side. So Mr. Lee will say, "Start rattling shots off of his head. And don't forget to work your defense." That's bobbing and weaving and circling. Semicircles with your upper body, under and up to get out of the way of punches.

Mr. Lee is sixty years old. He looks younger in the face, but the hands don't lie—they're wrinkled with age spots and with zigzagging bulgy veins. His body is fit and his chest and arms have muscles under thin brownish skin, only slightly wrinkled, like a crumpled paper bag.

"Get your hands up!" Mr. Lee says at the starting bell.

Fighters move forward to meet at the center of the ring.

They're dancing now.

"Get in there," Mr. Lee says, "stay in there!"

They're throwing punches.

"Thread that needle!" he says. "Make him know who you are, son. Hit him in the kidneys!"

It's the blood I hate. I cringe when I see its color. Recoil like I hear it screeching, full of sounds.

Esther and I sit face-to-face, both of us holding an envelope with both hands. After weeks of job applications, I've been wanting to see what kind of work I could do. Esther still wants to act, still wants to be a star, and if Hollywood was smart, she'd costar in their next talkie. But I'm betting on the theater for her. A lead at the Orpheum. I'll walk to Ninth and Broadway every day to see her.

"You tell yours first!" I squeal at Esther, both of us smiling hard and holding our separate letters like reins, opened but folded.

"No, you first!"

I read over the letter quickly. "I got the job at the *Times*!" I say. Esther shakes my shoulders, celebrating my hair loose from its barrette. "Officer Adams wrote me a recommendation letter!"

Esther's joy flattens. "That guy . . ."

"What? It's the beat reporter job I wanted."

"Then I'm glad he's finally helping you."

"We'll see the whole city together! Pick you up from the college theater stage and we'll use my press pass to get into whatever event you want. The big fights! The Olympics opening ceremonies are next year. We can watch the buildup."

She carefully opens the letter in her hands. "I'm moving to Europe, Lou," she says.

"What?"

"Touring five cities," she says. "Vienna, Prague, London . . . I've been cast in *The Mikado*. The leading role. Calls for an Asian. I'm her!" She screeches with joy.

"Does your father know?"

"Lou? I'm going to Europe." She waits for my good reaction. I want to be happy for her. But I don't want her to go.

She folds her letter and shoves it in her bag. "Anyway, I'll be home in a few months," she pauses. "Let me be the one to tell my father. Don't steal that from me too."

The bell sounds below us, three dings, and both fighters go back to their corners, and immediately, in tandem and as if on cue, we sit up straight together and cover our noses with our dress sleeves against a smell like charred toast and burned oil and vinegar feet that's snaked through our window, mixing with sweat in here.

Screaming immediately follows from across the street and in through our window; an apartment door is smoking. It's Mrs. Rubio's place again. It's not the first time. She's caught things on fire before when boiling jalapenos with carrots and onions to pickle.

Esther is already outside on the sidewalk helping Mrs. Rubio out of her building. I can hear the bells of the water wagon not far away, but it's not a real fire they're coming to—it's smoke—and when the firemen get here, they'll see and remind Mrs. Rubio not to leave food on the stove, ask her for a jar of peppers and about her daughters—the ones she left with her husband—and if she'll join them in Mexico. "This is my country, my home!" she'll say.

I lean into the open window, ready to hear everyone deliver the same old lines. I don't know what Esther could add to the script except, "Look at me, some fancy-pants touring actor, abandoning her best friend for five cities that can't find their own Asians." I roll my eyes.

The firemen are coming down the street now, but they aren't the usual crew. The shield on the front of their wagon has a big number four. Not from Boyle Heights. They're all Black men from across the bridge. Four miles they've come from South Central L.A.

I run down the bleachers, watch them from the front door of the gym, amazed by them doing white jobs but Black like me. They stop out front, across the street. One of the firemen is speaking Spanish to Mrs. Rubio, telling her not to worry. He asks if there's anything she wants out of her apartment. He doesn't mention Mexico or her daughters. He stays with her while the other two disappear into the smoke.

Esther crosses back to me, leaving Mrs. Rubio with the miracle men. "You could've come and helped," she says.

"I will next time," I say. "Mrs. Rubio'll be fine."

Aaron, Mr. Lee's assistant, comes over to watch too. "There was a fire this time," he tells us, but we never asked him, so we just stare at him for interrupting our presence. "I guess they've already put it out," he says.

Aaron's a strange bird. Before Mr. Lee hired him, he'd turned him down three times and refused to train him. "White boys have other places to be trained," Mr. Lee said. "Many places. For us, this is all we have," and Mr. Lee wasn't going to waste space on someone who already had everything.

"Hello," he told me the day he came to interview. His greeting was unexpected.

"You talking to me?" I said. He only smiled. "Hi," I said, and hurried along. His favor toward me wasn't going to help him with Mr. Lee.

But Aaron's become close to Mr. Lee since then, always up under him. Aaron's here before daybreak, gone after midnight. He might even live at the gym, but Esther says he has an apartment nearby. She saw him walk into a place on our way to Mr. Lawrence's house off Central, where these firemen are from.

"I swear he's the spitting image of the rabbi I see at Canter's," I told Esther. "Ashkenazi Jew," the rabbi told me. "Same as Albert Einstein," he said, and it mattered to the rabbi where he was from—somewhere in Eastern Europe—but I don't care. I don't even know my own origin. It's been almost a year and it doesn't matter. I'm here now.

A loud crack comes from the canvas like halving an old baguette in your hands. Me and Esther cringe at once. It is the unmistakable break of bone and now the screaming fighter.

Aaron and Esther run to the ring. Mr. Lee joins them there. I only look on from afar—don't need to live with the sight of a splintered human bone piercing through the skin like it should be an earlobe.

Aaron fills a white towel with ice while Esther rushes outside, hailing the firemen before they go—a faster ride to the hospital.

I walk to the ring when the arm is covered.

Stand on the ropes.

There's nothing to do but wait.

Three firemen come with haste, too fast. The back of the helmet of the one out front reads J. CLAYTON.

He kneels next to the fighter, who's writhing and holding his arm, and draws his lips in and makes a whistling sound. J. Clayton waves his yellow-gloved hand and calls to another fireman for help. His eyes gloss past mine and my body becomes pig iron at the bottom of the ocean.

The room stops, except for him. The whistling stops. My presence weighs everything down.

J. Clayton looks at me again. Looks past me. I see his eyes. Everything around me is slow and floating in water like a bubble escaped from one nostril, ascending to the surface of the water. I can see him. Really see this J. Clayton. I take him in and recognize him in my lines, the ones I've drawn—my wrists feathering the downward slope of his eyes. His lids bigger and puffier—an allergic reaction—the same as they are now.

The contour of his dark freckles lies lazily in a strip across his nose like where a bandage would be if he broke it. I could never draw his jaw line, always made it with shadow. His nostrils flared, perpetually with a look like fear. His chin lighter and more pinkish-brown than the blush of his cheeks.

He's out of proportion for the artist's standard at school, his nose slightly wider than where the inside edges of his eyes should be—one eye slightly askew. And he's taller than the average human—eight heads high—but he's neither average nor an ignorant standard that somebody adopted as truth.

He is perfection.

"There you are," I want to tell him. "I remember," I want to say. A dream, right in the daylight, while I'm fully awake. It's cold now in the heat of this gym, against these ropes. The hurrying of those around me blurs like seeing underwater. Except for him. There's gravity in this moment pulling me under, dropping us through the floor, somewhere below the canvas, a basement room, barely lit, where we're swimming. No, I'm swimming and he doesn't see me. He's calling for gauze. The others join him at the canvas again. They are the haze, replaced now with a memory of a dream. It engulfs my present. A trick of time and I am inside a memory, not a daydream, and I am not afraid.

I am standing in a darkened theater. It's me but not me. I am a Senegalese-born German woman. It is Berlin and I've long completed architecture studies at Technische Hochschule in Dresden. The city is electric with possibility, a golden age for artists, for social extremes fueled by competition and a new reality. Berlin is now the third-largest metropolis in Europe, behind Paris and London.

At night, the bourgeois and the urban rich—rich in spirit and adversity—walk together under the green glow of streetlamps. It's why I came. To be broken open. To be overcome with color, and color expressed in art. My uncle lives here. He takes care of me. A professor of science, he believes that women should live free.

I want to dance. To pursue what I've always desired, to be who I was always meant to be. Late, but when you think it's over, that you've gone as far as you can, "Take one more step," my uncle said. I'm doing it at last. Ballet. But I am old. I am thirty-two.

Stage lights from the front of this small theater are covering me. The lights are not for me. This is not ballet. I am in the crowd, a face in the audience, but I arrived only a moment ago, an hour late, and the readers have begun.

My eyes adjust to the darkness and I can see that all the seats are taken. I can't find the friend who invited me, so I move unsteadily through the standing crowd into an opening between a pair of strangers, lean against the sidewall, and let my shoulder bag slide down my arm.

A donation pouch moves through the crowd and I take stock of my bag. See if lost coins are ready to be recovered. This bag has my whole life in it: ballet shoes, old event programs, and, yes, dull coins.

The room has become one creature. They applaud together, then fall silent, every head moving simultaneously now toward the stage for the next reader. No one is moving now, not talking, only waiting, affected by whatever they've just heard. I want what I've missed, to be of one mind with a writer and her words.

The sparkle of light through his glass of water is how I first notice him in the audience. The glass is raised to his lips and his head is craned back. He's sitting across from me. A young man. No, a boy, about seventeen or eighteen years old, and he looks like my first love but that was fifteen years ago. This young man would have had to walk straight out of my memory, un-aged. I smile at the thought of it—he's giving me another chance and in this chance he's still brown and beautiful. But a poet now. My man could never find the right words. Especially on paper.

The young man sets down his glass and he's called up to the stage to recite his work. "This is new, so please bear with me." He's smiling now, lifting me with his charm. His poetry is intelligent and measured.

He seems kind and says something funny, but my chuckle is short because I don't want to miss a word. As he speaks of love, I see fire rise behind his melody and hide. Too late. A wet stream of bright orange and yellow swims through the audience, searching. It's here with me now. I step in it. Let it undress me, shirt first, as I listen. I feel exposed standing next to these strangers. Blushing. Treading in warm water. Can they see me?

My imagination flows without restraint now, a memory within this memory, and I remember a different past, further away. How he smelled of heated sugar. He glowed like Swiss caramel in dim lights, the rosacea on his cheeks, his neck, reminded me of a garnishment of rose petals.

"There might be a salve for that rash?" I told him the first night I was introduced to my man. I needed something to say. His sister, whom I'd known for only a few weeks, had left us standing in front of the bakery while she collected day-old bread.

"It's a birthmark," he said, already moved on from my question because he'd been asked it many times before. I would later learn that the red blush was deeper than his skin's surface, maybe deeper than the bone, and when I pressed down on it, it remained unchanged, like it was sitting on the other side of a windowpane.

"Can I touch it?" I said.

"Are you a doctor and not a dancer?" he laughed. "So you've lied to my sister?" I loved the warmth of his smile. It was a bright crescent moon on the shelf of his jaw, rolled on its back, edges pointed to his eyes full of stars, dimpling with constellations.

"Just let me see it," I said, shyly but more forceful than was my nature. I noticed his body was flat and with no dimension, a wire hanger for the clothes he was wearing. I was curious.

"Alright," he said, watching me fumble around the top button of his shirt. He should've walked away from me then.

Until that moment, I couldn't stop myself from touching this stranger, my mind was already set in its ways toward him, to need him, to expect that he'd let me do what I wanted—a small measure of control—and what I wanted that time was only to move his collar. To let me see his rash properly. Six months later, he'd tell me he was "attracted to my erratic behavior." I was a game to him, and in his game his job was to stop me. No, to make me wait. So that night, he caught my hand in his, then smiled and said, "I'll let you see it. But only if you promise to kiss it when you do."

A week later, I remember sitting on the floor while he played short bursts from his trumpet and his music cried.

I remember our conversations about life and who we were. His theories on how Egyptians were able to build the pyramids. "On rollers or low gravity," he theorized. He was good at making bullshit captivating.

Now, here on the stage as this lookalike reads, I am feeling love for this stranger. So handsome and poised in his new clothes. Not him—my man would have never worn those.

The young man returns to his seat to applause—not mine, because now my memories have progressed, and I'm caught in the loneliness again. Standing in the rain, knocking on the front door of his sister's house outside of the city. The countryside.

Through the window, I could see them at the table eating dinner. I begged him to come to the door. "Just talk to me!"

I remember being sorry. So sorry. Why was I sorry? I thought we had an open relationship, at best. "Loyal to what?" I said. "When were you going to tell me?" I said. "I don't even know what *this* is," I said, because he never let me be secure in him.

So with my cheek pressed against the peeling paint of his sister's closed door, I whispered, "Because . . . I love you."

I was drenched in falling rain. I surrendered to his no answer when I heard his sister's voice, "Please invite her in. At least be a gentleman. She's your friend and it's raining."

He didn't.

I walked toward the station in the rain, coughing from a cold I'd been fighting, and I remember being silent to everything else but regret and shame. I remembered all the things I wish I'd said. Or said louder. Things I wanted him to say to me so that I could be sure this time. Be sure that this was an ending.

Then right in the middle of this remembering, I'm startled. I'm in the theater again. The young-man-lookalike-poet is standing next to his chair just in front of me. He asks if I want to sit down and I am amazed by him. This memory alive.

I stutter, "No . . . no, thank you," and feel a phantom burning in my throat, prompting me to cough and cry but I won't. "Thank you for asking," I say, and wish he would have asked me that fifteen years ago.

The heat of this gym confuses me. *This is real. This is now.*

My stomach lurches from unexpected time shifts of memory, of place, of being regurgitated from the pit of the ocean. I don't know anymore.

J. Clayton is lifting our fighter to his feet now, the fighter's broken hand cradled against his chest. And I watch him leave—my past and this present in one.

Without me.

THIRTEEN

-◄(O)►-

LOU, 1931

Mr. Lawrence was walking from the parking lot to his classroom and stopped in front of a light post there. A man walking by said he caught sight of Mr. Lawrence waving for him to come over. He thought to say hello since Mr. Lawrence had once taught his daughter. But before he got to him, Mr. Lawrence fell against the fence post. He was coughing strangely and taking deep breaths. His eyes rolled.

The man tried to help, pressed on Mr. Lawrence's chest, sat him up, then down, but his aid was useless. Mr. Lawrence was having a heart attack, and he died before he reached the hospital. A terrible thing for a stranger to witness and worse for me to know. But I'm glad Mr. Lawrence didn't die alone.

By the time I got home, Mrs. Miriam had already returned from the morgue. She was in the kitchen washing dishes with her back turned to me. I took a step forward, opened my mouth to speak, but when I heard her sniffling, I just turned around and went to my room.

I'm sorry. He was good to me too.

I've learned that death for heart attack victims doesn't have to be inevitable. So I've decided to write my first article for the *Times* on the first successful open-heart surgery in America, which was performed in 1893 by a Black surgeon, Dr. Daniel Hale Williams. Maybe it'll foster hope for people. It's what Mr. Lawrence would have wanted for his students. It's the least I can do for him and Miriam.

Three weeks we prepared for his memorial service. Before we left the house, Mrs. Miriam looked over all her children—me, the foster—as we darkened the doorway—Black—and were all dressed in black. She rubbed her son's collar to straighten it, then rubbed and straightened it like she was automated even after it was fixed.

When she finally got a hold of herself, she wouldn't look at us. She told us we shouldn't mourn Mr. Lawrence the way other people would. "His children should celebrate his life like he would've wanted." And now, we stand side by side in the church, my brothers and sister between me and Mrs. Miriam—honoring her wishes, tearlessly, like dry statues. His children pocket their tears and let them overflow back inside themselves, drowning while standing.

The pastor is already at the front of the church, a beautiful young man, newly married, maybe twenty-five. He's sitting in a throne of a seat at the back of the riser, a church stage, and below him in front of the stage is Mr. Lawrence.

His casket is like a narrow black piano with the top open and a body inside. It's him. Bunches of blue flowers line the casket where piano keys would be. I can see his face from here—the tip of his nose.

People are walking up to the casket, some gazing on him lovingly, for too long in my opinion, holding on to the side of the coffin, mumbling words to his painted face. Why would anyone want to touch a coffin with a dead person inside unless they were paid to?

A line has formed now, five deep. A mother and father are holding the hands of two children, maybe eight and nine, their eyes widening as they get closer to the front of the line. I bow my head and pretend to be praying when Esther joins the line.

I don't dare to turn around to see if the church is full or to take attendance—who came and who didn't—it's not my business to know. But a woman has rushed to the front, holding Mrs. Miriam's black-gloved hands. I don't look at her face.

I close my eyes and pretend to be praying again. The woman holding Mrs. Miriam tells her she was Mr. Lawrence's student eight years ago. She's going to law school now.

My hand is pressed by someone standing next me, uninvited. It's too moist to be Esther's so I don't open my eyes.

A man's voice—a white man's voice in a room of Black low tones—says, "I'm sorry about what happened to your father." I wish I wore gloves.

By the time I opened my eyes, he was gone, and a song began on the organ and the whole church stood at once, their feet together, a whoosh of one hundred single steps at once.

Goldie sits on the organ bench playing. "Nothing sad," Mrs. Miriam had told her, and they decided on "It Is Well."

The pastor on the stage closes his eyes and begins singing along.

I like him. But I think he's too young to hold his role at church without sinning. The mourning single women here in our front row are proof, myself included. We watch him closely as he mouths words to the song, his suit jacket open to the dents of his chest, his shirt snuggly fitted. He buttons his coat's middle—we don't need the hymn book cause we're reading him. And what is sin anyway? A finger-wagging, holier-than-thou killjoy, nitpicking small personal misdemeanors while ignoring major injustices?

I've thought about this.

Well, him. And my prepared excuse for our future moral failing. I shut my eyes to help me quit my honest thinking.

As the song closes and the pastor takes his place at the podium, all of us ladies smile at him, almost forget it's a funeral. I can't tell you what he's saying about Mr. Lawrence or the ever after. He punctuates his lips and his last sentence with Mrs. Miriam's name, pulling me from enchantment. It's her turn to deliver a few words about her husband.

She looks out over the church and, judging from her wide gaze from left to right, there are many people behind us. "Thank you for attending," she says. "My husband would have been pleased."

She tells us she'll read a poem, one written by an English priest, Henry Scott Holland, because "This is Lawrence's homegoing celebration. Death is just a transition to a better place. We transition twice. Once when we're born, something we have no memory of, and again when we die. Both should happen with excitement and not mourning."

She unfolds a sheet of paper that had been tucked inside the wrist of her glove. She reads:

Death is nothing at all. It does not count. I have only slipped away into the next room. Nothing has happened. Everything remains exactly as it was. I am I, and you are you, and the old life that we lived so fondly together is untouched, unchanged. Whatever we were to each other, that we are still.

Call me by my old familiar name. Speak of me in the easy way which you always used. Put no difference in your tone. Wear no forced air of solemnity or sorrow. Laugh as we always laughed. Play, smile, think of me. Pray.

I don't know how Mrs. Miriam let go of him so easily.
I know how I did.
I let him go of Mr. Lawrence by beginning to forget him already.

FOURTEEN

LOU, 1931

This is what it must be like to be a Black woman and lose. To not be able to grieve publicly when tears are called for. To not be comforted by someone who'd hold us as if we were as fragile as a white woman. We're expected to be strong, denied of gentleness. *She can take it. Just leave her alone.*

Maybe it would worry people to see a Black woman crumble. Would be the most pitiful thing. *I haven't seen Mrs. Miriam cry yet.*

I've only seen her anger.

She told me I can't do another drive-along with Officer Adams. Can't bake him cookies with her money anymore. "He harasses Black people. He doesn't deserve what you give him," she said, claiming I give him more attention than I do my own family. But Officer Adams said I'm like a daughter to him. He said I'm like family no matter my race or my past. Not Mrs. Miriam. Before Mr. Lawrence passed, she was still following up on leads about who I belong to, talking respectfully to somebody over the phone,

"Well, if you hear anything else," she said, "you can reach me here," like she was trying to get rid of me. Mr. Lawrence never would.

This morning, she invited me to sit at the table with her even though she says I've been sitting around the house too much since school ended. "Find something to do," she's been saying.

I cleared the breakfast plates this morning and walked the children to school before eight. I have been *doing*.

But since I've been home for an hour she's been sitting where she is, at the table in Mr. Lawrence's chair. She just called me in here, too, so I'm in my same seat to the left of her, where two stacks of newspapers are nose-height on the table before us.

"You need a pencil?" she says.

"No, ma'am, I got a pencil," and lift the one from my dress pocket. The one she gave me the first day I came.

"You have your scissors?"

"Yes, ma'am." We're clipping coupons, and the *Los Angeles Times* is on top. I'll start work there next week.

I place my first two clippings between us—a dozen eggs on sale for ten cents, potatoes fifteen cents. She picks up the last coupon I cut for cookies on sale—a box for ten cents—and she crumbles it into trash. For the boys, I'd thought.

"We don't need store-bought cakes," she says. "Just circle the ones you think we need."

I find oranges on sale, twenty cents. That's five cents off. I draw a square around it. Cross it off because branches of the neighbor's persimmon tree reach over into our yard. That's citrus enough.

I run the lead softly down the left side of the gray page of advertisements, leaving a faint line down its center. I circle cantaloupe. We don't have melons. Circle raisins and cheese but cheese is cheaper at the dairy. We can always use flour.

"You're a grown woman now," Mrs. Miriam says just as the snipping of her scissors stops. "Got your high school diploma. Educated."

"Yes, ma'am."

She starts snipping again.

The right side of the page is selling cars. Buick, Ford, the Plymouth Model 30U. They are a marvel. Can't live in the sprawl of Los Angeles without one. Henry Ford was a genius, you ask me. First to mass-produce cars on an assembly line, creating something affordable for most Americans. I trace his new model shown on the page: FORD V8 CABRIOLET, 65 HORSE-POWER. CAN OUTPERFORM EVERY COMPETITOR. COMING SOON!

I put a whole circle around it, and again and again, because I've heard if you want something you should circle it seven times, the way Joshua walked around Jericho in the Bible before the walls came tumbling down and the city was his.

Mrs. Miriam reaches into her left pocket and pulls back a barrel of dollars, wrapped round themselves. I only glance at it. She says, "This equals a fraction of Mr. Lawrence's pension."

I circle bread.

"It's six months' rent for the apartment on the corner. Mrs. Devore says the tenant's moving back east and it'll be available by week's end. It'll help you get started. Start saving for your own property. Women need property of their own. Even if it's a parking lot." She keeps the money out in front of me, wags it in front of me. I know what she's trying to do now Lawrence is gone. I don't reach for it.

She drops it on the table.

She starts clipping again, harder and faster than she needs to.

My sinuses throb like they're fighting a cold. My nose runs and I don't give it the dignity of tissue. I wipe it with the back of my hand. It's blood. And it's left a shiny red streak across my skin. I wipe again.

"You should take care of your nosebleed."

"It's fine." I put down my pencil, rub my hands over the blood till it's gone. I say, "You and Mr. Lawrence promised to adopt me."

"He can't keep that promise now, can he?"

"*You* wanted to adopt me."

"And you didn't decide, did you? You didn't say yes to us. Just wanted to play a game with us."

"I just asked for more time is all."

"To do what? Did you even look for your family?"

"Mr. Lawrence wanted to help me. You said—"

"We said *we* wanted to adopt you. Together. He's gone!"

I've never heard her yell before.

"I can't afford you on my own," she says, "and you need to make a life. Your own family. Can't have two mothers here."

She pushes the money toward me. "There's your fresh start."

I look down at my paper and circle the car a fourth and fifth time. Six and seventh. I don't want my car to get away from me. I circle it again. Harder than before. Restart my count.

"You want all his money, is that it? You want what you haven't worked for? What's for his children? I'm helping you."

"I can help bring in more income. Help with the children while I work my new job."

"What are you doing to that paper!" she says.

I look down at the table. Paper's shredded—words and car and all—crumbled into a gray and black pile. I drop my pencil, the graphite is done, its wood splintered into my writing fingers, a ragged hole torn down to the dinner table, my place setting ashes. I didn't realize. I brush it away.

"I'm not leaving," I say.

Her breath shudders.

"I have a job coming at the *L.A. Times* and I'm not leaving."

I go back to the coupon for oranges. Circle it.

She rests back in her seat, reaches in her left pocket again, returns with another fiver, and lays it on the pile of money. Tears are already streaming down my face and I don't look up to beg, "This is the only family I've got."

"I'm not your mother, Lou," she says, hurting me. "And by law, Lawrence wasn't your father. And now that he's gone, I got to pick up the pieces and count what's left."

I'm on my own.

Again.

FIFTEEN

LOU, 1931

Esther drove me to an apartment with Miriam's bundle of money in my purse. She told me not to look yet when she took my hand and walked me up the cobbled stairs to a wood landing.

I heard the front door before I opened my eyes. "Don't open 'em yet," she said, so I balled my fists, stood jittery there, and for a moment wondered if the landing or if something might surprise me with a knock to my big forehead. Maybe I'm always worried about my head. My mind.

Esther draws open the curtains, running them along the rail. "Now!" she says, "Come in," and takes my hands, pulls me toward her. "Look outside," she says. "Take in all of Boyle Heights."

My breath catches.

The blue skies are like water, washing its tint over the city and smells of Sunday stew.

The empty field across the street is green and fenced. Young boys are kicking a ball. Street cars below run in both directions, the streets wide enough for drivers to make grievous errors and survive. Each black car is shaped like a duck's bill with four wheels, each holding one man only, occasionally two, inside. There—a woman in the passenger seat stares straight forward. "I love it," I say.

"Isn't it to die for?" she says.

Four miles from South L.A., from Mrs. Miriam and her sons who aren't my brothers.

"Take your coat off, this place is yours," she says.

"Mine? But how?"

"You're prepaid for the year," she says. "I hope you don't mind. Mrs. Miriam asked me to help."

Heat flashes across my chest and rests there, spreads over my body and dissipates with her excitement. She wanted to help.

"Come see," she says, waving me over to my kitchen. "You can bake all you want and for whoever you want."

"How did you get the landlord to lease to you?"

"Who said he leased to me? Having a man's name helped you. I was merely the agent for my client Lou. Here are your keys, Mr. Lou Carter."

"Carter?"

"You didn't want to go by Mrs. Miriam's name anymore, did you? And I liked Carter."

I can't believe it.

"Close your mouth, sissy. Here are your keys."

I don't know what to say.

"Open this cabinet. Go ahead. Open it."

She disappears to another part of the apartment when I open the blue-painted door. Inside is a single plate and cup and bowl. She opens the bottom door—a baking pan, kettle, and pot. In the drawer are utensils.

"Furnished," Esther says from another room. "What are you going to do for protection? We both know you can't fight."

"I've got my cap gun."

"Still?" she says.

I follow her voice into the bedroom, where she's opened a curtain.

"My good luck," I say. "In the right light, my gun looks like a .22. I'll keep it under my pillow!"

"You know what they say about pointing a gun at somebody in L.A. You should be ready to kill 'em. And sleeping on it is worse. You'll shoot yourself in the face."

Esther sits on a small table in front of the window, posed with her ankles crossed, her short blue heels like gumdrops.

"Who said I'd want to kill anybody?"

"Well, you can't now, can you? With a cap gun, you can only threaten 'em to death." She taps the wood tabletop. "You like it?" She spins round and puts her feet on the back of a bench seat. "Well, come on," she says. "My family's housewarming gift to you."

I've never had a writing desk of my own. Its legs are iron.

"My mother thought it was perfect. My father said it's true." She stands to the side to let me through. "One of a kind. An antique from Georgia. 1850s."

"It's beautiful," I say.

"Go ahead and sit down." My hesitation is my delight. *One of a kind.*

I pull out the bench and scoot in, run my hand along the oak top. It's smooth. This bench is pine. Its fragrance rises with my movement. Even dead wood lives.

I tuck my hand in the compartment under the desktop where papers and pencils would go—plenty of room. I don't have any pencils. "And this is from me," Esther says, holding a small box out in front of her smile. I take it, and she leans back against the wall. "I didn't have time to wrap it."

When I lift the lid, the sweet water smell of new pencils rises and shades the pine. "Yellow pencils," I say, touching every one with the tip of my finger. Mine have never been painted like royalty.

"Legend has it that the color yellow used on pencils represents wealth in China where the best graphite is from," she smiles. "But those are from Jersey City. A close second."

Light from the window strikes the razor sharpener, drizzling white lines inside the box.

"The paper's acid-free," she says. "The clerk from the art store promised this stationery will last a lifetime."

I get up and hug her, run into her with my arms and body. "I don't want you to go."

When I finally release her, she throws up her hands and I see the tears in her eyes. "What's a few months," she says. "You'll be head of the paper by then, you hear?"

I smile.

"So you'll have to promise to keep me in the headlines. Make me a star."

But she already is—the truth. And she leaves for Europe tonight. Truth.

I stand in my new apartment window with this thin glass between me and city life, caught alone behind the pane. Tears roll down my cheeks without me giving them permission, a bad weather pattern stirring inside me, raining down on Esther's gift of place and the precision of sketching tools and I'm sorry for it.

Esther stands behind me, wraps her arms around me, her embrace speaking to me in a language I've never heard. She's my family and she'll miss me too.

SIXTEEN

SARAH, 2103

What is it I'd want to tell you about jail, the food? That's not something to remember.

But there are some things to keep hold of: Trust. Respect. Loyalty. Respect, above all. If women in here behaved the same way people do on the streets—their threatening behaviors like driving angry and cutting people off, a random middle finger flung in the air, an inconsiderate remark, a foul tone, or some other casual insult—they wouldn't survive in here long or survive well. Even *we* know the basic requirements of human decency.

I've decided to practice kindness and to live. Live actively. I've written enough about death and cruelty to last me lifetimes. There was only one time when I thought I could change things. Spark some insight. Lou's stories sought to do that, make people care, make them notice when one life passed from this realm.

Can you imagine thinking that writing could change the world? It's what the young believe. What my first brother believed. And maybe I still want to believe again too. Maybe it's why I can't abandon my yellow pencil, scrawling my memories on these prison walls, the highest corners already filled with lost languages. They're my confessions that'll never be understood now.

I learned to write this one when I lived among ruins in Spain. That time, the year was 1507. First Brother and I were hiding together, our Moorish brown bodies golden under the Spanish sun. He was fifteen years older than I was—a father, an uncle, my mother all in one.

Moors, along with Jews and Gypsies, were being hunted down and killed because the land was losing its kings. There would be new royalty, and Muslims had had their moment, they'd told us. For six hundred years we had subdued the land but by then our claim to the land was gone. It belonged to their god, they said. But my brother said our god was their god too. I disagreed. I said the land belonged to itself.

First Brother has always walked with a limp. He was born with his hip askew, dislocated in the womb after his ankle tangled around his mother's heart during labor, he said. She died offering her organ so he could escape her birth canal alive.

I remember eating rice with First Brother in our room above the plaza in Triana, Seville, not far from the river. Triana was abandoned during the fighting; its cobbled streets were speckled with colorful tile, not blood. "None of this is ours," First Brother told me as he limped toward an opening in the bricks where we could see our brightly colored city through the wall. "We'll leave before winter," he said. "Before the flooding comes."

We were the only ones left in the city. Our cousins, my other brothers— forty-seven of us had dwindled to three and my aunt had been gone for days by then. "We should have left with the Jews when their homes were taken," I told First Brother.

"And where would we have gone?" he said.

"Better than wandering, afraid, in the remains of other people's riches."

First Brother and I spent our days committing words from a book he called important. Not holy. He carved the copied words onto a bone. A horse's femur. I kept mine on a tablet he risked his life to wash and dry, exposing his presence at the river. He told me, "Every time the future speaks our words, our language—algebra, alcohol, alkaline. Chemistry, cipher, checkmate, influenza, typhoon, orange—they are resurrecting us. Not our bodies but our minds."

I had purpose in that life, those transcribed words and caring for him after we didn't leave by winter. And I failed him. I'd been working on the tablet inscription for almost a year. First Brother trusted me with it, but after two hundred and ten days of writing, it shattered while I carelessly danced by candlelight. Even now I can't unsee his heartbreak for me. All of the heartbreaks we shared.

"Everyone is gone!" I said, collecting the broken pieces.

When I stopped crying, he laid his hand on my back. "We still have this one," he said, holding up the femur. "You can know how many seeds are in an apple. But you cannot know how many apples are in a seed."

In the coming months, floodwaters rose in the city. For many lives I didn't remember First Brother. Being reborn was an erasure.

LOU, 1931

It's been two months of death at the *Times*. My beat as a new employee is to report on the tragic deaths of colored people—all shades of brown: Chinese, Japanese, Mexican, Indian, Native American, and, depending on our country's mood, Irish Catholic.

Death should be front page, center, for the way it changes survivors. Tragic death is bad for the dead, yes, but for the living left behind, death changes everything. That is what I try to write about.

My office is in the basement. Officer Adams said it's cause I'm new, not cause I'm Black. "Not everything is race," he said. "That's what the trouble-makers want you to believe. Truth is, people like to keep their distance from death, the paper too. Who wants to acknowledge the inevitable?"

I think he's right, and I think people who work in hospitals and traffic enforcement should know best. Maybe it makes sense for them to want to keep Black patients separate from white ones. It's to keep us near Black doctors . . . who are separate from white doctors, and doctors need to get to their patients quickly. Health and safety workers must know how fragile life is, don't they? How how is life here one moment and gone the next for everybody. Most of us only *hear* that a person has died. Unless it's a spouse, or an imposing mother-in-law, or, sadly, a parent, or a séance of children standing around a hospital bed, we don't usually see people when they go. Makes me wonder *if* they really went at all, trusting what other people tell us. Trusting the reports.

Even as we walk by closed caskets, we have to trust that there's a body inside and that the weight the pallbearers bear is skin and bone. And on the occasion we do look inside, we see a person transformed by somebody else's makeup, somebody else's hairdresser—by someone who never knew the man, woman, or child. Her hair not right, the nose and eyes not right. It's her dress, yes, his suit, yes, but our friends and family are not looking like themselves in these death masks, in their own clothes. And on top of that, we're fooled into thinking our dead have shoes on.

They don't.

What else are we lied to about? What else are we assuming? It could be anybody in there. And without even the dignity of their traveling shoes.

Today, I'm writing about Mrs. Olivas.

I take my notes out and lay them across my desk and write: *The car was a 1923 Chevrolet Superior, notorious for its fragile rear axle. It could've been leaking oil. She pulled her five children from the burning wreckage before being caught in the door.*

Mrs. Olivas had been burning for so long and so thoroughly, without help, that when the firemen pulled her out the next day, she was only a frame of blackened bone: a hero to her children with no place to pin a medal. Not even a thread of red hair survived. Nothing red that could be mistaken for her dress or the lipstick she wore the night before to meet her husband.

She had gone to Raymond's Pharmacy & Soda Shop in South Pasadena, ordered a pop and a sandwich for herself and for each of her children, and laughed with Mrs. Tanaka, her family friend.

That night in Pasadena, I write, *Mrs. Olivas and Mrs. Tanaka were there to celebrate Mr. Olivas's homecoming. He had been in South America doing business deals and ran into an old business partner in South Pas. He asked his wife if he could stay behind and said, "I'll be just a minute." Then kissed her goodbye.*

Mrs. Olivas drove home, hoping to get the children to bed early so she could spend time alone with her husband, but on the way, a tree walked right into the road in front of her car just as she had turned to swat at her arguing children.

The tree must have wanted to look inside their black metal box, to hear what the children were arguing about. Something silly, the tree must have decided, because just after that, and just after the ensuing accident, the tree returned to its spot on the side of the road.

No, that's not true.

I erase my last paragraph and start again. The tree never moved. But my first version sounds better to me than her swerving off the road, distracted, and hitting it head-on. A tree that would take her life and scar the lives of her children forever. I want to change it back. But we have no power over death. These bodies have an inevitable appointment.

My editor, Morris, called me to his office. All eyes were on me as I dragged myself inside. "Close the door," he said. I did.

I waited at the door. He said, "There may not be a such thing as objective truth, but a tree moving is plain fiction, Lou. Do better. True and truth must meet somewhere." Then he laid my second story across his desk. "This, I like," he said. A story about a Negro and his unfortunate death in the San Fernando Valley of Los Angeles: Tarzana.

In 1916, I wrote, *Merritt Adamson Sr. and his heiress wife, Rhoda, whose parents were the last owners of a massive Spanish land grant in Malibu, built a state-of-the-art dairy in the valley called Adohr Farms. Adohr was Rhoda spelled backward.*

Rhoda's clean-cut Adohr milkmen competed with the milkmen from dozens of dairies. These food Santas delivered perishable necessities and sweet treats to thousands of customers on hundreds of routes. Bread, milk, and ice cream. And like their cousins the postmen, Adohr's milkmen braved dogs and flirty wives, and on occasion they'd have to maneuver around car accidents that always accompanied California rain.

Carl was a Black man and on his first day as a delivery driver he failed to pull out of the lot. Dead as dead on takeoff. The excitement of his new job and new income for his family proved to be too much for the Philadelphia-born boy who'd already invested in the day with his clean white coveralls and new haircut. His heart stopped right there in his driver's seat.

I titled his story "People Die Every Day in L.A." But seeing it on Morris's desk made me think I should have called it "Carl the Driver."

"Where's your heart, Lou?" Morris says. "You write something decent and kill it with your title."

The Death desk is the most important desk in the room for colored people, Morris once said. He told me I could make Black lives important: rescue them from the past and help them live again.

Morris has been the editor at the *L.A. Times* for thirty years. He hired me because he said the *Times* needed a change and my writing was good enough. "You are teachable," he said, and then made a point to tell me that he was doing the whole Black community a favor by hiring me, by giving me a chance. I'll be honest. The same can be said for white folks. I'm not sure who he's giving a favor by hiring white people with no experience who can't put a sentence together.

Like Metal Wally.

Metal Wally wants the job I've got. Not just because I'm Black but also because I'm a woman. He's healed from his impediment of metal braces and the name I gave him—now he's just Wallace Stone, a blond white guy who speaks with authority whether he knows what he's talking about or not—but to me he'll always be Metal Wally.

We've been out of school less than a year and he already pretends not to know me. The first time I saw him in the office, he had the gonads to ask me—no, demand—I bring him coffee, like I was his disrespected wife or a poorly treated colleague, not a friend from high school.

It's like his mind was erased through one of his conspiracy theories that I used to think were harmless. He spent three weeks of summer in the Midwest with the father—the man who'd left him and his mother for a new wife, the wife his parents wanted his father to marry before he chose his momma.

I heard Wally tell somebody else that he saw his father happy and with new kids—twin boys—the ones his father should have had all along before he made the mistake of marrying his momma, and now his father has a steady job, he's going to church and living a right life—a different man and father than the one who raised him.

I imagine Wally came home feeling like he was a proven mistake. How else could his father be living such a good life now?

My guess is Metal Wally is trying to prove himself now. Make a name for himself and become whoever he thinks is greater than his daddy. And that man, it seems, would not be friends with Negroes. So we don't talk anymore. That's a good thing, since his conversations to others are more of his conspiracy theories, lacking the complexity and empathy that the high school paper tried to teach us—didn't work on me either. But between us, Metal Wally is the worst.

His whole train of thought has been reduced to simple themes. "The world is simple," he'll often preach to the reporters. "Every story is simple. Every solution is simple. It's intellectuals and politicians who complicate things." He'll summarize what he sees as a problem, then give a short answer. "Immigration? Simple," he'll say. "Mexicans stay home." And "Inalienable rights?" he'll say. "If Blacks and women get all the rights that I already have, then life will be worse off for me—simple."

I've seen him pull up a chair at somebody's desk and explain, "If somebody's getting more of something, it must mean I'm getting less." He went on to say in his longest explanation yet, "Two groups can't be getting more at the same time. You can't add people to your dinner table and expect you'll have more food. Simple. Rights are not a real cause anyway." But before he finished his statement that time, a war vet who'd surrendered his legs in the fighting near France lunged at him. I caught his wheelchair, kept it from rolling away.

The newsroom is loud now. Reporters from all districts, columns, and specialties yell and disagree about politics and life and water rights and Hollywood stars and Europe and the president and the president again; what the starlet had on, what actor married who. "That's what readers want," Susanne in Entertainment argued, wanting to bump China from the front page again.

"No, important issues only. Route 66 is progress," another reporter says, then claps his hands together. "Boom! Finally, a way to drive a straight shot from Chicago to L.A."

Route 66 has been called America's Main Street. And the Mother Road. And more than half of it lies in Indian Country—roughly 1,372 miles. Tribes had used those dirt paths for generations before the government paved them over and called it a highway.

Now, it's traveled by automobile, motorcycle campers, adventurers, and immigrants fleeing the Dustbowl and Depression. Members of New Mexico's Acoma Pueblo and other tribes are expected to sell pottery from roadside stands. It helps everybody, they tell us. Route 66 *will* be built. The only issue now is what path it'll take.

In all proposed outcomes, Route 66 will knife a smiley face across the mouth of America, extending its natural edges from Illinois down to Missouri, then farther down to Oklahoma and Texas, then upward to New Mexico, Arizona, and then California. It'll bring more money and jobs to the city, but whole communities will be displaced; our colored and poor communities will be displaced. The people who are fighting are fighting to keep the path from running over their bodies.

Chinatown would be moved to make way for Union Station. The Chinese graveyard would be uprooted and moved to Boyle Heights. If the Depression has shown us anything, it's that racial tensions are the inevitable result of scarcity, the same as it was with no food and no jobs. The niggers and immigrants *must be* the ones responsible for any lack. And by "immigrants" they don't mean the obvious—that they are too. The only people not immigrants here are Natives, millions of former American slaves, and their descendants.

So jobs will be taken by the new white people coming to town, and they will be promised protection against *us*, sold a bill of goods that we're all vice and sex, uncivilized. That means new neighborhoods will have to be built for them while ours become zoos; housing segregation, which the mayor just calls "the housing restrictions," means Jews, Blacks, Mexicans, Chinese, Catholics, and Eastern European are at risk. I feel most sorry for the white ones, if you could count them victims too. They're white-skinned but not white enough yet to be embraced. White Anglo-Saxon Protestants only.

I didn't notice Metal Wally standing next to me until I heard his voice near my ear. He points to one of the torn pieces of paper at the top of my notebook, just another drawing of a face, a mindless doodle of, if I were honest, the man who I know now is J. Clayton. "Is that a sketch of a suspect?" he asks. I tear it out and crumple it in my fist, then lean back against the wall. I let him finish his water so he can go.

Generally speaking, no one pays me much mind here in the back of the room, except for my editor. He's told me that he doesn't care that I'm Black so long as I can do the job. "But God cares," I said. "He made me brown on purpose. He cared that you were white on purpose. And cared enough to make rainbows. God likes color, and my skin color is not unnatural."

I haven't asked Mrs. Miriam to visit me here. Not yet. How does someone reinvite somebody back into an intimate space after an estrangement? But she and I talk often. We write letters that walk themselves the four miles between us. And anyway, I wouldn't want to have her sit in this old earthquake damage and see her disappointment in me—not married, not taking care of my own home and family, not living in service to a husband who doesn't consider himself a gift to me too.

Jagged lines cross my walls here in the basement. The foundation of my office is cracked so unevenly that the floor is two heights. I use the higher part of the broken floor as my chair.

I take one of Mrs. Miriam's letters from my bag and read it. She's been traveling more with the boys since Mr. Lawrence died. His daughter from the first marriage wanted to stay behind with her auntie so Miriam left her.

They went back east to see family, and she says she's kept her joy since the memorial. I asked if she misses him. She wrote, "I'll always miss Lawrence. I haven't let him go. But I have to allow myself to live life and tell myself it's alright to still wish he was here." These are the stories about death that no one gets to read about.

I sit at my typewriter, which sits on a stool, a light dangling from a cable above it. I roll up my skirt from the knees till it's a tire of cloth around my waist so I can move better. There's no way to sit like this in a pencil skirt without it ripping up the back. Nobody'll come down here anyway and see my legs out. Esther would've. She would've said, "Congratulations, this is a hole!" and I would've still been proud 'cause she was in it with me.

Morris warned me on my first day not to hang anything on the wall. "You don't want to tempt this office to collapse on you."

I try my typewriter. "This is L.A.," I read aloud as I type.

"This is Los Angeles," Morris says, correcting me, the bass of his tone startling. "Where everything can collapse any minute."

I didn't see him come in.

I hop off my seat, roll down my skirt.

"I thought I'd check on you," he says.

I straighten my blouse with quickness. My sudden movements knock loose the light fixture above my typewriter, its bulb shatters on my seat.

Morris covers his face.

Glass slices a deep gash in my thigh. It bleeds at once.

My reflection in the downed silver fixture shows the blood. I cross my legs, but it's too late. Morris already sees me bleeding.

I pick out the shard.

"Is that blood?" Morris says, cringing and staring too near to my crotch.

"Only if you're asking because you have an extra sanitary napkin."

He looks away. "We'll get you a new office as soon as we can," his hip bumps the dented doorframe as he turns on his way out.

My skin only needs a few seconds to scab and heal anew; I still have no explanation for this. All I keep thinking is what if everything Metal Wally believes about Black people, about me, is true and I'm unnatural? Because there is nothing natural about a body that does not carry its scars.

—

Morris is yelling out assignments to reporters now and some are mad: especially the world news ("real" news) reporters who think they deserve the big stories (Europe) and not the animal shelter or the groundbreaking for such-and-such, or the story about the brick wall going up around La Brea Tar Pits. I'd die to tell the story of the dinosaurs who were swallowed up and became tarry ooze in the eighteen pits of Hancock Park. Or about the brick wall and bridge being built by the City in its effort to keep Tar Pit sightseers from falling in and adding themselves to the body count.

The other reporters walk up to the front, grumbling as they yank the white sheet assignments out of Morris's hand. "Lou," he says over the newsroom commotion, "I want you to take this one. Officer Kerry Adams. He thinks highly of you."

The room quiets. "Officer Adams?" I say.

"He's joined the City Council panel. Elected to the at-large seat, deciding on this Route 66 project."

I walk to the front. Metal Wally eyes me while Morris shuffles through the other story tickets in his hands. He pauses at one. "Wait, I want you to take this one too. The fire station. On Central," he says. "Engine Company Four. The Negro fire company."

The reporters start chattering again.

"Did someone die there?" I say when I get to the front and take the ticket.

"They're having a celebration in a few days, honoring Sam Haskins, the first Black fireman employed by the City, and our relationship with the coloreds is tenuous. See if you can get an invitation to the celebration. You'll meet with the fire captain. Jefferson Clayton," Morris says.

My whole body stiffens.

"He's a hero to the coloreds, and he can tell about you the colored perspective on this Route 66."

Two months ago was the last time I saw him. Every time since when I hear the whine of a fire truck siren, I turn and walk away, covered in chill bumps. It's like when Mr. Lawrence died. I'd be standing in a crowd somewhere and I swear I'd see Lawrence back from the dead. Once, I chased a man with a head shaped like his. When I caught up to him, I'd planned to laugh with him and say, "I knew you were playing possum!" but it wasn't him. Mr. Lawrence is dead. And this man—J. Clayton—is from my dreams. Never living and never dead. Just a doodle on my page, now real and alive. That's not something to run to.

"I have two other deaths due next week. I'll pass on this Clayton one," I say.

"Get some of their complaints," Morris says, not asking, and using *their* as if I'm not Black too. "Captain Clayton's family . . . his wife and his four-year-old boy are delightful too."

He has a family?

"They're from the South and should appreciate how good coloreds are treated here. So give the story some life this time? No walking trees. Just the living, breathing story."

I take the ticket from Morris and say, "I've only worked on stories about death."

"Which have always been stories about the living," he says.

SEVENTEEN

-◄O►-

LOU, 1931

The dead white woman's door makes me uneasy. I stand in front of it, considering its lacquer shine and size, common for motel buildings. I'll bet this was a conversion—some two-story plantation house turned into ready-to-rent rooms, by the day or by the hour. That was before the Depression stole the hope of a thriving motel business after nobody had money to travel. It's two levels of apartments now.

The stairs on each edge of the building lead to a landing that goes from one end of the building to the other—three apartment doors upstairs are protected by a guardrail to keep the drunks from stumbling off the ledge to their deaths.

I stand in front of the third apartment. This door is wide enough to fit a woman carrying a baby on her hip while holding her toddler's hand—a whole family coming to L.A. on vacation, their father, a military man, home from overseas.

But I'm alone now.

Someone could open this door and pull me in without me bumping the doorframe. No one would know.

Someone is vacuuming inside. More than one person. A team of cleaners, judging by the noise—sucking in and, strangely, blowing out the mess. A dusty exhale into some collection bag, I'd guess. One I've never seen. But cleaning machines are being enhanced rapidly these days to keep up with the changing young families. Women are encouraged to take more time for themselves in L.A.

I knock.

A wind catches my scarf, and it rises like a cat's tail, balancing. I smooth it back down.

White children are playing on the first floor, squealing as they run past the stairwell, laughing now, headed toward the palm trees next to the parking lot where there are swings and bad ideas—an unattended merry-go-round for kids to fly off and a metal slide heated by the sun that'll brand the backs of their thighs on the ride down.

Another white kid, maybe seven, is at the bottom of the stairs looking up at me. I smile. She doesn't. I knock on the door again.

The 2:00 p.m. sunlight seems to have stalled between the buildings, shadows unchanging, like the length of time for those hard on their luck. Dozens of families, new to the city, are housed here. Temporarily, I'm told. That was the intention. But when the government is responsible for hospitality, something is always lost.

The curtain on the window next to the door rustles, then stops. "Hello?" I say. No answer.

A darkness inhabits the window now—a white man with stains of dark circles under his eyes. "What!" he says to me.

My voice quivers. "I'm Louise with the *L.A. Times*. I'm here about Mrs. O'Malley."

"Speak up!"

"Louise . . . with the *Times*." The curtain shuts.

A moment later, I hear his voice again: "Nigger's at the door," he yells to someone inside. The vacuuming does not stop.

I wait.

The door creaks open. The man from the window has opened it and, without inviting me in, he turns and walks away from me. He has a baseball bat in his hand.

I stay in the foyer a second longer, long enough to realize I should follow. "Close the door behind you," he says.

My eyes adjust to the darkness inside the empty great room—no furniture, no images on the wall. I pass an open door on the right and shiver when I see another man, a big man, sitting close to the carpeted floor on an outdoor lounge chair, a broken Adirondack—it must be from the East Coast. His hands are inside his jacket and a glass drinking cup is on the armrest, a plate of food is on his lap. His radio is next to his foot. "You lock it?" the man in the room says.

"What?" I ask.

He sets his plate on the floor and gets up to lock the door, but he knocks his glass over, spilling cider. "Damn," he says. But at least he didn't shatter it. The man with the bat keeps walking without cleaning the spill and I follow behind him.

We stop at a door at the end of the hallway. He knocks with one knuckle, then opens it. The vacuum sound is loudest now.

The man tells me wait and I do.

Finally, he nods me forward and moves out of the doorway. There, at the back of the room, is a man-sized metal cylinder, a cream-colored barrel, half the size of a car, laid on its side and resting on a stand that looks like a cot. It has an opening for the head of the man who's lying inside. There's an opening for his head but not for his feet. His double chin is girded at his neck like bunched clothing; the rest of his reddened face is severely swollen, like a two-day-old balloon with a third of its air escaped so if you squeeze the bottom, all the air inside would rush to its over-inflated head. I imagine his whole body matches this.

The cylinder he's lying in is the source of the vacuuming racket. I see now that it is his breathing machine. He moves his head from facing upward to the ceiling to the side to see me where I am. The machine rattles.

"Are you contagious?" I say.

"Polio's transmitted through community pools, so no. Not to you."

I can't take my eyes off his machine. I've never seen one this close.

"Do you know why you're here?" he says.

His frizzy brown hair is like combed-out soft curls. "Because your mother passed away," I say, and I wonder what those knobs do. "I've been assigned her story."

"Do you know why you were assigned to write about my mother's life?"

I didn't want to tell him because it'd be rude to remind a grieving son that his mother's non-Protestant religion puts her squarely at the bottom of America's whiteness. So I say, "Because I work the Death desk."

"No, because I requested you."

"Me, sir?"

His face holds a firm expression now, and it makes me feel like I should be paying closer attention to him, so I surrender my curiosity over his machine and look him in the eyes. He's a pink elephant of a man, I think. Swaddled like a baby in a blanket of metal.

He begins barking like a hound, not a cough but hearty laughter. He can hardly breathe from laughing. He coughs and brings up a massive amount of phlegm and moves it to the front of his teeth, and the man who let me in goes over to him, pinches it away, and dabs his mouth with the tissue.

"Did I scare you with this device?" he says, chuckling now. "I wonder what people think when they first see it. Cost me fifteen hundred dollars, more than most people's houses."

The lung inhales and exhales. I talk over it. "I . . . I've never seen a device quite so grand," I say. "An iron lung in someone's house? I've only ever seen them in hospitals."

"I had Danny there encourage the doctor who treated me to give me one. You see, the polio virus paralyzes muscles in the chest, isn't that right, Danny?"

Danny, the man behind me with the bat, doesn't answer.

"Polio patients can't breathe. That's how most people die from it in the early stages," he says. "I'd been waking up in the middle of the night and couldn't breathe. Doctor said it wasn't because of polio . . . but what do doctors know? He just didn't diagnose me yet. Too early."

"Can I touch it?" I say.

"Come on," he says.

I walk next to it. He shifts his eyes toward me, hardly moves his neck. I lay my hand flat on the shiny metal and feel my delight rise within me. I say, "I've read this can maintain respiration artificially until a person can breathe independently." I'm in awe. "People who survive this stage usually recover most or almost all of their former strength, usually takes one or two weeks. Not long."

I run my hand over the knobs, but I don't turn them. Two small and greenish circular doors are on the side of the metal cylinder, just large enough for a man's arm to reach inside the tank. I open a door. "Is this alright?" I say.

"Go'n," he says. "I'm dressed." A hospital gown.

It's hot like an oven inside. A cookie tray. A smell of disinfectant steams off him and it reminds me of jail.

"Can you move my arm while you're there?" he says. I feel around till I find his arm inside the tank and I adjust it. He thanks me. Something cool touches the side of my palm. A melting icepack that somebody put in place.

"Is this your first or second week inside it?" I say.

"What is it, Danny? One . . . two . . . two years?" he says.

"A year and half," Danny says, correcting him.

"Nothing keeps people breathing better. Longer than this machine. I plan to live forever," he says.

I close the door, step back.

On the front is a latch you'd have to squeeze to open the entire lid. "Can you get out from inside?" I say. "If you wanted?"

"A coffin," he says, "You see the latch there. Hinges are on the back along my left side, next to the wall." He lifts his head, shows me he's stuck. "That's why I've got Danny."

"That sure is a lot of trust."

"Boy's earned it," he says. "Sit," he says, and Danny pulls up a chair behind me, one high enough that he and I can talk face-to-face. "My name is Vic O'Malley. My mother was Helen O'Malley."

"Louise," I say, and rest my purse on my lap.

We study each other up close. He has dark freckles on his cheeks underneath his eyes, like he dotted his whole face with black eyeliner. I turn away to study the room. It's spotlessly clean.

"Shall we begin?" I say.

"Wait a minute," he says. "Before you start asking questions, be a doll and flick that switch."

I do. The vacuuming stops.

"I can hear you better now," he says. "And you didn't answer my question. Do you know why you're here?"

"To help let the community know about your mother."

"What do you think they need to know?"

"Let's start with the day she died?"

"Danny, what was it? The sixteenth or seventeenth of last month? No, it was the nineteenth. She died right there where you're sitting. Her heart gave."

"I'm sorry," I say, and squirm in my seat. "You were her caregiver?"

"I'm a man," he says, disgusted by my question. "She had girls. Was hard to care for too. Fired everyone. Kept most of 'em at a distance. Those closest to her she treated like slaves. Jump when she said jump. Sit, sleep, feed her when she said and not on schedule. And if they did those things, after a while, she'd give them more responsibility. But people were in and out."

"So she had a hard time trusting people?" I write that down.

"No, it means she didn't trust anybody she couldn't abuse. Are we going to have a problem here with you mincing my words?"

"No, sir," I say, and line out his first statement.

"Dan-nay!" he calls out, and Danny comes. "Git me another sack of ice, would you?"

Danny brings it in and puts it under his neck. "Some ice chips too."

I wait for him to get comfortable, start writing my next question, reframing it.

"Who's your people?" he says.

"Black people."

"Naw, your family. Your parents? If we're going to talk about my family . . ."

"I'm a foster."

"By who? Who fostered you? The church?"

"A man named Mr. Lawrence and his wife, Mrs. Miriam?"

"Lawrence!" he says. "No shit. That man went through holy hell trying to keep me. No cross-race fostering, they told him. But they couldn't find an Irish family fast enough. At eight years old I already had a reputation," he says, proud of himself. "They couldn't keep me in jail, could they? Juvenile hall was always packed with child robbers and fighters, it was survival, a sign of the coming Depression. You get yer ass kicked for a cookie. My social worker needed to get me out of there, and at the time, Mr. Lawrence still believed that all a child needed was love and discipline. No matter race. But the problem was me. I was a pill."

"They let him keep you?"

Danny brings him a plastic cup filled with cold water and ice chips. He places the straw on Vic's lips, lets him drink. Vic pushes the straw out with his tongue. "The juvenile courts," he says, "were always going round Lawrence's house, asking for reports about me. And he'd have to lie for me. If he didn't, what kind of life would I have had?"

"Not a good one," I say.

"I admit I wasn't easy, but what child is prepared to be abandoned by his parents and, to be fair, foster parents aren't ready either. Thank God my birth mother rallied. She got herself together. Credited it to her Catholic faith. And she got me back. But Lawrence. How is he?"

"Died," I say.

Vic's eyes close. "I didn't know," he says. "See, another reason we need to tell people how we feel about them before it's too late."

On the wall across from where we sit is a poster canvas, hand sketched in pencil. It's a castle with a twin tower, square openings near the top of each one for peering out.

"That your art?" I say.

"My mother's," he says. "That castle haunted her. She was six years old when her family came to America from a small town on the River Barrow. Muine Bheag.

"Ballyloughan Castle. She said it felt familiar to her." He signals to Danny for more water. "What else do you need to know about my mother?"

I glance at the questions I'd prepared in my notebook. "I'm just going to ask you a few questions about Mrs. O'Malley. If there's something you want off the record, just say so and I won't record it."

"Then erase all of that I said about my mom and her castle and our dad. Off the fucking record."

"I will," I say.

"We're from the same place," he says. "I can trust you, and I want to tell a different story about my mother. She used to bake bread for us. Apron and all. Wait for us to come home from school." He looks at my blank pad of paper. "You writing this down?"

I write his name at the top of the page. The date.

He begins telling me stories of his mother and over the next hour explains why she had to do what she did to survive. Immoral activity, he called it. But she managed to keep him and his sister. Every time he gets too emotional, he says, "Off the record," but it's still nothing in comparison to what he allows. I say, "Do you want that off the record?"

"Why?" he says.

Danny disappears from the room, called back to the front door by new knocking at the front door. A moment later, he yells back toward us, "It's a dago and a beaner. No, two dagos. One's a burned pizza."

"Italians," Vic says, and we sit quietly. He tells me, "Flip on my switch."

We let the vacuuming sound relax us as we wait for the guests to join us.

The doorway fills with a darker-skinned man and a lighter one. For a moment I wonder why the criminally minded are obsessed with racial slurs. For me it's either black or white. Italians and Irish are white, but for white people it might be more nuanced and tribal than that.

The darker one is smaller. Young, maybe sixteen. He's carrying a black plastic bag over his shoulder like Santa.

"Who's the Jane?" the older one says, referring to me.

"Your mother," Vic says. But it sounds more like "ya muva." "The fuck you asking me questions for. You got something for me?"

Vic gives me a head signal to flip the switch again. The vacuum stops.

Without a word, the young man lobs the bag from over his shoulder, and clothes spill out on the clean floor. The boy kneels and begins separating them.

The older one says, "I got a load of clothes to sell. Half price."

"Where they from?" Vic says. "Not interested if they're not stolen."

"A clothes shop," the older one answers. "One of the good ones down on the high street."

Vic asks the boy on the floor, "You steal 'em or did someone else?"

The boy doesn't answer. The older one says, "He stole 'em, and the boy doesn't work with anyone else."

Vic eyes the boy and says, "Then if anything comes back to me, I know it's you."

"No," the older one says. "You'll know it's me and I'll know it's him."

Vic moves his head to see the clothes better. "Are there any for fat people?"

"He's got all sizes out in the car," the older one says. "I'll bring 'em in if you want to buy."

"How many pieces?" Vic asks the boy but the boy still doesn't answer. "How much you want for 'em?"

"Two a pair," the older one says.

Vic moves his head in a circular motion. "I want all of 'em," he says. "Danny, get the boys paid."

Danny goes up the hall behind them. Strangely, I feel like I need Vic's permission to leave and it seems to me to be a good opportunity to do so, but I don't move.

Vic and I talk for another hour after the salesmen leave about Mrs. O'Malley and her fantastic adventures in the old country and I wish I could be there to see it. He tells me he's done talking and I can go.

Before I leave, he says, "On the record, I don't steal from people. I capitalize on what's been stolen. Isn't that the American way?"

I don't want to argue.

"I hope to see you again soon," he says.

It sounds like a threat.

EIGHTEEN

LOU, 1931

The story about Mrs. O'Malley ran today and I can't wash her son out my mind. He's my foster brother, I suppose. Existing here before I did. Before I knew that he was. Before we shared a father figure in Mr. Lawrence. I can't stop wondering whether I'm wrong for not wanting to know where I came from, who my family is. What good did it do Vic when every day he lays in his coffin, afraid to die?

I pace in front of the firehouse, wiping and rewiping the sweat from my hands on the hips of my dress. I walked for over an hour to get here from my apartment. Four miles shouldn't have taken an hour but it did because I was dancing with my nervous thoughts. They spun me back when I turned to go home, undipped me when I sat on the curb too long. The rest of the walk was a partner-less slow shuffle. I took my time up Central Avenue, where I threaded myself through neighborhoods, doubled back. We're all Black here, all of us dancing afraid, like any minute our legs will be kicked from under us. The three- and four-bedroom palaces of houses, bigger than Mr.

Lawrence's, with wider and deeper green lawns and palm trees lit by sunshine, give me comfort. But not enough that I'm not afraid of standing here.

The firehouse is wood. More like a barn except for the roof and its decorative concrete finishings up there. The building's like a woman going out for the night and has two different thoughts about evening wear. On the top, she's fancy-dressed for a ball, but from the waist down she's wearing men's overalls and house slippers.

Hand-carved signs hang on the concrete top of the building: ENGINE CO. 4 and 1892. The barn doors are open to the street.

My hands are shaking. I crush them into each other. I'm going to go in, I tell myself. Just one more minute.

"Hello," a man says from the doorway, drying his forearms with a red rag. He's old enough to be my father—no, my grandfather, if I knew him or drew him and didn't imagine him frail. This one's got perfect teeth, unstained by age spots of coffee or tea, and his silver hair is full.

His muscled body is pressing through his young man's uniform. If a woman a third his age closed her eyes and felt up the wall of his chest and abdomen, she'd say he was twenty-one.

I stop looking at him.

"Can I help you with something," he says.

"Yes, sir," I say, walking toward him, my hand extended. "I have an appointment with Captain Clayton. I'm Louise Willard from the *Times*."

He smiles and a dimple in his left cheek deepens. "And I thought you were here to see me."

My face flushes.

"From the *Times*, eh? I suppose I should give you a tour?" His demeanor seems to loosen with his words. "Come with me," he says, and I follow him up two flights of stairs. He runs ahead of me, taking two steps at a time. He throws his hands in the air at the top of the flight. "My body's seventy-four," he shouts, "but Sandy Paul is twenty-two!"

He waits for me. Helps me onto the last step. "Thanks, Mr. Paul."

"Sandy Paul," he says, correcting me. "Both are my first names."

He points over the railing, to the room below. "That's where they used to keep the horses," he says. "They were our fire engines."

I cough, still catching my breath.

"Take your time," he says. "It's the dust. I'll get you water and we can finish a tour some other time."

When we reach the second floor, Sandy Paul asks me to wait in Captain Clayton's office, said the captain wouldn't be but a minute. My stomach lurches at his promise. But I nod, left to a room occupied by a person from my imagination.

He has books on his shelf. The edges of pages are worn. One is stamped with the words *Los Angeles Public Library*. The sight of these makes me happy because my imagination is a reader. One who might also steal books.

A plaque is laid on his desk without a screw to hang it. IN RECOGNITION OF YOUR SERVICE, it begins.

His voice from over my shoulder startles me. *My imagination has a voice.* "I brought you water," he says from the doorway. I fight my spine to keep it from bowing.

"I didn't intend to be late," he says, coming around his desk in front of me, but I don't look at his face. Only his hands. The hands I could never draw.

"Please, sit down," he says, and places the water in front of the seat I should take. I lower myself into it, across from his desk. We meet eyes. Yes, it's those eyes. *What am I doing here?*

I remind myself that I'm working. I'm conducting an interview. I become aware that I have not said a word to him yet. All my words seem to be caught below my tits. No, lower. My belly. No.

A look of curiosity passes over his face. He says, "I've been looking forward to meeting you."

I don't answer.

"Let me get you a pitcher of water for later," he says. "Chipped ice?"

My face flinches.

He disappears through his door and moments later returns with a pitcher of ice water. He sets it on the other cork coaster on his desk and falls back into his chair.

"I'm so glad you were able to make it—"

"You don't have any photographs of your wife or your son here," I say in an accusatory tone I don't mean, but my strength to say anything was forced up from my feet and overshot the observation.

He looks around his office as if noticing the absence for the first time and nods. "No, I don't guess I do. I'll have to fix that."

"Louise," I say, and exhale a smile. "Louise Willard. But just call me Louise."

"Pleased to meet you, Louise. Captain Jefferson Clayton, but just call me Jefferson." He laughs. "The man whose family is missing"—my expression flattens—"from the office photographs."

I look at the clock on the wall and mark the hour. One o'clock. I say plainly, "I want to be respectful of your time. My office advised me that we have one hour."

He shifts in his chair. "We can take as much time as we need. I've got nothing planned after this." He pauses. "I'm sorry, I'm sure you have friends. Family?"

"I've prepared questions," I say, finally looking up at him but not directly. Instead, I look off center, at the side of his face, between his ear and his eyebrow. He must think I'm cross-eyed. "I'll jot down notes as you speak," I say. "And I'll also be listening, so it's alright to keep talking even if I'm not looking at you."

"Alright," he says, then shifts in his seat again. "Should I be concerned about my words? The things I say? Not that you would twist them but . . ."

"Just tell me 'off the record' if you want. Like safe words before or after you say something you think is questionable."

"Safe words?"

"Safe," I say. "And I'll be sure to remove it. And I'll also send you a copy to review before it goes to print if you change your mind."

"Louise," he says, and my name on his lips feels brand new. "I didn't mean questionable. That I would say something questionable or wrong. I'm . . . I guess I'm just asking your permission to be myself."

We meet eyes now. And hold on. He smiles at me—my sketch alive—and considers me like he knows I was his creator.

I don't want to ask a business question anymore. I want to know what he's thinking.

"Have we met before?" he says.

My neck heats instantly.

"I'm comfortable, is all. I'm not usually with this sort of thing. Can I ask about the photo on your desk?" I say.

He turns toward it and lifts the frame. In it, two young boys are smiling, standing next to pedal bicycles. One boy is a foot taller than the other and he's hugging the smaller, proud of him.

"My younger brother," he says. "And me." He sets it down. "Where are you from?"

"Where was the photo taken?"

He leans back to eye the photo again. "Somewhere in Alabama," he says.

"You don't remember?"

He smiles.

"Who put the bell on your bicycle?"

He picks up the frame and holds it close to his face. "Would you look at that? I've seen this photo every day for years and this might be the first time I've seen the bell."

"Is your brother a fireman too?"

"He's in prison," he says.

"I'm sorry."

"It's alright," he says, and turns his head right around to show me the scar at the back, a thin line curved into a semicircle where hair doesn't grow. "We were in an accident together. He was driving, had been drinking. Didn't see the woman who was walking on the road that night. Our car flipped at the same time she lost her life. Killed instantly."

"I'm sorry."

"I'm sorry for her and her family. I was luckier than she was."

"So you were running away?"

"Wouldn't say running. I was drawn to L.A. Two years after my miracle awakening, eight years ago. Had lost my mother and father within nine months of each other, natural causes."

I want to tell him we have something in common. We're both orphans.

"I'd just married," he says. "If I was running, I guess it was first to her."

He's such a good-looking man. The kind of man who if he weren't Black could have everything.

"Toward love," I say.

He nods. "And to Los Angeles."

"Did you know anyone when you arrived?"

"My cousin, Cliff, and his wife. I met Sandy through him. In fact, Sandy was the second person I met in L.A. Tried to sell me a used car after my cousin set it up. Said I'd need a car if I was going to make L.A. my home, and Cliff sells cars."

"You and your wife stayed with Cliff when you came?"

"We'd saved, and our church took up a collection. We bought a house a couple blocks from here."

"So we've lived this close and God never let us meet before now?" I say, and I want to take every word back.

He smiles at me. "Maybe God was waiting for the right time. For this interview. The universe has a way of bringing people together. Those who are meant to meet, do."

"You believe in that kind of thing?"

"Absolutely," he says. "What's the point of all of this if you don't believe in fate?"

My face reddens, my sight blurs. I flip the notebook page. "Your— your cousin, Cliff?" I say, using my words as a reversed magnet to him, distancing myself because turned around might mean a hopeless collision. "Did he help you get on the fire department?"

"Indirectly," he says. "It's how I met Sandy Paul, did I say that already? And he was on the department."

I write that down. I want him to keep talking, to keep me pushed away. "Oh?" I say, an evasive maneuver for the science he's turned on in me.

"Cliff told me he'd just got in a new four-door Buick Series 40 Phaeton, that he'd sell it to me at a discount, twelve hundred dollars." I write it down. "Had four-wheel hydraulic brakes, a radio and heater, a smooth shape. Said he'd bring it by my house for me to look over, but it wasn't Cliff who brought the car. It was Sandy Paul. He was my cousin Cliff's partner."

"Partner?" *Keep talking.*

"In business together. But from the start, it was clear to me that the car Sandy brought was not a new car, so I asked him, 'This a new car?' and Sandy said it was, so I lifted the engine cover to take a look. Looked under the wheel arches, then in the trunk. I opened the passenger door and climbed inside it and I said again, 'This a new car?' Sandy promised if I'd drive it, I'd see for myself, but I wasn't going to waste more of my time, so I picked the car's silver medallion from the floorboard. It was almost hidden under the seat. I said, 'This ain't a new car. For one thing, this emblem goes on the hood of the car, not here on the floor, and there are joins rewelded in at least three places, new paint on the inner wheel arch, so it's been replaced. Same for the paint near the engine. There's new welding in the trunk.'"

He laughs. "You should've saw the look on Sandy's face."

I don't look up when I smile.

"I sent Sandy off with his used car, hoped I'd never see him again, but as it happened I ran into him the next day at the post office."

"The next day?" I say, another encouraging maneuver.

"When Sandy saw me, he said, 'Let me get you another car to look at.' And I said, 'I'll never buy a car from you. You tried to cheat me.' And that's when he tol' me he and my cousin Cliff were in the business of repairing wrecks and reselling them. Their mission was to put cars in the hands of colored people. He said Cliff told him I was looking for a car and Cliff asked him to say it was new. Offered Sandy fifty bucks if he sold it to me as is. A finder's fee. So see, it was my cousin Cliff who tried to steal from me," he said.

"But Sandy Paul didn't say no," I say.

"But that's business, doll. And I didn't know Sandy yet. I knew my cousin but not Sandy."

"And you still trust him?"

"He's looked out for me since then. Put his life on the line. So yeah, I trust him."

"You believe it's possible to turn distrust into trust?"

He thinks about it.

His eyes smile. I've never drawn him with smiling eyes. "I believe strangers can grow together. Especially when they're meant to. Don't you?"

NINETEEN

◀○▶

LOU, 1931

I write: *The Endurance Flight Girls: Edna Mae Cooper and Mrs. Bobbi Trout
landed at the Los Angeles Municipal Airport this week after spending 122 hours
and 50 minutes in the air.* It was a new endurance record for women and
Morris said I could write the story. I'd begged him. Just one story on women.

A crowd of five hundred people met Cooper and Trout at the airport
when they landed and when they were asked how they felt, Edna said,
"Guess we may have lost a little weight, but we feel fine."

Mrs. Trout, the transport pilot, said, "I wouldn't want to go up again
tomorrow, but I hated like the deuce to have to come down. I've never felt
better."

Their mood was pleasant, and they seemed physically fit.

I reread my last line, *Their mood was . . .* It's not right. I scroll down the
typed page a short distance and fold it over my typewriter so I don't have to
remove it. I take my thin, flat eraser disk and rub its abrasive edge over each
typed letter, one at a time, carefully—Morris hates spots on the paper where

it was scraped of errors. I use my eraser brush to shoo away the crumbs and paper dust and keep them from falling into my typewriter. Even a small buildup could cause the bars to jam in their narrow grooves.

I retype the line: *Despite their cheerful mood and physical fitness, they were rushed to the California Hospital for observation.*

That's better.

I tear it out of the typewriter like a tooth from the gums of a child and hold it out in delight. *Morris'll love this one.* My best work!

I lower it to my desk and see a man in my doorway, standing behind my page. It's not Morris. *How long has Jefferson been standing there?*

"Looks like a good story," he says, and I don't know if that's a question. Or what I'm supposed to do now.

He sits across from me on the chair somebody stored down here and I wonder if it's really him there. Should I draw him again? Is this a vision so I can draw him right this time?

"Can I read it?" he says.

He must be a dream—brown vested, tartan pattern, repeating grids of navy and black laid over his long-sleeved button shirt, his coat flung over one shoulder like a brown model in his Sunday best on a Thursday. Out of place like a piece in the wrong puzzle. He belongs at the fire station and places related to him, not in this basement with me, voyaged across his oceans and onto my island.

"Can I read it?" he repeats.

I look down at my unnumbered pages. *He's real.* "It's not very good," I say.

He smiles at me and it forces mine. He says, "Morris said it'd be alright to come down and chew on your ear about the Route. Maybe an op ed you could write?"

"The Route?"

"City plans to destroy our neighborhoods. I swear to God, Black slaves who were brought here against their will and Natives are the only ones who should have any say on where the Route goes. We're not immigrants."

I feel hot around my neck.

"I'm sorry, I shouldn't have sworn."

"You can swear," I say. His cheeks come alight with my words, forming a new smile. One I've never drawn. My voice deepens on its own. "You can do whatever you want."

He clears his throat.

I cringe at my words and stack my story pages on the girls like there's more than two pages—a whole novel of phrases—switch their order and then write a page number on each. *1.*, I write. Then, *2.*

"Here they are," I say. "Take your time."

He reaches for them and I can't let go. We hold them together like a communion wafer, holy, his spirit speaking to me in tongues I can't decipher.

I let go.

"Any chance you can come to the station tomorrow for the Sam Haskins celebration?" he says. "First Black man hired by the Los Angeles Fire Department. You can cover it for the paper. I can ask Morris for you specifically."

I want to nod yes but I've made enough errors.

"Will you? For me," he says. "I want you to come."

We meet eyes.

He's my dream alive.

The engine is on display at the center of the fire station. STATION 4 is painted on its side in gleaming gold. From here on the sidewalk, I can see him between the red-painted wheel arches and the folded hose. I'm an hour early. Miscounted the time it would take to walk here from home in heeled shoes. Apparently, I could run in these.

He's rehearsing his speech, and his voice is leaving my stomach in shambles, my legs lead-weighted.

Quiet now. He flips through the pages of his speech and they crumble and slice air.

Two men, including Sandy, are shouting to each other on the side of the building. They're washing a second engine, preparing it to go outside along the street where lamps are strung with decorated paper—bright red, white, and blue, the colors of our flag—for parades, for pride. An American flag drapes this engine's bonnet. The Fourth of July is in just a few days' time.

Jefferson's voice begins again, booming loudly without a microphone, and his tone kisses me, leaving trails of goose bumps up my back and along my arms like the footprints of tiny dancers.

He isn't dressed properly, wearing his cream-colored work trousers and white t-shirt, untucked above his hanging suspenders. The cut of his arms is like a boxer's. I can see the shape of his chest through the thin white material.

"Is someone there?" he says to the empty hall.

I raise my hand and step out from behind the engine wheel where I'd moved. "It's me," I say shyly.

"You made it!" he says, walking toward me, excited, and I can't help but smile. My skin flushes.

"Am I the first one here?"

He points to outside through the window, where Sandy is fixing the flag on the engine and talking to someone. Women in white aprons are walking in and out of the building behind them. "Food preparers," he says, and sets down his speech. "They won't be in the dining hall for another few minutes. We can talk about Sam Haskins there if you want?"

"I don't want to get in the way," I say. "I'm early . . ." He takes my hand and I let him.

We go to a back room, a large hall where already-prepared food is covered. Chairs have been set in a circle around the space, leaving the center for dancing.

At the far side of the room, behind a short wall, fresh-squeezed juice and water pitchers in buckets of chopped ice are out on a long counter. We stop there behind the wall, where he pours himself two waters and gives me one, then hops up on the countertop and pats the place next to him. Our thighs touch when I join him.

"What d'you wanna know about Sam?"

"Can we start with your story of becoming a fireman and move into how Sam's legacy allowed you to be here now?"

He nods as he drinks from his glass. Sets it down and begins with a story about his father and uncles, who fought fires in Georgia. It was there that he knew he wanted to be a firefighter, but the older men would tell him that this was a young man's game and he'd dismiss them. "I thought I could do this forever," he says, "but now I know what they meant. Having to get up at any time of the night when there's a call, the weight of the equipment, getting up on the truck. The weather. Thirty-two and my body is already feeling like it's time to retire. I'm not like Sandy," he says.

"It's not the death?" I ask him. "That's not what makes you want to retire? Seeing it all?"

"Why?" he says, refilling his water glass. "Natural selection. I see death almost every shift. Everybody has to play their card." He finishes his water in a few gulps; his lips are wet. "If I ask you a question, will you answer?"

"Sure."

"How old are you?"

"Seventeen or eighteen." When I'd arrived, my social worker had settled on sixteen and I don't know if I believe her.

"Or?" he says, laughing. "So, in other words, you're afraid to share things with me?"

No, I want to tell him everything.

Footsteps move at a smart pace in the hall, coming toward us, jogging. Sandy Paul leans into our space. The way he eyes me and him together makes me feel guilty for doing my job.

"Time to get ready, boss," he says, and Jefferson hops down from the countertop, shakes my hand like ending a men's business meeting, and walks out with Sandy. I don't know whether to stay or go.

I slide off the counter, straighten my dress. Sandy Paul circles back and tells me to eat something while I wait.

The hall is filled now with life and music and dancing, like a low-budget Hollywood party in South Central L.A., but the last Hollywood party I snuck into was with Esther. The Hollywood Hills. Esther said, "If you're anybody in Hollywood, you need this invitation." And she had it.

The party wasn't like the whites-only parties in Santa Monica. There, all were welcome. Jews, Blacks, and anybody else with a gift or charm. Albert Einstein. Charlie Chaplin.

The driveway leading up to it was a giveaway to its glamour. Lit like glowing candy floss, and Mary Pickford couldn't have chosen a better color. Blue. Mrs. Pickford and Douglas Fairbanks had been silent film stars and, true to their art, their home was extravagance in sign language. "Welcome to Pickfair!" the young men said that night, opened our car doors and continued in their glee even after they saw we weren't white.

Esther and I stumbled past the front door, where we were washed with glints of light reflecting from crystal chandeliers above us, hanging like rain drops on silvery spider webs.

Mary and Doug were two of the four founders of the motion picture studio United Artists. But before they were lovers, Doug was one of the founding members of the Motion Picture Academy and hosted the first Academy Awards ceremony in 1929. His father was a Union soldier during the Civil War, a lawyer from Pennsylvania who was Jewish. But after his father left, Douglas's mother changed his surname from Ullman to Fairbanks but that's only the rumor. And, anyway, this is L.A., where anybody can be whoever they say (and can pass for)—by name or appearance—and nobody worth knowing requires confirmation. Before his fame in Hollywood, he published a self-help book called *Laugh and Live*, and it lauded the power of positive thinking as a means to raise one's social prospects.

Clearly, it worked. Their palace was proof. Hors d'oeuvres were pedaled on sterling trays in the hands of white help. Skinny dancers with flat chests swung and bobbed over the music while Esther spoke differently with different people. With agents, producers, actors, and other "important people," she offered broken English that also sounded guttural, like Cantonese, but with others she'd use a drawl-free midwestern accent that wasn't hers either. It was her game.

When the tune "Maple Leaf Rag" exploded from the belly of the piano, everyone in the room squealed and rushed to the floor, their bodies jumping, the pianist tapping his fingers wildly across the white teeth of his piano, missing the black ones.

The crowd whooped and hollered and clapped between the melodies, added their own notes. Esther pulled up her dress to show her legs and feet, was sure-footed, spinning and wild like the hair of the man playing piano, his blond strands like hay circling in a bunch like propellers, like Esther. Jaunting, jumping, leaping. "Come on, woman!" Esther told me, and grabbed my hand. But the crowd was wild, as if dancing to the song of their lives.

They created a circle, standing side by side, and made an opening on the dance floor. They did small bouncy steps as they waited and watched couple after couple go into the center and perform dance moves. The risky ones summoned cheers.

"Come on! It's our turn!" Esther said, yanking on my arm.

"I can't go in there!" I told her, and just then another couple took their turn inside.

"What are you afraid of?" Esther said. "You can dance."

"I'd rather just dance here," I said. To this day, I wish I had said yes and charged in. But I didn't.

"Oh, don't be a pansy," she said. "And for once in your life, don't be a bystander."

Inside this station, music is as electric as it was that night with Esther. "There you are," Jefferson says, his voice a chiming alarm, like we'd had an appointment. "Knock knock," he says.

"A knock-knock joke?" I say over the music.

"Come on. Knock knock?"

"Who's there?"

"Wendy."

"Wendy who?"

"Wendy hell, you gon' come from behind this wall and dance with me?"

I can't help but laugh. "We can't just dance!"

"And be the only ones who aren't?" Around the room, folks are dancing moves that haven't been stolen yet, almost everybody partnered indiscriminately, friends with friends; even food servers have been roped in. "At my party," he says, "everybody dances."

I won't be a coward this time. I slide my shoulder blades slowly downward. Roll my hips, circle my wrists in slow turns with them. I flick the bottom of my dress, raise the seam from the floor, show my legs, my feet, and these new shoes.

"I thought you'd be at the colored paper by now." Another man's voice rises behind me like tires screeching before an accident. Metal Wally.

"You don't have to stop dancing," he says.

I wasn't gonna, but I am straightening my clothes. "I'm sorry to hear the layoffs didn't go well for you. I'm still at the *Times*."

"Don't be sorry, I took the severance, wanted to leave anyway. See." He flicks his badge. "With *L.A.'s Snooper* now. The real heart of the city. I chose to put my talent on something that matters. You must be Captain Clayton?" he says to Jefferson. "You're my first assignment."

"Then I'm honored," Jefferson says.

"I'll work my way up, see," Wally says, and leans into Jefferson like he's telling a secret. "Truth be told, was tired of waiting for my chance at the *Times*. They should be called *Behind the Times*. They don't have any vision. So watch yourself with her. The Jews run that paper anyway. Trying to take over the world."

Wally's eye catches a person more interesting than us across the room, and to see what he sees prompts a hush; the music is background noise. The Black woman is standing in a delicious form-fitting dress, her peach heels like rubber stoppers at her feet, holding in all that sass. Her face is like a European white woman's, tanned honey, more movie star than commoner. Jefferson doesn't say "excuse me" or "bye" before he leaves my side for her and does it with haste, like an ocean wave ready to drown her in himself.

"Isn't his wife a doll?" Wally says.

I watch Jefferson hold her. They fit together. Of course she's his wife. They're both the kind of people who'd spend their lives wanting for nothing. And she's the woman who changed the path of her life for him. Her heart's possibilities in exchange for his.

TWENTY

SARAH, 2107

I was asked by my public defender whether I killed the man because I flew into a jealous rage.

"Is that your defense?" he said.

I didn't answer.

If I killed a man, it wouldn't be for jealousy. Even if he cheated, because I don't believe in adultery.

That it's all bad.

But saying so is not other people's permission to be human. To lie. To cheat. To steal from the one who loves them. Or from those they've pledged their monogamy (or some form of it) to.

What I do believe in is the gift of pain and grief that adultery brings. In pain's power to ground us inside the consequence of our choices. Our partnering. To make us inhabit ourselves long enough to ask, What am I doing with my life? Few actions can plunge people into a personal free fall the way adultery can. Make them look at their smile on the outside and vice burning on the inside of their contradictory selves and ask why.

Like murder.

Presuming you get caught.

Presuming you'd care.

And presuming you'd want to know why you're lying and breaking promises and hurting people.

But justice isn't about what *you* want.

You don't decide.

Your community does. Your victims do. No matter how much you try to manipulate, they'll remember their memories, not yours, for the rest of their lives.

How many lives, how many deeds, can I still remember? Are there really thirty-six people in the world who are supposed to be righteous and stay righteous, to justify the existence of the world in the eyes of God? I've heard there were eleven. I've heard fifteen.

No matter, I must not be among them. Jury found me guilty using cir- cumstantial evidence, which means they guessed from the bits of evidence they were given and determined—as fact—that I'd been overcome by the heat of passion and killed him.

I've been called "emotional" before.

What woman hasn't?

But all humans—men, women, and other—are indisputable emotional beings, though we associate reason and rationality with order, calm, and control, emotion with chaos and unpredictability. Rational behavior is de- pendent on emotions.

The brain motivates us based on what it's learned—what's helpful or hurtful—so emotions rise and roll before we've made what we think is an emotion-free, rational, and reasonable decision. So I guess I was emotional when I killed him.

But which emotion? Fear?

And what does it mean to act in self-defense when you can't die or be wounded for long? Defense of being inconvenienced? Like fighting against wearing a mask in a pandemic because you—personally—will likely recover if you get it? Forget other people you pass it to. If they die, it was because it was their time to. So for the man I killed, I was merely an instrument of natural selection.

No, I wouldn't lie about that.

I have self-control.

I have my mind. It was my decision to act and it was also an accident. I'm not a killer.

Anymore.

LOU, 1931

Her name is Leticia Thomas, and this is her house. Her husband passed on three months ago. I read the details of his death before I came. I'm sure I just walked over the spot on her porch where her husband went—the third step. There were handprints across his face, but the official report was heart failure caused by a lung condition.

Mrs. Thomas has no grass for a lawn. Instead, it's planted with palm trees and yuccas, orange trees and jacarandas. A tropical paradise that prompted W. E. B. Dubois, during his tour of Los Angeles a few years ago, to say that Black Angelenos were "without a doubt the most beautifully housed group of colored people in the United States." But her house is not like the other houses off Central—palatial bungalows and Spanish-style stuccos. Her Craftsman is not made of wood. It's mostly brick. The windows along the side of her house seem older than the house, reused from some place that was burned down or demolished. I knock on her front door and wait.

No answer.

I knock again.

Nothing.

I walk along the left side of the house next to the driveway, knocking on those windows, in case she forgot I was coming and can't hear the bell. We had an appointment. Ten thirty, and most people are up and out and back home again. "Mrs. Thomas? It's Louise from the *L.A. Times*."

A beautiful garden of white flowers blooms near my feet, in a square where the concrete was carved out and potted with soil. The white heads of the flowers are tilted up with mouths open, waiting on rain. "Mrs. Thomas?" I say, going to the next window, knocking on glass. "Mrs. Thomas?"

"I'm glad you're here," a woman says from the far end of the drive, behind a wood paneled gate, tall enough that only the crown of her head shows. I go to her and she wiggles the latch, struggling a little to get it open. I put my purse over my shoulder and grab the top of the gate and pull. No use. "Our appointment was for eight," she says.

"I'm terribly sorry," I say, and stagger my legs to give myself more power. She pushes, I pull. "I was told ten thirty. We can reschedule if another time would work better?"

She pushes her body into the gate, and with a hard shove the gate comes undone. "Come on in," she says with a smile. "No better time than now. Can I get you a cup of tea or a pill to relax you? Or coffee?" She waves me in. "It's kindness to keep a pill or warm brew for friends and company." She stands to the side so I can come through the gate.

I follow behind her as she weaves a path through her thigh-high grass. "Your home is lovely, Mrs. Thomas."

"Leticia," she says, and points to the far back of her yard. "My husband built the garage." A pile of nicely stacked bricks is hidden in thin reeds and from it she picks up a small, scooped trowel. Next to it wet mortar is drying in a gray clump.

"I'm sorry to hear about your husband's passing," I say.

"I'm just glad the *Times* is interested in David's life. He lived a good one."

"Resting in heaven now," I say.

She turns, corrects me. "He's all around us." She picks up a piece of timber and throws it to the side of the path. I cover my mouth as we make our way to her back door, our movement agitating wispy insects.

"Can I ask you a question?"

"Is it whether I believe in God?" she says. "Because I didn't say he went to heaven? Was it right to assume I'm Christian because I'm Black? Is that what you were about to ask?"

"Not if the question offends you."

"If you're talking about a god who hates the poor, immigrants, and homosexuals and gives less preference to Blacks, Mexicans, and women, then I'm atheist. I don't know that god and I certainly don't believe in him."

I want to ask her more about it, but I don't. This interview's not about my personal questions. It's an excavation of her husband. I follow her to her back door.

The foundation of her house is earthquake broken, like my office. It's raised, so it's much higher than her yard. Mrs. Thomas has to reach up to turn the doorknob to open it. We step up toward a tiled kitchen, but she stumbles, scrapes her knee on the jagged edge of the step. The step is red. It's been bled on before. I reach for her.

She holds up her hand. "I'm fine. Do it all the time," she says, brushing off her knees and the dust there, strangely uninjured.

Assorted buckets and sponges are in the way and she pushes them over with her foot. Rags lie on the floor and are hung over the countertops. "Excuse my mess," she says. But I don't see mess. I see beauty. Murals and mosaics are completed on the kitchen wall and tiles are affixed everywhere—floors included—but most jobs here are in process. The wall behind the kitchen table is only partly done—blue and white and yellow and green mosaics, like an incomplete jigsaw puzzle glued to the wall.

"Some think I've got too much," she says.

"No . . . no, it's nice," I say, and look around the room. No wall is untouched by ceramic. There's a section of blue tile on the back wall. An image is painted on it. A green field and poppies, behind it a castle on a hill.

"Ah, that castle," she says. "You like it? Castles are defenders. They take care of the people inside their walls."

"Beautiful," I say.

A partly eaten sandwich and today's newspaper on the table. A cup of cold tea contains a thin skin of milk lying like a continent on the surface. There's mail on the table too. It's a lived-in work site.

I touch the tiles behind the table. The mosaics are saturated with color.

"It's a Californian invention to put tile everywhere," she says. "My husband preferred the textured matte glazes of Ernest Batchelder. But I like the brilliance and balance of the ones you're looking at. Malibu Pottery's my favorite."

I take out my notepad and set it down on the table to look in my purse for a pencil. She gives me hers. "I've got a million of 'em." She asks me to hold a paper-size sheet of plywood against the wall like a shelf. She wants to use the edge to level a tile so it's straight. She places a new yellow mosaic on the wall, no spacer. She eyes the distance between the last two and this new one to keep them equal. "The tile boom created more than a hundred tile factories in L.A. California took the nation by storm. My husband was on the first wave."

From a bucket under the table, she uses her trowel to spoon wet mortar, lumpy and gray like discolored pancake batter, and spreads some on the wall and a bit on the back of her tiny tile.

She picks up a rubber mallet from the floor. "The mines," she says, "are what triggered his bouts with breathing. Inflamed airways and all the mucus. I suspect there's something in those clay deposits. Or in the tiles he cut at the factory for fifteen years."

A little mortar drips on the floor.

"You don't want to use too much of this stuff. It'll bubble up around all four sides of your tile and you'll have to clean it out or else when you add your final touches, the grout in the spaces will look terrible. Excess mortar's easy to clean out when you have just a few tiles, but with a hundred and twenty? I'm not that patient."

She takes the plywood sheet from my hand and lays it over the yellow mosaic; she taps the ply with the rubber mallet, flattening the mosaics underneath. She lifts the wood away. With a small wedge tool from the table, she cleans the mortar from the four sides she'd put up before I came but leaves what's oozing up from her new one. "It's better to let it harden first before you clean out the cracks and joints. Hardened but not dry." She reaches out her hand for another tile. I take one from the narrow box on the table. "Blue," she says.

She lays her cheek on the wall and closes one eye, trying to see better across its surface. She rubs her palm over a patch of wall like she's brushing off dust.

"So there's not a god who's angry at us?" I say, finally asking the question I wanted to before.

"Yes. No. Maybe. Imagine God's a violin maker and we're the players who have choice, and now she's watching us use her lovely creations as tennis rackets. Whatever that feeling would be. Hand me another tile." I do. Then I return to the box, captivated by an image.

Next to the box, a framed photo lies face up. Leticia's in the image, a few years younger, standing in front of a makeshift nurses' tent. Military. A red cross is on her uniform. "Turkey 1917" is handwritten in black at the bottom center of the photo. There are four other Black women nurses with her, a radio resting on the table next to them.

"You were in the war?" I say. My voice rises with excitement in knowing *we* were there. Black women.

"Stationed in the eastern part," she says. "Americans were associated powers supporting France, the British Empire. Russia."

"Allies?" I say.

"Not allies," she says. "We were avoiding foreign entanglements, is what they told us. Our support was loose," she says. "I was sent with the nurses. Came home and Los Angeles still won't allow the county hospital to train Negro nurses."

I pick out a yellow tile and give it to her.

"Then what's the radio for? And the second one in the photo, the one under the table?"

She leans back and considers the photo. "Would you look at that?" she says. "Double duty. Nurse and a pattern finder. Sometimes a code breaker. Sometimes just listened to conversations over airwaves."

"What were the messages like?"

"They taught me. They taught me that when you can recognize a pattern, you can change an outcome. Change a pattern in your own life, you change your whole life. But I tell you the truth, the only pattern worth repeating is kindness."

I wish I could just listen to her talk, unguided and unhindered by my questions. But I need to write about her husband. "Have you always lived in this house?" I say.

"We started in a car in L.A. after Kentucky. Homeless for six months, when all we had was love," she says. "My husband used to say we could all love harder. Till love was all gone, he said. As if *gone* were possible."

"That's sweet," I say.

"He was," she smiles. "And then the tile came. A perfect fit for an artist at heart. His art could make money. But then the war came."

"And he went?"

"I did," she says.

She holds the plywood up against the wall herself. Tilts it straight. Takes the pencil from behind her ear and draws a bottom line between two lines of tiles that will meet in the middle.

"Did they treat you poorly over there?" I ask. "For being Black?"

She pushes a yellow tile into the tiny space. It clicks in. The fit is too tight. She flicks it out and starts sanding down the corner of the tiles that are already hung on each side. "It was the bloodiest war in history," she says. "A million people died in less than 150 days. It wasn't just the deaths that exceeded anything people had ever seen before. It was the first time certain weapons were ever used: machine guns, tanks, poison gas. The injuries were brutal and new. We didn't know how to treat them. By the end of the war, twice as many soldiers were injured as were killed. An unprecedented scale. Unprecedented severity. So, no. It didn't matter my skin color. I couldn't let it matter. People I saw were hurting, I was a nurse and couldn't let how others behaved affect how I treated them. Even the cruel ones, I treated with—"

"Mercy?"

"Not mercy. Respect," she says. "Compassion," she says. "Mercy assumes you have power. Something you can decide to give or not. Compassion is kind anyway. What we saw humbled us. There were things we couldn't treat if we tried. Shell shock, for one. The nightmares soldiers had, their terror, outbursts. The new treatment—electromagnetic therapy—didn't work."

"I know somebody who had that," I say. "She's better."

"Better how?" she says, reaching for a tile in the box next to her.

"How?" I say, thinking more about it. "Well, she hasn't harmed herself. Not even after she lost the third baby to miscarriage."

"Three babies?" she says, pushing the tile back into the space. "Sadness can be the hardest thing to let go of when there are no visible scars. Scars are the only proof a person has to show that something went terribly wrong."

She shifts the tile in the space, straightening it.

"What was the weather like in Europe?" I say.

"Europe's a big place," she says.

"I always wanted to travel out of the country and eat, see the sights, take it all in. What's the thing you remember most?"

"That people died," she says.

We're both quiet now.

A blue tile falls off the wall. I pick it up and its corner is chipped. She fingers the tiles in the box and finds a new blue square. Blue again, not yellow or white. I can see it now—the pattern on the wall that first seemed random. I pick up the pencil from on the table and hold it out to her. "I see a lot of death at the paper."

"I saw a lot of murder," she says. "For borders, politics, race." She searches through the box of tiles. "But no one thinks herself a bigot," she says. "It's 1931, and even now, with all of the race separation by neighborhoods, jobs, marriage and churches, with police, no one will see herself a bigot. She'll simply point to someone more bigoted than she is and say, 'See, there's a bigot.'"

Leticia brings a new blue tile close to her eye. She spreads mortar on the back.

"What are you afraid of?" I say.

"I'm afraid to grow old," she says. "My body will go. My mind. My husband's family will come here to stare at my empty husk, listening for the health of my sentences. I'd rather get it over with. Move on so the universe can reuse me the way it reuses everything and let me live again some other way."

"Again?" I say.

"It's impossible not to." She presses her blue tile on the wall without the help of a drawn line. It is perfection.

TWENTY-ONE

LOU, 1932

Esther only wrote me three times in eight months and her Christmas card hardly counted, since she only signed her name to something Hallmark could have written. But I won't ruin our reunion with it. She'll be here in an hour, and when she walks in I want her to breathe in the warmth of melted brown sugar, vanilla, and butter and feel covered in caramel, not complaints.

I haven't slept right for three nights waiting for her. I watched the sunrise again this morning, holding her incomplete letters in my hand—she couldn't say it all—but I hope her conclusion about Europe is she hated it.

In her last letter, in January, she sent me newspaper clippings from Germany and said she quit drinking on account of her puffy face; the article featured her mug to prove her condition. She drew an arrow to her swollen cheeks then wrote *Horror in Großstadtschmetterling*.

Her new show was getting all the buzz. The article read *Pavement Butterfly: Silent Film Turned Stage Play. Esther Lee as Mah is an actress of transcendent talent and great beauty.* I already knew that.

I shopped for a gift for Esther, a dress with pockets. She likes pockets.

Cleaned this apartment and recleaned. Got my pie crusts in the oven, open the kitchen window to let the heat out but outside feels as hot as inside. March and ninety degrees is perfect weather for a reunion party and a barbecue.

Down below, Sunday drivers take their time along the usually busy two-lane, ditching church for sunshine with nowhere to go because every business is "Closed Sunday."

I put my hands in the flour mixture and swear I hear the distinct sound of Esther's car, too early. Mr. Lee said her flight wasn't to land till three.

I look outside my window. Nothing. No, louder now. Must be about a block up the street, gears screeching, engine revving, grinding, and crumbling like it's about to fall out.

Esther's car rolls into view. That can't be her. It's slow, like the end of a carnival ride, the power shut off, rolling to a stop curbside. Smoke rises from the car's undercarriage.

I wait in the window to see who's getting out of the car. The waft of the burning clutch tumbles up and in.

It's her red lipstick I see first.

I stumble out of the kitchen with my fingers covered in flour, white handprints explode and chase me to the door—a bomb where I held the counter, held the wall, the table. I wipe my hands on myself to get to the door—a grenade.

I scramble down my steps and she sees me. Wordless, we serve each other hugs while an unexpected rain falls from the blue, unclouded sky, and it occurs to me how odd it is that water can develop from air, untethered from a rock or spigot, and fall like magic, the air raining on us. This moment *is* magic.

"Have you heard about the Lindbergh baby?!" she says, like we haven't missed a conversation or day together.

"Isn't it wild!"

Somebody gets out of her passenger door. "You know my sister Melanie," Esther says. They look alike, but the face is a limited palette. "Well, come on," she tells her. "Let's get out of this rain."

Esther and I rush up the stairs into my apartment. She plucks her wet hair dry with her fingertips, throws off her coat, makes a beeline to my kitchen. "How do I turn on your radio!" She flips it on. "They say it was a burglary gone wrong," she says. "You think it was a burglary? Or you think that Lindbergh man is hiding the baby for publicity? It's horrible is what. Bad things aren't supposed to happen to white babies." She pauses. "What are you wearing?"

I tie my big apron tighter and straighten my dust cap.

"Are *you* baking?"

My front door opens, and Melanie is standing there, almost forgotten already. Esther keeps tuning the radio through whirs.

"Melanie?" I say, then choose my words carefully so they are slow and clear and understandable. "Esther's said in her letters that you've been in China."

A puzzled expression flashes across her face.

"How did you enjoy your time there?"

"I speak English," she says.

Esther moves the radio from the kitchen counter to the window ledge, adjusts the antenna, and fidgets with the knobs, whirring from one station to the next, Spanish, English, static, English again with static on top. I join her in the kitchen. "I wish you weren't baking sweets," Esther says. "You know I can't eat sweets. It'll age me and put on pounds that'll keep me unemployable. Hollywood hates fat people and old women, more than they hate Asians."

"You look no more than twenty," I assure her.

"Yeah, but if another director puts me in a kimono and I have a pudgy face, I'll look matronly on the screen."

"I can help with whatever you're making," Melanie says. I nod, though I wish it were Esther. I say, "Are you older or younger?"

"Guess," she says, friendly.

"Hmm?" I say. "Hard to tell with brown people, too. After about twenty-eight, we shape-shift with weight gain and loss till about sixty. Forget aging."

"Two years older," she says.

"For the custard," I say. "Five tablespoons sugar. Three tablespoons cornstarch. Large pinch of salt. And toss those ingredients in here." I put a medium saucepan on the stove.

A man's voice finally comes clearly through the radio, saying he doesn't understand the hoopla around housing restrictions in all the new suburbs. "Why would anybody want to live where they're not wanted?" he says. "As an American, I should have the freedom to have my children grow up in a lifestyle my wife and I choose, without foreign influence, Negroes or Mexicans."

Esther turns the station, settles on a new one. A jolly voice comes through the radio. "Welcome to AM 900, home to your CBS radio network KHJ. And I'm your host, Ross McMahon."

"Can you listen to a different station?" I say. "McMahon is always trying to get his guests to disagree."

"It's the only place I can get real news," Esther says, "without listening to idiots who think they're not foreigners here too. It's not McMahon's fault that his guests misbehave. They're lucky to be on his show. He has thousands of listeners."

"Aren't you going to help us?" I say. "Your sister's doing all the work."

Esther leaves the radio, washes her hands. "One and a third cup of half-and-half. Four egg yolks."

While she measures in the milk and cream, I whisk them in the mixture and turn on the flames under the pan. It feels good to have her near me, familiar.

The static on the radio returns as Esther pours in my already-separated yolks, one at a time. "Get more of the half-and-half ready because the heat causes it to get lumpy fast. If it does, we'll pour in more to keep it creamy and smooth."

The voice of a soft-spoken woman sputters through the speakers. McMahon, the host, tells listeners the guest is Aimee Semple McPherson. "Turn it up," I tell Melanie. "She's one of those crazy church ladies."

"Welcome, Mrs. McPherson," McMahon says.

"Aimee," she says. "And thank you." I can hear the smile in her voice. "Pleased to be here."

"And Mr. Fighting Bob Shuler!" McMahon announces the other guest in the studio with excitement. "I'm glad you could join us too. A busy man these days. The school to run and a church."

"A pleasure," Bob says, firm as a handshake.

Esther talks over their conversation and goes in the living room, sitting on her knees in front of the radio. "You think they're going to talk about the Lindbergh baby? They need to talk about the Lindberg baby. Even the mob is involved in the search. I'll bet that baby's dead. Wouldn't that be sad? Who would kill a baby?"

I say, "I hope whoever took him wasn't a Black person. God, I pray he wasn't Black. We've got enough to deal with."

McMahon says to Aimee, "You're the founder of the Foursquare Church. Have a fifty-three-hundred-seat church right here in Los Angeles, the largest in the nation. An icon in your own right. And you're . . . a woman."

"It's God's church," she says calmly, humbly. "I'm just His messenger."

"Outrageous, is what!" Bob, the other guest, says. "Unorthodox." Bob's annoyed. "Women should not lead a church. And this woman's on her third marriage!"

"Happily married, I'm sure," McMahon says, blocking the jabs for his guest. "Happily . . . for the third time?"

Now me and Esther and Melanie sit together on the sofa and lean in, hover next to the radio.

"Yes and no," Aimee says.

Bob jumps on it. "See, this is the kind of degradation of morality we're getting used to in our country and I'll keep speaking against. Truth is not negotiable! Ask her about what she does at their church. Demonic activities."

"Well, hold on, Mr. Shuler," McMahon says.

"Quite alright," Aimee says. "He's referring to the spiritual encounters some members experience. Physical healings and miracles—"

"Catholic!" Bob says.

"We're not Catholic. And Catholics are Christian."

"Oh, forgive her, Lord," Bob says.

"Esther," I say, not taking my eyes off the radio, "can you grab the extracts from the table and take them in the kitchen?"

None of us move, staring at the Bakelite radio, paused now, waiting for the static to clear. And anyway, Aimee's not answering.

Esther gets up.

McMahon finally says, "Let's change direction a little from these 'experiences.' Twentieth-century Pentecostalism? Would you agree that the Azusa Street Revival here in Los Angeles is responsible for the spread of the faith?"

"Led by a Negro," Bob interrupts, as if to clarify.

"God uses everybody," Aimee says. "Even a broken vessel like me. Like Peter. Like Paul."

"I won't have a woman preaching to me!" Bob says. "What's relevant is her failed marriages and shirking her duties at home with her husband, which is no doubt why the first left her to be adulterous twice over."

"Twice?" McMahon says. "Once someone is married, she's always married so long as her spouse is still alive. Her relation with her new husband is adulterous."

"Esther?" I say. "Since you're over there, go'n and pour in a half-teaspoon of vanilla and a half of almond extract. I'll get the chilled whipping cream from the ice tub in a second. It'll take a half-cup in the end. Will you whisk it in for me?"

McMahon says, "So, Aimee, you're happily married now and leading a church?"

"My third husband and I are . . . separated. So no, I'm sorry to say, not happily. It was a mistake from the start."

"I'll say," Bob says. "You should be ashamed calling yourself a woman of God!"

"I'm not ashamed of the Gospel," she says. "Jesus's death, burial, and resurrection in three days."

"Three *days,* not three husbands," Bob says. "God intended for marriage to be between one man and one woman. That's two people. The *same* man married to the *same* woman forever, not this rodeo of one rider, different bulls. You've made a mockery of marriage, sitting here smiling."

Aimee says, "They break my heart too, Pastor." There's no smile in her voice this time. "My failed marriages," she says.

"*You* divorced them!" Bob says.

There's silence from the radio. Inaudible mumbling by Bob.

"All abortions should be mourned," Aimee says. "Even the ones we choose."

The men gasp.

"Lou, turn it off!" Esther says.

"And let me be clear," Aimee says. "I'm not talking about the abortion of a child. I'd never choose that. Even someone empty would be filled with hope at a chance to adopt a beginning-baby."

From the kitchen, Esther yells, "Maybe the baby doesn't want to be adopted!"

Melanie says, "But that doesn't mean a baby wouldn't want to live."

I flip the radio off on my way back with the cream because the radio's anger is contagious. I say, "I told you—that station is always so salacious. I swear they just want people to fight on the program and say things they don't mean to get ratings."

"They're saying what they believe," Melanie says, her voice soft and unexpected. "They should be able to share their thoughts so we know who they are."

"Sure they can," Esther says. "But as a woman, if she's not careful, some man who's not a gentleman might hurt her for her words."

"Hurt her how?" I say to Esther.

"She's still young," Melanie says. "Life's nothing to lose when you're young."

TWENTY-TWO

—◄(O)►—

LOU, 1932

"The carefully planned kidnapping of the Lindbergh baby remained a mystery to the outside world tonight," the *L.A. Times* reads on March 3, 1932.

Twenty-four hours after the infant son of the famous flyer Colonel Charles A. Lindberg was snatched from his crib, there is an air of expectancy inside the brilliantly lit mountaintop home in the isolated cedar back country of New Jersey as the search halts, waiting for his son's ransom.

Lindberg, haggard and distraught earlier in the day, appeared calmer after nightfall and was known to have expressed confidence that his son, ill from a cold and clad only in a light woolen sleeper when abducted, would be returned safe.

In the meantime, from his county jail cell today, Al Capone offered a reward of $10,000 for the safe return of the Lindbergh baby and the capture of his kidnappers. "It's the most outrageous thing I ever heard of," said Capone, whose own name has several times been mentioned in Chicago abductions.

"The dastardly and cowardly kidnapping" of the infant Lindbergh, as it was described in Congress by Senator Barbour, brought a shock to Washington today that quickly steeled itself into a determination that the federal government join the search for him and his abductors.

Actor and comedian Will Rogers wept from his home as he describes his last visit with Baby Lindbergh just two weeks ago Sunday. Will bounced Baby Lindbergh on his knee. "He's the cutest little feller you ever saw. His hair is just like my wife's except more so because he's got hundreds of golden ringlets all over his little head." In his letter to the *L.A. Times* editor today, he added, "Why don't lynching parties widen their scope and take kidnappings?"

Reading Mr. Rogers's words make my stomach turn the second time this week and not because I don't like children. Death must be getting to me. And this month marks the four-year anniversary of more death and no justice, when thousands of poor people, dressed only in their pajamas, were snatched away in their sleep.

Three minutes before midnight, on March 12, 1928, the St. Francis Dam presented itself like a fat man playing dress-up in six-inch heels. He tilted and slipped and the dam failed.

Twelve billion gallons of raging water and debris tore through San Francisquito Canyon, thirty miles north of Los Angeles, and nobody could help him up. Their neglect would cost them their lives.

Just a mile down the road from the dam, Alvin Ram had been sleeping with his family when the sudden stillness woke him. He set his feet down next to the side of his bed and rubbed and cracked his neck. Strange, he thought, to hear no birds, no mouse chatter. Only a distant rumble with no quake.

He checked on his daughters, still asleep in their beds, then pulled his suspenders over his shoulders and walked out into the pitch-black dark. He breathed deeply, took life in. He was grateful, he thought.

It was a relief to hear the dogs. Their barking, however, became furious. The racket woke his girls and they joined him on the porch. He grabbed his pistol and trained it into the dark.

They all noticed the strange white mist in the air. His youngest daughter, only five, lifted her hand and pointed to what looked like a giant silver web rising to ten stories high in the distance and getting closer.

No, it couldn't be.

Before any of them could make out what the gleaming veil was, God seemed to blink, carrying the whole family away in his lashes. A roar followed. Sirens screamed desperate warnings in the distance. Electric wires snapped, and Power Station Two reported that Power Station One was gone. "I repeat. It's gone."

Chunks of concrete from the station and the dam were now racing down the canyon in a two-mile-wide deluge, swallowing houses, bridges, livestock, and sleeping human bodies. The crippled and infirmed had no chance. The flood had fifty more miles to go.

Telephone operators frantically called ahead, trying to outrace the water to wake as many people as they could. And even as the flood sped toward their own towns, two women operators, Reicel Jones in the city of Saticoy and Louise Gipe in Santa Paula, bravely stayed at their posts, calling residents in low-lying areas, urging them to flee to higher ground.

Motorcycle officers rode into the path of the flood and knocked on every third house, warning people and telling them to wake their neighbors.

Many residents rushed into the hills, where they watched as the muddy water took more prisoners and turned west into the Santa Clara Riverbed, where it flooded the towns of Castaic, Fillmore, Piru, Valencia, and Bardsdale, then continued through Santa Paula in Ventura County, where it would empty its wreckage into the Pacific Ocean fifty-four miles away. The worst American civil engineering failure of this century.

"St. Francis is down" were the words that followed the midnight call to a mansion in the hills above Los Angeles.

"Did anyone die?" quivered William "The Chief" Mulholland, still in his pajamas.

Within the hour, he was dressed in a suit and tie and chauffeured to the former site of the dam he'd built, where water was still trickling. Mulholland remained there, stooped and stupefied, for three hours; the open mouth of the dam presented itself like all the teeth had been knocked out except one. A single piece of concrete in the dam wall didn't fall. That piece would be named the Tombstone.

Mulholland hoped that the cause in fact of the break would be sabotage by those radicalized farmers who he'd battled with for years in the water wars. But it wasn't.

Investigations would determine it was his hand, his construction missteps, that would lead to over twelve hundred homes being destroyed, orchards ripped from the ground, thousands of livestock and animals killed, and more than four hundred fifty people dead or missing—the real number unknown because migrant workers weren't counted.

"I envy the dead," Mulholland said. Among them may have been his best friend. Tony Harnischfeger, his dam keeper, one of two people whose call he'd answer day or night and drive an hour from mansion to mud in response. Mulholland had built a cottage for Tony and his family just under the dam.

Tony's wife had left him, so in the house with Tony was his new girlfriend, Leona, and his six-year-old son, Coder. His wife kept their daughter.

Tony was so well positioned in Mr. Mulholland's life that whenever the dam wall sprang a new leak, Tony would call Mr. Mulholland, who would take a thirty-seven-mile slow drive from his mansion in Los Angeles to Saugus, where they'd stand in the canyon, staring up at the 195-foot dam.

Mulholland had no formal engineering training, but to his self-trained eye, the structure was safe. "Leaks," he said, "were to be expected with a dam of this size," but he encouraged Tony to keep him informed.

Ranchers and townspeople who lived downwind of the wall would joke, "See you later, if the dam don't break." And it was a joke because no one would believe it could happen. That it would break. Mulholland was smart, they thought; he had so much money, and the city had given him all this power, absolute power, to build it, inspect it, manage it. Why would Mulholland walk below the dam if it wasn't safe? He'd hike in the canyon with Tony's six-year-old son. Mulholland wasn't looking to die.

Tony had built steps up the canyon hillside, next to the dam wall, in case the unthinkable happened. But it *was* unthinkable. The reports from motorists who complained about the new potholes in the road next to the dam wall were pesky at worst. Including the report from one motorist on March 12, 1928, earlier that day, that the roadbed near the dam was sagging more than a foot.

Mulholland inspected the cracks, as he did every time Tony called. He determined there was no need to grout the cracks, as he sometimes ordered, and declared the dam safe. Then Mulholland headed home. Just twelve hours later the dam wall would fail.

Just minutes before the dam broke, another motorcyclist driving on the road above the canyon would report seeing lights, though the dam had no lights—there was only Tony's flashlight that he'd share with Coder.

Their bodies were never found.

Tony's girlfriend, Leona, believed to be the first victim of the dam, was pulled dead from the mud. Although rescue volunteers first reported having found Coder, his mother confirmed the freckled redheaded boy in the morgue wasn't hers.

Mulholland would resign seven months later and pay no fine or penalty even though the investigation showed the dam was built well below civil engineering standards of the time. In the formal hearing determining his guilt or innocence, the jury found that "the construction and operation of a great dam should have never been left to the judgment of one man, no matter how eminent." The City took responsibility and set up a one-million-dollar reparation fund for the victims. But not all lives were created equal according to the U.S. Constitution, so nonwhites were paid less.

Some say Mulholland did pay. Not with a single dollar but with his reputation, his body, and mind. In the days following the tragedy, his speech became slurred and his hands trembled. It was the cost of surviving. And this tragedy was only four years ago.

When I presented the final story about Mulholland and the St. Francis Dam to Morris, he fell silent after he read it. I wasn't sure whether to sit or stand. Then he finally said, "Why did you write this?"

I sat in his chair, trying to understand his question. "Because, Mr. Morris, it's about death and there are colored people in the story, and because there's something I think we can learn from it."

"We did," he says. "The City has teams of people on all construction projects now. Engineers. Scientists."

"Maybe there's something more? The migrant workers who lost their lives? The equal value of all life . . ."

"The man is sick, Lou. Dying. Right now in his bed." Morris shakes his head, puts his hands on his desk. "You know, you never struck me as angry, Lou."

"I'm angry? I'm not angry. That's the story."

"Certainly a tad rebellious, if you ask me. The story reads like you're transferring your anger onto this poor, sick man. Is it white people you're angry with? Me? I've heard of an angry Black woman, but this is low, Lou, and to be a gentle lady like yourself showing no compassion. Migrant workers, really? Given a chance, these people wouldn't stand up for you."

I fold my arms. Let him finish his argument with me without me. I guess I am angry. Now.

"I want you here, Lou. Really. I do. I've supported your work here, haven't I? Is . . . are migrant workers even something you care about?"

"I care about life," I say.

"Then what about the story on the vegetable markets in Little Tokyo you abandoned? The canals in Venice? A Black man built that community. What about Willa and Charles Bruce? Their Negro beach resort was shuttered and wrongfully condemned by the city a few years back?"

"Then why didn't *you* write it? Am I required to only write about Black people?"

"Required? Is that what this is? You bringing your lukewarm attitude to a city we're passionate about at the *Times* and to you it's a requirement?"

"I love this city."

"Do you?" he says. "You know where lukewarm gets you? It's like trying to heat old bathwater with boiling water. They both get cold. You need to care, Lou. To be on fire for L.A., too, bring your fire to L.A.'s fire. You've become a bystander, and this article you wrote is no more than lodging a complaint. Where's your interview with migrant families who lost someone? Bodies are still being discovered every year. Where's your investment?" He leans forward. "There's the greater good to consider."

"Whose 'good'?" I say. And in my mind, I dare him to answer "Society." That answer is almost always self-serving.

"This is my life, Lou," he says. "My city. Not just a job. You're halfheartedly doing a job that could hurt someone's legacy. That's career ending."

He studies my face, but I give him nothing. Nobody loves Los Angeles more than I do. It's the only thing that's mine.

He takes a deep breath, rubs a hand across the back of his reddened neck. "Los Angeles," he says, "will remember Bill Mulholland for making it possible. Without his work, his vision and inventiveness, Los Angeles couldn't have grown the way it has. He built the longest-running aqueduct in the world here, made sure we had water. Over two hundred miles from the Owens Valley to Los Angeles and he did it. He deserves credit for that and more. So when we eulogize him, we'll tell the story of how Mulholland was a self-taught immigrant ditch digger who became one of the richest and most powerful men in L.A. That's America. That's the miracle and the man we'll remember at the paper."

"Even if it's not the whole truth?"

"Because it is the truth too," he says.

Morris turns my flat white pages into a wadded ball of paper, and I don't complain. He's right, I don't care. And I don't care about his heroes. It's like he said about the workers—his heroes don't care about me either.

TWENTY-THREE

LOU, 1932

My city and its water feel good over my body.

I promised myself to never see Jefferson again, but he invited me to the beach. Not just me.

He rang me at the office and asked if I'd join him and the group of second-graders he volunteered to tutor in swimming. I told him I don't babysit. He said, "Naw, just come." Said he wanted to show me how to get over my fear. "What do you mean, afraid of water? Like bathing afraid of water? Or drinking water afraid? What about rain?'" he said, laughing. "Bring your swimming cap."

So now, I float alongside my second-grade pals in the Inkwell, the only stretch of the Pacific coast in Los Angeles where Black people are allowed, our toes on the edge of the future, ready to live differently.

"Don't bend," Jefferson says as I hold both of my arms around his one. "Trust me," he says, like a lullaby "Just lie on your back. You can close your eyes."

The flat of his hand is a life raft below me. Five feet of water and he's another foot above it. "Relax," he says, and I let myself sway and dip like a buoy, unafraid now because I'm with him. Unafraid of his touch. "Who wants to go again?" Jefferson says, and in a sing-song the children shout, "Me!"

And I understand what it means to be us. To be wanted and excited, to be in danger yet unafraid. To be in a place you have to forget you don't belong.

The last two miles of the ride home from the beach with Jefferson have been in uncomfortable silence. It's not his fault. It was the sight of the setting sun that triggered in me an unexplainable fear. A haunting feeling rose with the shifting landscape as we moved toward the horizon where both dawn and sunset mimic a cracked egg, the Santa Ana mountain range its jagged break, side lying, spilling yellow and red light from the haphazard line. The sight of it closed my mouth.

I pretend to be resting against his door, my eyes closed, keeping my fists clenched to hold my fear in my hands. He asks me how I enjoyed the day, and I don't answer as if I'm sleep.

And now, the closer we get to Boyle Heights, the farther I feel from him, distracted by my own countdown. He'll pull up in front of my house in what I'd guess is ten minutes and we'll say goodbye. I don't know if or when we'll ever have another time like this.

"It's been a long day," he says to himself. "Thank you for helping with the children," he says in case I'm listening.

I hear the mariachi bands playing in the plaza, welcoming me and every driver back home. I wish this music could be a beginning, not an end.

I recognize the antiseptic smell of the drugstore, Fourth and Mott. It's sanitized every morning to keep polio away. Jefferson slows. "Lou," he says, a gentle hand on my shoulder. "You're home."

I feel sick.

I look out the window and see I've left a light on for myself upstairs and force a natural smile. "Thank you," I say.

"I'll walk you to your door," he says, already out of his side of the car. He opens my car door and I pause in the moment, wanting to remember it. He reaches out his hand and I take it.

He walks me to the base of my stairs and we both look up the steps to my landing. He doesn't move.

"I'll go from here," I say, and he nods, kisses me on the cheek like a gentleman—those new kisses, right side then left side, hello, goodbye. "European," they're calling it. It's been all the rage. But when it's his turn to kiss the left, he doesn't. I lean forward, and in the confusion we linger. There, between the left and right side, paused at the center, inches from each other's lips. I feel the warmth of his breath. "Good night," he says.

Upstairs, I collapse on my sofa—*coward.* Outside, young children are playing hopscotch in the warm dark. They're counting in Tagalog. *"Isa, dalawa, tatlo,"* they say, one, two, three. They argue in English, as if in two minds. And it occurs to me that I can give myself permission to be of two minds too.

I leave my coat and purse on the sofa and take a seat at my writing desk with Esther's pencil and paper, try to sketch our sunset moments that make me afraid of them being both the beginning of something and an end. If only I can draw it, it can stay my present—the car ride, the mountains, Jefferson's face.

Then, I realize I can't remember the shape of his eyes.

Like forgetting a dream while waking. My images are stick figures with curves. I tear out the page, the next, and again scribble him wrong, wasting good paper. *Not him.* I try again, then circle my poor imitation one, two, three times around. Tunnel through the paper to the oak desk on purpose. Four—

The underside of my hand is streaked with silver dirt from sliding sweaty over my own pencil marks. I'm drawing Jefferson. I'm forgetting his face. I'd recognize him if I saw him, of course, he just left me, but to remember him to draw him is like lifting the heaviest stone. Every sketch looks more and more like rounding a stick figure, and I can't get the fear out of my mind that this paper is my memory; if I can't draw him, I won't remember him. I try again and again. Sketch his closed eyes in a semicircle. The arch is too high. I open his eyes and make them rounder and deep. Sketch his neck, his temples, his forehead. The result is a man with a death stare.

I flip the page and draw him again. Not right.

Again.

A shadow moves across my room. I stop drawing. Hold my hand still. It's not unusual for shadows to take shape near the edge of the bed when you sleep in the city. The subtle movement could be my own breathing.

I hold my breath.

Something moves.

I finger the razor in my pencil box, pick it up with my right hand, slide my hand in my desk and take the cap gun in my left. I turn in my seat and sit eye-to-eye with a figure of a man in the corner of my room. I thrust my razor between us, threatening the darkness. "Take another step and I swear I'll gut you like a pig."

He puts his hands up. "Don't you have to shoot a pig?" he says, and stands. Lowers his hands. I point my gun at his neck.

"Lou?" he says, like we're friends.

"I swear to God, I'll kill you!" He raises his hands again. I flick the gun barrel toward the lamp. "Move over to the light where I can see you."

He steps over slowly.

I see him. Aaron slides his hat from his head.

"Why are you in my apartment!" I say, holding him in my line of sight, still somewhat relieved it's him.

"Are you going to shoot me?" he says.

"I dare you to move again."

"Lou?" he says. "I know you won't shoot me."

"You don't know me."

"I know that's a toy gun. I was there when you stole it from that woman in the alley."

"Get back!" I say. I drop my gun, take the razor from my other hand and push it out into the space between us.

"Don't you remember me?" he says.

"Why are you in my apartment!"

"Do you remember me, Lou?" his voice calm and measured. I see him as if for the first time again. Like we haven't seen each other since we lived in the old country, years ago—strange and familiar because this is the only city I know. "How did you get in my apartment?" I say. My elbows buckle as if the razor's heavy.

"Esther's key," he says simply. "She left a set with me in case you ever needed my help."

"Help for what?"

"A lockout. Leaky toilet. An overflow."

"A break-in?" I say. I feel lightheaded.

"Can't be too careful," he says. He reaches out for me and gently takes hold of my cut hand, sliced from gripping the razor too tightly, but I still won't let it go. Blood covers my skin like it's from a source other than me. He smears it away, ready to care for it the way he does one of the fighters, but it's already healed. I pull my hand away.

"This must be confusing, I know."

"I need you to leave," I say.

"I can answer any questions you have."

I rush my razor to his throat, hold it there. Press it so he can feel it. "Don't come to my house again. Don't speak to me. Don't look at me. You understand?"

He nods.

"Give me Esther's keys."

He hands them to me and gets up. I follow him into the living room, then to the door. "I'm sorry to have scared you," he says. "I only wanted to help. When you're ready, we can talk again."

I close the door and lock it twice.

TWENTY-FOUR

—◄O►—

LOU, 1932

If Route 66 has its way, it'll come right through our Black neighborhoods, move our cemetery, even remove Mr. Lee's gym from Boyle Heights through eminent domain—a concept that means the government can take somebody's property and give the person some money, what the government think it's worth. Forget what it means to you or your community. And then destroy it.

The City isn't mapping the suburbs for the Route. Their focus is on us, where the people are "foreigners"—not white enough, not Christian enough, the destruction of neighborhoods akin to raising border walls between the equally vivid colors on the paint pallet on the city. The haves and the have-nots, heritage, religion, white collar versus blue collar. But people are here today to fight to preserve this community. Morris has sent me.

City Hall is already loud and packed with bodies even though the meeting doesn't start for another half hour. Tonight's the second consecutive meeting and protestors, like the wall, have risen to the occasion. A group of men and women are holding signs that read MEXICANS KEEP GOING, WE CAN TAKE CARE OF OUR OWN.

One of the women holding a sign raises her fist and shouts, "We will not be reverse colonized!" To the left of the room are banners that read CALIFORNIA IS FOR EVERYBODY and IMMIGRANTS ARE AMERICA.

More than a handful of fighters from Mr. Lee's gym are in the crowd; some have their young sons beside them holding tiny American flags. The gym is beloved.

I should be happy to be here with these passionate people, but what I want desperately is to find Jefferson, to be in his company. He's not here.

There's great anticipation about a speech to be given tonight by Cyrus Avery, the father of Route 66. It's been reported that Avery said he'll be damned if the highway isn't approved.

I take out my pencil and paper and write that Route 66 will bring money and fresh blood to the city, a continuously paved highway from Chicago to Los Angeles.

"You look like shit," Esther says, coming in next to me. Her long plaid dress is wearing her, black gloves covering her hands.

"You made it," I say, relieved.

"My father made me come. Wanted to make sure I saw this circus . . . this process. Democracy at work."

"Don't take the innoculation!" a woman yells from the front of the room. She's with her husband, and his t-shirt has a circle and a strike-through of the words POLIO VACCINE. She is carrying a baby on her hip.

"The government wants to make polio vaccines. They want to make us sick!" he says.

"Isn't that . . ." Esther says.

"Yeah, that's Bertha. From high school."

"She barely passed science."

I give Esther the sheet of paper Bertha handed me on the way in. "Here's the flyer she gave me about the innoculation."

Bertha is telling someone at the door, "I researched this."

"Did she say 'research'?" Esther says.

"It's normal to have questions about a new innoculation, isn't it? Even if you're not against them. They believe what they're saying."

"They're holding themselves out as experts. Neither one of them could hold a candle to doctors and virology experts anywhere in the world."

"It's submission. A lot of people have a problem submitting to authority. They only trust themselves."

"Are you kidding me, Lou? They're raving! Can't even rationalize with them. Have you tried? I have. And it feels like telling them to calm down in the middle of their panic attack, and theirs is an extended one. They just don't know it. And they sound convincing because they've convinced themselves."

"A healthy distrust of the government is fine."

"Lou, they use fragments of the truth that can hurt people. Keep people from getting help. We're repeating mistakes we should have finished making a century ago. Or at least decades ago, with smallpox."

"Vaccines have eggs in them!" Bertha's husband yells. "Are you allergic to eggs? No polio vaccine!"

At the front of the room, fifteen empty seats raised a couple feet from the floor are waiting for the City Council. The middle seat is higher, for the mayor. Security is posted around them, eyeing the crowd. The council, when they're ready, will walk out together, pour their bodies into their seats, lay their papers on the desk in front of them together.

Two flagpoles shoot out from the wall behind the council seats, each holding a different flag: California and the United States. Behind them on the wall is a golden plaque—the State of California golden seal, a bear and oats.

"You want water?" Esther says. "I need water." I shake my head, and she shimmies among the crowd, headed toward the ice water pitchers.

I move to the back of the hall and stand with my notepad in hand. The unnatural light above is yellowing my paper like my page has been smoked over for days. I write what some are shouting: "The city is getting more deeply divided by race," a white man says. "For what?" he says. "For white southerners and midwesterners to feel comfortable here? Maybe we don't want *them* here."

Others are calling for further repatriation of Mexicans to Mexico, demanding Mexico take care of, provide opportunities for, and keep safe its own people. Hard enough to take care of our own families.

"Race hate!" someone says.

"No one's checking the Canadian border for aliens," another man says, and I cringe at the word *aliens*. It's what they use for Japanese cantaloupe farmers in the Central Valley, a word for all the things called "illegal" or "vice" for want of imagination and baseless morality, like antitattoos and antihooch. They've criminalized self-comfort so the only comfort we're allowed is what we can pay for *from them* in state-run doctors' offices that discriminate against us or their pharmaceuticals. "Aliens," I say to myself, and write it down, and it occurs to me that race hate is not a deal breaker for a lot of people who consider themselves good . . . unless they've decided that they're the ones being persecuted—real or imagined.

I say to the young white woman standing next me, "Excuse me, ma'am? I'm with the *Los Angeles Times*. May I ask why you've come today?"

"Yes, ma'am," she says respectfully. "I'm here to do what I can. To find out what I can do. I don't know what help looks like."

I ask her name, Katherine, and then her age, twenty-seven. I see her race in her skin tone: straight red hair and blue eyes. I ask her religion. She tells me Mormon but that's not what brings her here. "There are so many good, kind people in the world," she says. "People who just want to do good, kind things. I want to be one of them. I'm here because I'm not powerless."

"No borders!" another woman shouts, and everyone seems to just stare at her. She clears her throat, nods her head, resolute. "No borders," she repeats.

The engine of sound starts again around the room. There's much to talk about. These are the final days before the vote to approve the destruction or life (and for whom) the Route will bring.

The room falls silent when the mayor comes out of his chambers. He announces that Cyrus Avery has fallen ill and won't be able to join us tonight. A swarm of loud sighs circles the hall. Shouting now. Security holds up their hands for quiet and to keep people back. The mayor says, "We all want to do what's best for hardworking Americans." I write it down and think it must be beautiful to be an American who believes that every good thing that happens to him and is denied to others happens because of his hard work and good morals.

"You're Louise, right?" a Black woman beside me says. She's a tad shorter than me and looks like Mrs. Miriam but more yellow. She's wearing a press pass for the *California Eagle*. "You're from the *Times*?" she says. "Charlotta Bass." She holds out her hand to shake and I'm starstruck. I know who she is. Charlotta Bass from South Carolina. First came to Los Angeles for her health but stayed for the love. Founded the *California Eagle*, one of our city's race papers for colored people and Black people. Word is she's on the slate for the next presidential election. Vice president of the United States. She'd be the first Black woman to do it. A hero. I shake her hand.

She takes out her camera and flash, and I don't know how she does it all. I only have a pencil and notebook.

"We sure could use another good reporter at the *California Eagle*," she says. "We're up to four now. A funded paper. Not a big budget, but there's pay and you're already trained. There's a lot going on, more with Route 66 on its way."

"You think they'll approve it?"

"Unless somebody can show why white people will lose money. Money is power and only fear is greater than that."

"I'm just filling in today really. I'm usually on the Death desk."

"You're from Boyle Heights, aren't you? Are you covering the TB outbreak in your part of town?"

Another man's voice from behind me says, "TB outbreak? Now that's news. A colored's disease." His voice is instantly annoying and familiar. Metal Wally is all bundled up around the neck with a tartan-striped scarf like it's cold out and wears a gray wool blazer. He leans against the post. "You got a cough?"

"I don't have it," I say, flipping my page.

"Let me guess," Charlotta says. "You're Wallace Stone."

"You know your business," Metal Wally says. "You know my work?"

"I've heard you're the new reporter for the *Snooper*."

"Was tired of waiting for my chance at the *Times*. They should be called *Behind the Times*. They don't have any vision. The Jews run the paper anyway. Trying to take over the world."

"That so?" Charlotta says.

"I've got something real to say. The country's going down the drain. I'm after corruption for the *Snooper*. The criminal element. All kinds of vice that the mayor is in on. It's part of their agenda." He whispers, "A cabal."

Wally's eye catches a person more interesting than us at the front of the room and goes toward it. He snaps a photo from near the mayor's seat and a man in a black suit rushes him, escorts him out. NO FLASH PHOTOGRAPHY, the signs here read.

Charlotta says, "If you want to come off Death, you should come by next week. Let's talk about what the mayor is planning for this Route. He ain't gonna do it today without Avery here. He's got people all worked up in here thinking something's gonna be voted on."

"Are you sure?" I say. "It's on the schedule to discuss the Route."

"There's only one voice this Council cares about and it ain't ours. Or theirs," she says, pointing to those holding signs, IMMIGRANTS WELCOME.

The mayor knocks his gavel and brings us all to order. The City Council members take their seats. After a moment of silent attention, the mayor announces the council is tabling Route 66 until next month. "We are adjourned."

TWENTY-FIVE

LOU, 1932

The driver saw the red ball but not the Black boy behind it. It's why Jefferson didn't make the City Council meeting seven days ago. That afternoon of the red ball, neighbors went running. For the boy. Then for his momma. We were told there was no drinking involved. Jefferson's station was the first to arrive on the scene to give aid till the ambulance arrived.

Morris asked me if I'd cover the story, but I told him I was too close to it and what would come from me would not be journalism. But maybe I should've reached out to Jefferson. To his family or to his station, but I didn't. I read about it in the paper like any stranger would.

The *Times* said that Jefferson's wife had been inside her house laughing with friends when someone called for her. "Come quick! Come quick! We think it's your boy."

She must have dropped the pan in her hand. Was baking at the time, wearing a flowing dress. Her radio was on.

Her girlfriends held her tight as she collapsed after seeing her son's red ball and then the matching red on the road—I've seen red on the road.

Today is their son's funeral. Esther and I walk in a procession of three hundred brown men and women and children and officers under the waterless skies of L.A. This stretch of Pico Boulevard is named after a mixed-race Black man, Pio Pico, the last governor of Mexican California but not the first. Los Angeles was first settled by a group of *pobladores*—most of them African Spaniards—who were on a long journey, not to conquer and take but in search of a better life. And in 1781, when these African Spaniards made the decision to call this place home, they named the city after those they found there: *Los Angeles*, the City of Angels.

But everything disappears here. A permanent boomtown, Los Angeles is always resetting and replacing its angels.

A woman at the front of the line begins singing "Didn't It Rain," a song about hope for the future, for better times we can't yet see. Her voice seems to call down heaven, calls down a halo and it grounds itself in our path, standing on end. We mourners walk through its circle, comforted, healed; Esther and I join in song. But somewhere along the road, Jefferson's wife, positioned between a church sister and Jefferson, is letting go of their hands.

TWENTY-SIX

LOU, 1932

Charlotta's home has been converted into a self-publisher's dream. A printing press is at the front, three typewriters at the back, two hundred books holding each other up. This is her home. When her husband died, he left his share of their business and all of this to her. Her secretary let me in and asked me to wait here in her office.

A framed photo of them is hanging on the wall, and a matching one is on the desk in front of me. I don't think I'll ever be a wife. To be a wife, it seems, is to forfeit every gift God gave you to serve your husband. Sure, you repurpose yours for his but usually that means for children, so I don't blame Jefferson's wife when last weekend after the funeral, as our procession passed Jefferson's house, she walked across her lawn and through the front door, packed her bag, and was on the bus back to Alabama by the end of that hour. And out of obligation or awe, Jefferson never broke the line. Now he's rumored to drink alcohol at work because he didn't go with her. And I'm sorry. I won't ring him, but I *am* sorry.

A shuffle behind me in Charlotta's office causes me to sit up straight; her voice follows. "You want something to eat?" Charlotta says, carrying a plate of food and talking like we were in the middle of a conversation. "Go'n fix yourself a plate. There's black-eyed peas in there. Corn bread. Don't nobody eat the hog head cheese but me."

There's something beautiful about being around women who know who they are, say what they mean with little effort. "No, thank you. I had a meal before I came." I lie because I can't eat and talk.

Charlotta slides a stack of newspapers across her desk. The *Los Angeles Courier*, a weak paper of conspiracy theories and articles from citizens with views I don't agree with. I say, "The publisher of that paper will accept any story. Everybody's got an opinion, and not all of 'em are worth publishing."

"Is that so?" Charlotta says, and picks up the latest edition from the top of her pile, opens it to center. She reads in silence, cleans her teeth with her tongue; it bulges behind her lips when she sucks something out of her teeth. I wait.

The collard greens on her plate are slick with ham hock fat. The bottom of her cornbread has soaked in its juice from the plate. My stomach rumbles.

"It's important to me to know who my employees are," she says. "Who the people in my house are because everything I have is here. The *California Eagle* is not just a job for me, it's my life. Was my husband's. So authenticity and honesty are important to me, you understand."

"Yes, ma'am."

"So, you want a plate of food? You hungry?"

"I-I just want to learn more about the job."

With the tips of her fingers, she taps the open page of the weak paper and says, "We live in a time where people think their personal opinions about facts are equal to facts.

"That's why I think it's a weak paper."

"Emotions and insecurities can get wrapped up in an opinion. A person without a formal education will tell the educated, 'You're not better than me because of your degrees.' And this is true. And the educated who have spent years in the process of learning will say, 'How do you not know that?' Distrust and ridicule are easiest for both sides. Nevertheless, that doesn't change the facts. We're all thinking people, formal education or not, but the devil is in the part where we're working from different facts and, sometimes, different goals. Not all of them good.

"So what do I value? Honesty. That you'll be willing to accept correction, and I'll listen for yours. If you're going to work for me, I want to empower you to be you. Not me. And I'll respect that for as far as I can without knowing better. So if you say you're not hungry or don't feel like eating, don't eat."

"Yes, ma'am," I say.

She flips a page in the paper, taps its face once. "Now look at this advertisement. That's pretty, isn't it?" she says. "Makes me want to buy a washing machine and I don't even need one. That's the kind of ad-man money we need behind my paper. Can you sell ad space?"

"I just write stories. Usually about death. I'm a journalist."

"So you sell your stories?"

"I sell the truth."

She's amused. "I'm glad you know who you are and what you sell. Then tell me . . . can you respect another person's opinion long enough to get the story?"

"Facts or opinions?" I say, and smile.

"It's all an opinion until you hear the right answer."

"Then, yes, ma'am."

"You're on the Death desk at the *Times*?"

"I'd like to do more than death. You don't have to pay me."

"I won't let you work free," she says. "Black women need to be paid for their labor." She opens her desk drawer, removes a sable leather pouch, and unzips it. "I'll pay you what I pay the other reporters. The same as the other reporters at your level. And if you're bad at your job or our personalities are such that our differences are irreconcilable and unhealthy, then I'll let you go. Here's a ten-dollar advance," she says, pulling the bill from the pouch, but I don't take it.

I push her hand back. "I'm not asking for your money, I'm asking you to teach me. That's my pay. Teach me how to fight."

"Alright," she says, and slides her money in her bra. "Then you'll owe me," she says. "The first rule I'll teach you is don't ask for my advice. Sure, ask me to teach you about something but don't ask for my advice about your problems. People who ask for advice ask because they don't want to take full responsibility for their decisions. They want somebody else to blame if things go sideways. So don't ask me to help you cope with your uncertainty. Second, fighting's easy because anger's the easiest emotion. That plus injustice is a spark. I can teach you organizing. Strategy," she says, sizing me up. "But I'll be honest, Louise. I haven't seen the part of you that wants to fight."

I look down at the paper.

"That, you've got to learn on your own."

TWENTY-SEVEN

SARAH, 2117

We like to make crime exotic. The mafia and thugs and drug lords. Forget the bloodbaths they've caused. Forget the real victims. We're relieved when we tell ourselves we're safe and aren't capable of those same things. But aren't we? If we're hungry enough—for power, for food? Denied righteous living enough?

And if we can't romanticize the criminal, we forget their humanity. Forget that their story is more than just their crime. There was a life before and after—even in the years behind bars.

I know what it feels like to carry the burden of the worst thing I've ever done. That's what it means to serve time in prison. That's what it means to be released into a society that reminds you of the worst of yourself on a public record. You've aged thirty years or earned your growth, a family, real change and redemption, so I won't share the details of my burden with you because I've already been found guilty enough.

Fifteen years was all the time I did for my life sentence. When I was convicted, I thought to myself, how many guards will I watch grow old and retire, how many wardens will come and go? Bragging about it in prison only made me seem delusional, but isn't that all of us? Unique in the ways we go mad, especially in America, where melancholy and sadness are not presumed to be normal human conditions. Here, there's a pill, a drink, a religion, a spiritual perspective with a diet plan for that. There's a tremendous amount of money to be made from treating the expressions of our distress and discontentment.

The Supreme Court overturned my conviction last year. I confess that "not guilty" is not the same as innocent and anyway, you don't have to punish a person with prison to hold them accountable. Sometimes the right deterrent is a loss that matters to the one who did it—status, position, money, family. Yes, sometimes freedom. But justice could be a permanent reminder of what you did—your dead child-passenger from your own DUI. Lou's was the life that held itself out in front of me—punished.

As for my crime, I still need to forgive myself for what I did—not guilty. For not seeing another way out on that day—not guilty. For seeing my victim's gun tumble to the floor—not guilty. For seeing its metal handle as a seduction and ignoring the open door—not guilty. For deciding that one bullet wasn't enough—guilty. I was fighting back and losing but not afraid to die. Death is not the worst thing that can happen to a person.

So that day when my victim's gun tumbled to floor, I saw its metal as a seduction, not the open door.

We have to forgive ourselves for who we were and choices we now know we got wrong. For the things we've done before that we wouldn't do now. Or do the same way. Say the same way. Even when there's nobody to apologize to. We have to own those mistakes. I'm working through mine. Lou would have to do the same.

PART THREE

TWENTY-EIGHT

SARAH, 2117

To be fair to myself, in Los Angeles we've all been suicidal. So many of us have survived the first expiration date we've given our own hands.

We are medicated.

We pop antidepressants when we feel joyful (not sad) because we don't trust our joy. Instead, some of us believe joy is a setup for a slap down because we haven't figured out how to live fully in the joy of a moment; so completely that there is no room to ponder what's next and what else also exists. Peace, anyway, is Black joy.

We have found religion.

We've found group classes where we can sit outside, cross-legged, in perfect weather. Our final postures like a fat ballerina stretching.

There is an irrational hope here too. Even now. Hope that a turnaround can happen in just an extra hour of living. But I don't have a choice to hope or not. To die or not.

So I'm sowing into the future.

Huey P. Newton once said, "The revolution has always been in the hands of the young. The young always inherit the revolution." So what I do today is for them. Those I can lift up and cheer for, those who might find some inspiration from what I leave and be restored. Or ignited.

I'm minding my integrity for them today. Because if anything I've done or said in this life is worthy, it won't begin to live boldly until after I'm dead. It's the truth of all greatness.

Which I am not.

And not dead yet.

LOU, 1932

If I'm going to learn to fight, why not here in the place the City wants to destroy? Esther will be proud of me when I tell her. I'll march out in front of this gym with a sign written with anti-this and anti-that. Then, when the going gets tough, I'll chain myself to the building. *That's good*. I'll have leaflets like Bertha had at the meeting and I'll shout, "Don't destroy our gym! Don't des—"

Two small white boys are standing beside the canvas, about to take the ring below me, readying themselves to enter. Aaron is somewhere behind the ring, out of the way where I can't see him. He's heeding my warning and now stays away from me.

The radio beside me squeals. It went from voices to a steady stream of static *shhhh*s. I hit the side of the box to strengthen reception.

One of the boys next to the canvas is a foot and a half taller than the other, his reach longer, and he's bulkier. The match will be speed versus power, but they're children, too kept-looking to be fighting. Both are clean-cut, their brown hair trimmed close at the back and around the sides, brushed to the side and parted, hardened with an egg-white rinse.

Mr. Lee has been extending his services to an afterschool program for disadvantaged children—not these—and teaching because he wants to hire a nurse for his wife, whose worsening physical condition has called for Esther, the youngest sister, to help. If you can't afford to pay for a caregiver for a loved one, it's you. Or your sister. Or brother. Youngest or oldest child. But Mr. Lee wants Esther to get back to her life and not keep forfeiting her jobs, her acting, her vacation, even a trip to the movies for fear of leaving her mother unsupervised for too long. But Mr. Lee's decided not to unsaddle his wife's caring on an L.A. County facility, so it's Esther. And anyway, Melanie has been too unreliable and unstable as of late.

The bell dings near the canvas. Some man shouts, "Don't make 'em fight! They're brothers." The tallest of the boys walks into the ring, the smallest doesn't.

My radio squeals again and I hit the side of the box, the static now transformed into voices. The jolly voice is unmistakable: "Welcome to AM 900, home to your CBS radio network, KHJ. I'm your host, Ross McMahon."

The bell rings inside the gym, beginning the boys' round on the canvas. I can still hear Mr. McMahon's voice over the shouting below. Finally, I hear Esther's hello and her smile through the radio. I smile back at her.

"And we also have in the studio Mrs. Pearl S. Buck," McMahon says.

I stare at the radio knobs and smile harder at Esther. I want her to feel me there. I want to tell her, "I'm here, Esther! I'm listening!"

McMahon introduces us to Buck. He says she is an expert on "the Orient" and wrote a book about the time she lived in China. Esther interrupts. "Mrs. Buck, my sister is a huge fan of yours. I feel honored to be here with you."

Below me, the boys' soft shoes dance on the canvas, scooting toward each other, then scooting back as they closed in.

My radio squeals, then there is laughter. "And you," McMahon says. "Do you ever feel used?"

"Of course I do," Esther says, her voice a melody. "I'm an artist. Being born an artist means you were created for other people's enjoyment. Maturity is deciding how others will enjoy you."

If there were a celebrity list in alphabetical order, with A being the most popular and most bankable, Esther would be a D, an actor whose face you can remember but not place in any particular film; an actor good enough for game shows and parade hosting but not an A—first to be called for a role—or B—second, or C—third.

What it means for her career is that she'll be called in a pinch by a studio or theater group but she may be the only Chinese vamp they have available. Radio and news shows might use her once a year to remind audiences that they treat everyone fairly but I think they're lucky. Esther deserves to be in every room, but not every room deserves her. And anyway, D-list actors have the best personalities. They're still gracious when you bump into them on the street corner.

Esther wants more.

Lately, to make up for the lost auditioning time, she's created a more direct path for herself; she's strategic with her time. She's been spending her free days in the Hills with some stockbroker-turned-Hollywood-director. He's used her ideas, and because of it, he's been named "The New Under 25. No better up-and-coming director." Esther, on the other hand, because she doesn't talk about her directing skills, only her acting, has met the destiny of so many talented women—to be some man's best-kept secret.

"You're a slangy thing, aren't you?" Buck says through the radio, a rude tone in her voice.

Esther doesn't answer.

McMahon follows up with another question for Esther. "Do you think you've changed since you've become more well-known? People recognize you on the street?"

"Sure," Esther said.

"Can you give us an example?"

"You don't have to answer that," Buck says.

"Thank you, Pearl," Esther says dismissively. "Friendships are what's changed for me. The friendships I've pursued in the past so desperately—and by *desperately* I do mean trying to prove myself a good and trustworthy friend over and over again—I stopped pursuing. In part because there's no longer time.

"Then a funny thing happened. Those people I once pursued now tell me, 'You've changed since you've become famous.' But I think only my requirement to be treated well has. I cherish proven friends. Like my friend, Lou, who I hope is listening."

"I'm listening!" I yell at the radio. "I'm listening!"

McMahon says, "And you? What is life like for you, Pearl? Since your book?"

"Friendships are not a measure for me. My life has always been consistent. I can't say I've ever pursued anyone or anything. In China . . ." She keeps talking.

On the canvas, the boys are dancing, neither one hitting the other. They're trying to look convincing, but I don't think they really want to fight.

"Aren't you afraid?" McMahon says to Buck. "Living in China with the Chinese? You've witnessed violence—"

"I have."

"You wrote that you saw children killed by the Chinese there. Your classmates."

"I did," she says. "But to be fair, some white people in China have done great wrongs to the Chinese. Not the missionaries I was with. They had done no harm and still they were killed, along with their children, who were entirely innocent. I was eight years old then and for me, a child, it was a frightful revelation that children could be killed because of their parents, who were in turn killed because some entirely different white people had been wicked."

"Why is it," Esther interrupts, "that white people can see other white people as individual and separate from each other, but they see the Chinese, the Blacks, the Mexicans, and others as having a single identity?"

Her boldness surprises me. But then, through the radio, a sudden commotion knocks around in my speakers. Something is happening in the studio.

"LAPD!" a man's voice says.

"We're live on air," McMahon says. "Well, hold on now. Hold on. You can't come in here! Do you know we're live?"

There's bumping, and I grab my radio and hold it tight on my lap, searching its screened face like it was a crystal ball that could show me inside the studio.

Esther's voice is raised. "Don't touch me! Don't touch me!"

"Let her go!" Pearl says.

"You're not supposed to be in here!" McMahon says.

And as I hold the radio to my face, hoping somehow I can see through it, LAPD officers walk through the front door of the gym. They're talking to the trainers. The boys stop fighting; they stare at me like I'm the imposter. The trainer and the boys point at me now. Aaron makes himself a wall between them and me, blocking them with his questions, slowing them with his concern about their right to be here, asking for a warrant, pushing back, demanding they leave. He's wrestled to the floor, flat on his stomach, a knee to his back. He cranes his neck up to see me, his shoulders an inch above the ground. His eyes hold terror for me.

TWENTY-NINE

LOU, 1932

I arrive where I began—LAPD Central Number One and nobody's told me why I've been arrested yet.

I ask the lady at the front desk if she would call Officer Adams to let him know I'm here. I've been arrested. Instead of disappointment, her face is alight. "Hey, you're the gal in the photo." She points to the poster on the wall—a large photo of me and Officer Adams playing chess that day outside of the Hall of Records. DO THE CRIME, DO THE TIME, is still there, alongside other posters of officers being heroic, one at a barbecue with a blond local family. One is of Officer Adams shaking hands with the governor.

"You two play chess together," she says. "You used to bring in those good roast beef sandwiches from—"

"Greenblatt's Deli," I say. "My . . . father and I used to bring them together."

"Oh, yes," she says. "How *is* your father?"

"He passed away. About nine months ago."

"Oh, deary, I'm sorry to hear that. What did you say your name was?"

"Lou. Louise. My father was Lawrence. My mother is Miriam."

The clerk holds up a finger to quiet me. She tells me he came in half an hour ago and dials. "It'll be just a minute," she says.

With glee in her voice, she speaks into the receiver. "Officer Adams, I've got Lou, the Negro, here to see you. Lawrence and Miriam's daughter. She's been arrested."

Her smile suddenly falls. She glances at me, then away. "Yes, sir," she says. "She's here in the lobby. Hasn't been put in a cell yet." She listens some more then turns her back to me. In a low voice, she says, "I understand," then swivels back and says loudly into the phone's receiver to whomever is on the phone, "Well, if Officer Adams comes in this afternoon, please let him know Lou has been arrested," then tells me, "I'm sorry, I thought I saw him come in. I was mistaken. When he arrives, I'll let him know of your predicament."

I woke up in a jail cell with Goldie and Esther and a woman we're convinced is a snitch. A jail plant who's asking too many questions. If she's supposed to be a troubled youth, her role was poorly cast. Even Esther would make a better Black woman, slum dweller, than her. Besides that, the woman's nails are clean, and her brows have been recently tweezed. "So, did y'all hear 'bout tha man who got beat down at Grand Central Market? He pro'bly deserved it," she said. "White man tryin' ta keep us down. Y'all do it? High five?" She raised her hand for us to slap.

We turned our backs.

And that's how I found out why we'd been arrested.

And why Esther, Goldie, and I decided it best not to talk while we're here, pretend we don't know one another. I hit the cell bars with my knuckles. Looked easier than it felt. The scrapes, of course, heal instantly but I'm used to that now.

A guard comes to our chamber soon enough, annoyed before I say any words. I smile and try my hardest to be polite behind the metal slats. "Hello, Officer. I believe there has been some misunderstanding. I'm with the *L.A. Times* and—"

"The *Times* is unfair to officers, you know that, right?"

"Oh. Well, I'm actually looking for Officer Adams. I'm sure he'd be concerned for me."

"What did you say your name was?"

"Lou. A friend of his. The girl in the poster out front playing chess."

"He's not here," he says flatly.

"Can you let him know—" He walks away. Esther takes a deep breath, pats the place on the bench beside her. It'll be a long day.

We were questioned for three hours about the beating of a white man in Grand Central Market downtown. Yes, we were there, but no, we didn't do it. We were just there with the rest of the neighborhood after word got out that King Eddy's Piano Store was letting go of some of its booze—a favorite of the mayor. Eleven miles of service tunnels lead directly to the basements of storefronts like King Eddy's on Fifth and Main and, as luck would have it, directly to Grand Central Market, where Goldie, Esther, and I sipped from glasses of tainted lemonade next to stands of price-per-pound chili vendors selling *chipotle, morita, yunam, costeño,* and *puya,* while we ate our dinner: grilled, chopped, and fried Mexican and Chinese food made on the spot.

Yes, Goldie left us for a few minutes, and we didn't ask her where she went, and yes, police officers stopped us later that night as we were walking home. Esther hid the wet crowbar under her long black coat while the cops threw Goldie over the hood of the squad car, but we weren't guilty of anything.

The officers were.

They snatched Goldie between her legs, saying they were searching for a crowbar involved in a beating at Grand Central Market. They let me sit on the curb because they said I didn't fit the description. Then one of the officers recognized Esther from her silent films and the talkies, seemed bashful he knew her face. "I've seen all your pic-chuz," he said.

So when Esther asked politely to lean against the wall instead of sit, he said yes and "Maybe later I can give you a ring." Esther said yes and gave him somebody's phone number and a kiss on the cheek, so he never doubted her.

After the officers let us all go, Goldie went her own way. Esther walked us to the concrete wash of the Los Angeles River, where she threw that crowbar over the side, took out a cigarette, and had a smoke. I'd never witness against her.

Of course it was Metal Wally who managed to get photographs of us near the market.

He sent them to the papers for money, then to the police. We were under his headline "Vice in the City." All three of us were recognizable in his grainy shots. *Co-conspirators*, it read, *aiding and abetting a criminal*. It meant we helped Goldie get away with a crime, but I didn't.

I sit in the square room, my legs shaking.

The detective leans back in his seat and says, "It would've taken thirty minutes for a woman to do that kind of damage to a man. He might have a permanent limp. Do you recall when Penelope Ellis left you for that length of time that night?"

"Penelope?"

"A.k.a. Goldie," he says.

"I would've noticed if she were gone that long. I would've checked on her in the bathroom or something. Penelope? Are you sure, Officer?"

"Victor O'Malley," he says. "Our victim."

My eyes widen.

"You know Mr. O'Malley?"

"I interviewed him for the paper once. Months ago. His mother had died. You say he was hurt?"

"He may have been involved in some criminal activity," the detective says, "but he didn't deserve what he got. Petty criminal out for a stroll. Just lost his mother, you said?"

"Yes."

"So you know what happened to him?"

I don't answer.

"Tell me about this razor," he says, throwing it on the table. "Among your confiscated belongings."

"It's for my pencils."

"Speak up! I can't hear you," he says.

"My pencils," I say. "I-I sharpen my pencils with it. Sometimes I keep it in my pocket."

"Thank you for your honesty," the detective says. "I can see you want to help us, don't you?"

I nod.

"Will you help us solve this crime and help an innocent man recover his life?"

I nod. I think I look cooperative.

After three more hours of questioning, the police had to let us go. They couldn't keep holding us for lack of evidence and no confessions. And worst of all, Officer Adams never came for me.

Esther was released to her father and wasn't allowed to take me or Goldie—no relation—so Goldie said she was walking home. Needed the fresh air.

I was last to be released, walked out of the station still handcuffed like a caged animal about to be set free at the edge of the woods. Wally was there. He was rambling off an explanation to me about being at the river on a different assignment—explosions at the aqueduct up north that killed some men—when he saw me that night and saw things heating. He did his job, "journalistic integrity," he said, and he never meant to hurt me. "Will you forgive me?"

I didn't wait to be unchained.

So with my cuffed hands behind my back and all my fingers free, I lifted my middle finger as high as I could get it, almost breaking my wrist.

What he's done could ruin Esther's career.

"Stay out of trouble," the guard told me. "We're watching you," he said.

THIRTY

—◀○▶—

Loss of freedom, like my stint in jail, even for a short period of time, is like grief. It has a way of taking and giving at the same time, like some wrong math. It steals things from you and adds weight at the same time.

I feel different. Angry. Betrayed. I'm supposed to go over the Route 66 strategy in the morning, but I won't go to Charlotta like this. For what? Even generosity—hers for me or mine—feels like a burden.

I open the side door of Mr. Lee's gym. Ten o'clock and this is my safe place, not my apartment. And like my last home, this could be taken away from me too.

All the windows creak like aged knees when the door opens, and it smells of sweaty men though it's dry and vacant, cleaned for morning. I tie my dress between my legs and around my waist like a diaper to keep it out of the way, stick my keys in a fold.

"I'm sorry, I'll go," Aaron says, appearing in the shadows near the bleachers. I haven't seen him for days. Not since he threw himself at the police to try and protect me.

"The cops the other day," I say. "Thank you for trying to stop them."

He nods.

"I got the key from under the brick out back. I didn't think anyone would be here. You mind if . . ." I eye the punching bags.

"I can help you," he says, and I shudder at his voice, recognize those words the night I first came and sat in the alley.

He hangs a bag for me, clicks it in.

"Why are you helping me?" I say.

He steps back. "This is nothing."

"The cops, my apartment. What do you want from me?"

"Let me see your jab," he says. I punch the bag slow, one handed: my right, then my left. Switch.

Faster.

Harder.

"His name was Stuart," he says. "Stuart Behren."

I stop, catch my breath.

"It was 1911 at that time. Germany was producing almost twice as much steel as Britain, and all Britain's fears of a competitive Germany were realized. Industrial maturity, they called it. Population explosions." I hold the bag to stop it swinging.

He sits down on the bottom step of the bleacher and runs a hand over his head, his eyes shifting side to side as if he's reading his memory. "Work multiplied in factories around Berlin. The working class neared four million people, half of them in socialist unions." He stops and looks at me as if he's waiting for me to say something, like he's asked me a question.

"My friend Stuart," he continues, "was one life. Unimportant to them but everything to me."

"You don't look old enough to have known anybody in 1911."

"We grew up together," he says. "Rock fights and bicycle runs. Stuart had a bunch of friends, worked at the AEG turbine factory, hundreds of employees. He helped me get a job delivering sandwiches to the factory."

"You worked in food service?"

"Essential worker," he says. "Like mothers. I'd only taken off work for a year to pursue academia.

"When I came home from school, I went to the factory to let Stuart know I was back, and when I didn't see him come out for lunch I asked where he was. Some foreman said, 'He's not in today.' It went on like this for months. Not one of my friends thought to tell me he was dead till Dicky. Dicky and me grew up together too, but we weren't that close. When I saw him at the factory, I said, 'Have you seen Stuart?' He said, 'Yeah, he's dead.'

"'That's not funny, he's my mate,' I said. 'Where is he?'

"Then he told me. 'You didn't know? He died. I'm really sorry,' he said. 'I thought you knew. I thought you were just messing about.'

"Everybody thought I knew. I was devastated. There I was just busy with life and he had been dead a year. I named one of my sons Stuart."

"Sons?" I say.

"A lifetime ago now. It was before you left."

"I left?"

He stands up and comes toward me now, too close. "No good thing is destroyed," he says, talking like a riddle. "Things are just liberated from the shadows."

I let go of my punching bag and let it swing. I hit it again as some kind of notice to him, a warning.

I wipe away the sweat from my forehead. He takes a step back and stays where he is.

"You and Stuart knew each other," he says. "More than knew."

I don't understand. I don't remember.

I don't know what he means.

"They never found Stuart's body. People saw him jump, but no body was ever recovered."

"I'm sorry," I say. "At work, I've interviewed a lot of people about what it's like for those left behind when a loved one vanishes. People usually know. They feel the absence."

"Does Jefferson remind you of Stuart?"

How would I know?

He takes a step toward me and covers my fists with his hands. "His death is why you left Berlin. To start again."

How could he know of my daydream, the moment I first met Jefferson? "You were there when he came. When the fighter broke his hand . . ."

"Doesn't he seem familiar to you, Lou? From some time before here?" He looks like he's begging me. "Your drawings!" he says like they're a key. "You've been drawing him for a long time, here and in other places. And then he walks right into this gym. Don't you wonder why that is?"

I shove my dress down from my waist and unfold it. Flatten the wrinkles. *I must have been speaking out loud that day. It's not uncommon to talk in your dreams. Even daydreams.*

"We need to be careful, Lou."

The key to the door tumbles to the floor and tings. I pick it up. Place it in his palm and walk away, back to the front door. He grabs me and pulls me into him, face-to-face. The colored parts of his eyes are like glass globes half-filled with liquid mercury. He says, "I don't know how much time I have left. I think we're in danger."

"I'm in danger? Or you are? You don't look well."

"I know you've seen it, Lou. Your shimmer. I've heard it . . ."

Heard it?

"Seen it in you. And if I have, others have too. It's why you might be in danger. I can help."

"Somebody wants to hurt me? *You* want to hurt me?"

"No, never."

"Then why try to scare me? You want to have me looking over my shoulder, being as strange as you?"

"That's not my intention. Not my purpose here."

"Then what is it? You creep around here, break in my apartment. Don't belong."

"I hope you'd do the same for me."

"Same for *you*? What are you playing at here?"

"Playing at? It's not a game."

"What's your purpose?"

He flinches. Thinks.

"It's the same as everyone's, I guess. Same as yours. To see yourself in everybody, then love yourself."

THIRTY-ONE

Aaron dropped me off in front of my apartment after I told him he could drive me home if he promised to shut up. He was scaring me.

His car was just a block from the gym. When we got here, he walked me to the bottom step of the stairwell in silence. Got back in his car. And what came next was nothing like the dreams I've had before.

I was halfway up the stairs when I had to sit down, violently shaken in an instant by a dream that started before I was asleep. It was the dream, not my exhaustion, that drew my eyes closed immediately, as if to start its show on time.

It was her face I saw.

A teenaged girl, maybe fifteen, lying on the shoe-scuffed linoleum of a liquor store located not far from here. But it didn't look like here. This was some future and I knew it.

Inside this vision, I was standing above this girl, then kneeling beside her. Blood was seeping from a gunshot wound at the back of her head. Her heart was still beating at a sluggish pace, but it wouldn't be for long. Her school backpack still hooked over her shoulders. Orange juice mixed with her blood.

She had been on her way home from high school, was wearing a front-buttoned sweater to protect herself from the coolness of a March day, and at that moment, her sweater was losing heat with her cooling body—a one-degree drop per hour. It's how the dead cool.

The bullet came from the gun of the fifty-year-old liquor store owner, a woman who was still standing at the cash register, her gun smoking.

The gun she'd modified with a hair trigger so that even a slight tap, not a pull, would cause the gun to fire. And that morning, her gun was placed under the checkout counter like a baited trap. There had been a liquor store robbery nearby, she had been told, so she was ready in case this was the day she might be confronted with evil. But none came. This fifteen-year-old Black girl did instead.

The girl was in the store with two other customers, strangers to her, but they were siblings—a nine-year-old brother and a thirteen-year-old sister seeking hair gel for their mother. They wouldn't have wished to become part of this history.

The nine-year-old boy will later testify to the following: When he and his sister went to the counter to pay, another customer was there, too, her dollars and coins bundled in her hand.

Say her name: Latasha Harlins. Her name echoes backward and forward through time and comes to me on the stairs. It was her face I saw.

The nine-year-old boy will testify that a bottle of orange juice was sticking out of Latasha's backpack. "You bitch," the liquor store owner would say, "you're trying to steal my orange juice." This, according to the boy.

"Bitch, I didn't steal your orange juice," Latasha would say.

Latasha would be grabbed by her sweater, hands on her body, prompting an escalation of violence. One that she did not cause.

Escalations against brown bodies, I knew, were often caused by those who already had plans to prey on those bodies . . . if the opportunity ever arose. Premeditated murder, where the premeditation happens long before that victim crosses paths with that predator, that cop, another patron, that customer—a murderer bent on starting fights while being secretly armed and having already decided to kill the victor, should he (or she) lose the fight they started. It's stand-your-ground cowardice, not stand-your-ground protection. It's what the liquor store owner will claim in defense. It's what other predators will claim when they prey on unarmed Black bodies.

The nine-year-old will testify that the two would exchange the word *bitch* with each other, Latasha held in place by her sweater.

Latasha would swing her free hand and finally break free.

Latasha would toss a receipt for the orange juice onto the counter before she'd turn to leave the store.

But what Latasha didn't see was that the liquor store owner had brought the gun with the altered trigger from below the countertop to the top, hidden under her folded arms on the countertop. It was aimed directly at Latasha.

Latasha didn't know then that the scuffle wasn't over.

Or that her life was.

Within days, Black people are running through the streets of this community, the Black community, knocking out the windows of storefronts, stealing and lighting businesses on fire. Lit it up the way Black churches burn in the South. The way football match celebrations around the world turn to torched cars.

These members of our community will beat windows the way exonerated policemen beat Black bodies. None of it would be the first time or the last time, not today or even sixty years from now.

In thirty years, a leader will be assassinated at the Lorraine Motel in Memphis, Tennessee, and my handwritten warnings before that day will be treated as the ravings of a madwoman. Another madwoman.

Only years before me, madwoman Izola Ware Curry stabbed the man who would be assassinated in the chest with a steel letter opener while he

was autographing books at his signing. Two of his ribs had to be cut in surgery, and the surgeon joked that women have always cost men ribs, if not
their hearts. And had that future-assassinated man sneezed, it would have
inched the steel tip of the madwoman's opener into his aorta and he would
have drowned in his own blood. She didn't intend to kill him, she'll say. Just
warn him. She had a pistol in her bra.

On the last day of the man's life, while he was still lying in his own
pool of blood, with a new wound to his head and a scar where his chest had
healed, his unpacked luggage will be unzipped and opened to a page in his
book *Strength to Love* by Dr. Martin Luther King Jr. and lying prostrate next
to his words will be his shaving cream and hairbrush.

But as I stand in this dream, at the liquor store market, I know that no
justice will come for this murder. That the liquor store owner will be convicted of manslaughter and ordered to pay five hundred dollars for killing
Latasha and be put on five years of probation. No jail. Because Black lives
don't matter.

When the forceful dream ended, I was sitting again on my steps, my
teeth clenched and aching. My eyes wide open and streaming tears.

I prayed to God for the first time. "If you're real, God, show me what
to do to change this. If you're real, God, take back this future I see for Los
Angeles."

Mrs. Miriam used to always say God is not a magician. Not a genie to
grant wishes, but I didn't care. Prayer to me seemed more like a gambling
woman at a bingo game. Win or lose, a girl's life.

Before I finished my prayer. Before I walked in my front door. Before I
finished with "Amen," I got my answer.

It's all going to burn.

THIRTY-TWO

SARAH, 2117

I used to think boxing was violence.

But it's not real violence.

Real violence has no warning, no time-outs. A bully stops when he's worn out or someone drags him off. But no one will drag him off. His size or his crazy will keep others from rescue. Real violence has no rules.

Boxing is between two people who expect what's coming. There's a bell. A referee. It's a gentleman's game. Like politics. It's dangerous people agreeing not to kill anyone.

In public.

Mostly.

But boxing will kill you just the same because rules never kept no one breathing. People do.

I have to remember the people. Remembering the centuries of violence would leave my mind in a bad place, a sick place, from overexposure, a place where I'd no longer be able to see the humanity in us. If I surrendered to my bad experiences with other people, I'd only see our biology on the outside—a weak frame.

Repeated images of the world's violence would be like watching decades of violence against Black bodies—beat and hung and shot and shot—being reminded of Black boys killed in the cities by other Black boys who are considered solely to blame, as if weapons grew from seeds in their neighborhoods and weren't delivered. Or white-on-white violence or other-on-other. It's strange to me how every race, across all these lives and all of this time, mostly kills their own.

If I let myself remember the violence against people for long enough, what I recall stops being people. Instead, my mind spares me, and what I remember are not people but something standing in for people. Like a birthday cake, a simple thing. Sometimes they have white or brown or colorful frosting on the outside, cream and strawberry filling on the inside. And in my memory, someone slams a fist down onto its perfection, smashes its delight; the red oozes out without much trouble, the pretty colors a blend. And I think, it was only a cake. Not a person. I'll have hundreds of other birthdays.

This is why I choose not to remember the days I was born anymore or the violence. Or else I'd be like the complicit monsters, like so many who watch and do nothing except make the rest of their day a fun day for themselves and their families. "Those poor inner-city kids shooting each other," they'll say. "Those poor kids running across the border (or trapped there), those poor people gunned down in their church, their synagogue, in the movie theater, at the mall, a night club, that restaurant, that concert, their school, or because they're transgender, or a woman killed on a military base, or people executed by the police for a traffic infraction or for sleeping in their car. Young gay people dying by suicide."

It's terrible to imagine, sure, or imagine that you could be a victim too. That it could be your children among those whose existence causes fear in another human being, enough fear to cause another to want to put them down like a rabid dog. Or "I'm young, I have rights, like the right to eat at a restaurant, even if being there perpetuates a disease that will cost an older person, a sick person, a disabled person, their life. Survival of the fittest." Not survival of our communities. That we're in this together.

Every mortal human being is only temporarily abled, is only temporarily without an ailment. If you live long enough, you'll see. So I don't want to be like those who can't yet find themselves in others. That some stranger's life was just a birthday cake that fell on the floor.

I have to remember our humanity.

LOU, 1932

Latasha Harlins is why I didn't fall asleep until almost 3:00 a.m., grieving, mourning, and terrified. Dead futures visiting me, forcing me to drink myself asleep, tricking my body into comfort, to forget jail or what Wally's photographs might do to Esther's career. To forget Aaron's "purpose" for me—he needs to just worry about himself, creeping around everywhere—so last night was a baptism of moonshine wine. One that didn't cleanse me but left me empty, which is worse.

My hair smells of piss and popcorn with traces of jailhouse bleach, and tonight is our community's last chance before the vote. Last chance to voice our objections over the path Route 66 will take around and through Los Angeles.

I open the door to the floor of City Hall and the air around me pollutes with voices. Picketers and churches. Men from the "Keep America White" clan, the Chamber of Commerce, the Elks Club. Goldie should be here to represent her father's church, Esther the gym, but I don't see 'em.

I walk straight to the speaking podium and flip through the papers there, the Council's agenda. I note that the mayor has made himself co-chair of the Council alongside the one already appointed.

Metal Wally is at the side of the room fiddling with the lens on his camera. I swear to God he better not come talk to me.

Houseless people sleeping on the streets are here too. Someone yells, "Bums!"

I move through the crowd and, in all suddenness, meet eyes with Jefferson.

I'm ashamed of myself. Since his son died, I haven't known what to say, and when I think of him and draw his face in private, my thoughts aren't to comfort him for his son but out of my own desires. I look away.

Goldie slides in next to me, bumps me with her hip, and smiles. I smile, too, but let it cool. She's the reason Esther and I went to jail. "What time are they supposed start?" she says. "I have to leave in a half hour. I already know how they're gonna vote."

"You speaking for the church tonight?"

"It's not in the path. I'm here to support everybody else. Thirty minutes' worth."

Wally catches my glance and raises his brows as if to say hello and starts his journey through the chasm of space in the room between us. Goldie sees him. "You see this asshole?"

Wally stops directly when the mayor starts the meeting with prayer. A hush falls over the room. The meeting is called to order. The first public-comment speaker is an old man who needs help to the podium and back. I wonder if Jefferson is speaking.

The next speaker spends his seven minutes yelling about water and war and hypocrisy. He yields the floor only after the mayor knocks on the gavel on his desk, not once but twice. And now, nobody wants to follow. We all look around the room at each other, the bold picketers now sheep.

My chest tightens when I see Jefferson take a step toward the podium.

He buttons his suit jacket, places a thick stack of papers on the podium—too many to be a speech. He doesn't look down when he begins.

"Good evening, Council," he says. "My name is Captain Jefferson Thomas Clayton and I'm pleased to be here today. I've been on the fire department for just under eight years. Before that, near Montgomery, Alabama. I inherited my passion for the department from my father. I've inherited this city, *we've* inherited this great city, from those who came before us, and we have a responsibility to it. And it's not always an easy burden for those of us who serve it. Like you."

He tells us about his knowledge of the neighborhoods. He asks the council, "May I approach?" with his stack of papers and he does, divvying his papers equally, a set for each council member.

"If it pleases the council," he says, "here are seven alternatives to avoid moving the Black cemetery. They include moving the old tile factory. It's vacant. Or the mill. A few acres of the orange orchard could be used for something other than new housing developments."

He speaks of his son who's now buried at the cemetery, and I wish I would've been the one he said that to, personally. If I'd shown up for him.

"We can value the loss of all the people there. For their families." His voice leaves him, the pause pregnant with silence, then reborn as audience tears, mine included.

He asks the council to imagine if their own children, parents, grandparents were lying beside the space where his boy is resting. "The living have a responsibility to the dead," he says, his voice quivering.

Jefferson grips the sides of the podium.

"Have you anything else to add?" the mayor says, flatly. "If not, we'll take your proposal under submission."

Jefferson doesn't respond.

"Is that all, Captain Clayton?"

And as if my voice has its own engine, "There are bodies laid to rest there!" I say. "Generations are buried there. His son!" My body is shaking. My hands. I search the faces of every panelist for something. Anything.

Jefferson turns around. Acknowledges me.

"Captain Clayton, do you submit?" the mayor says, ignoring me completely. He nods. "I concede the floor, Mr. Mayor."

"Swell, you've done a fine job here, Captain. Good *heart* work," the mayor says. "Now this council has to do the *head* work, do you understand?" he says to Jefferson, and I'm sorry for it. Sorry that these men are my elected officials and sorry my people can't vote.

"I've seen enough," Goldie says.

I grab her hand. "You can't leave."

"I told you I couldn't stay long. Choir rehearsal in less than an hour."

"But he needs us." I correct myself. "This could be history making."

"Isn't every moment?" she says, her voice softer and more tender than I'm used to. "Sometimes I'd rather read your version of our lives than be here to watch it myself." It strikes me that she was caring for me in that second.

She leaves me for the back door and pushes it open. It closes. Metal Wally follows her path through the crowd, pushes the back door open, but she's gone. He goes out anyway.

"No, I won't submit!" a bum shouts from the audience. "It's an abuse of power!" There are cheers in the audience for his bravery, then shouting and raised arms. A scuffle begins to the left of me and then the right. No one regards the mayor's gavel, so he raises his voice. He says, "Seeing as there's nothing more, I think we're ready to vote. All those in favor?"

"Aye," they all say together.

"Opposed?" Boos slither through the audience. "Hearing none, the measure passes." The mayor stands and knocks his gavel again, announcing, "The proposed path for Route 66 has passed with no amendments."

Gunfire outside—a rapid succession of shots, one after the other, pop,

pop, pop, pop, pop—jerks his head down into his shoulders. I'm already on the floor. "Gunfire!" someone yells. We all get low for cover.

Where's the shooter?

Four more pops.

I lie on my stomach. I don't want to die. I don't want to die. I don't want to—

Several men pull guns from holsters, there are *clicks* all around. *I don't want to die.*

"Nobody shoot!" a man says as tires squeal, losing their skin on the road. "Shooter's outside!"

THIRTY-THREE

—◄(O)►—

LOU, 1932

Metal Wally is lying face down on the pavement, his ankle and leg askew like a child's doll discarded from the window of a passing car.

Goldie's head is propped up on the passenger side of a four-door Plymouth, the window above shattered. Goldie is pushing herself up while people yell at her not to move. "Be still!" a woman shouts. A man kneels beside her. I reach them in a hurry, hold her head. Blood is seeping from her side, her dress a watercolor.

I tell her, "An ambulance will be here any minute."

"No, no hospitals. They'll let me die," she says. "Get me to the tile lady."

"Who?"

"Leticia Thomas."

The kneeling man says, "I'll drive you wherever she can get help."

As we went, I tried my best to keep Goldie's blood off the white man's back seat. A small puddle soaked in.

I knock on Mrs. Thomas's front door, Goldie hanging on around my neck and shoulder. Leticia opens the doors, regards us for a moment but isn't frightened. "Set her down on the sofa," she says. She immediately goes to a drawer in the back of the living room, returns with a wooden shoe box of materials, kneels on the floor next to Goldie, and splays open her box—gauze and bandages, green-glass vials containing liquids. Most read ALCO-HOL. There are cylinders of inoculation jabs. Only one reads MORPHINE. She fires its needle tip inside Goldie's stomach. I watch her, amazed. Her movements are rehearsed. Goldie's moans subside.

"Hold this here," she says, and I press the gauze against the hole in Goldie's side, stop her from bleeding out on the sofa. The body hates holes in itself. It wants its holes filled—puss, another person, its own blood. It would make a deep wound a well if it had to. Leticia explores the bullet hole with her tweezer-like instrument.

A shimmering reflection in Leticia's reading glasses draws my eye. It's me, my own face reflected. Another shimmer. This time above my cheek-bone, a slither of silver snaking through my eyes. A trick of light. A falling star through the window.

I lean closer to her lens, where the shape of Leticia's own brown eyes take form behind them, staring up at me and my shimmer.

She pulls a strip of tape and lays it across Goldie's gauze, from left and right. "That'll stop the bleeding for now," she says. "We'll need more sup-plies to close it."

Leticia lumbers up from her knees to stand and taps my shoulder with the back of her hand. "Come with me," she says, and I follow, glancing back at Goldie. "She'll be fine. Bullet passed straight through," Leticia says. "The morphine'll help her rest. My single injections are leftovers from the war."

On our way through the kitchen, she takes a flashlight from the countertop to help us see in the pitch-black night, and we step down from her back door into the garden, where she shines her light on old red bricks and discarded yellow and blue tiles, dried mortar. For a moment, it's like it's not night; her torch light peels away a film of darkness on everything it touches.

We stop at her deadbolted garage, where a white mattress is laid against the side, ready to be thrown away. "Wait here," she says, and walks around the side of the garage, returns with a crowbar. Not a key. It makes me nervous.

"What's in there?" I say.

"A dead body," Leticia says flatly, then laughs. "Hold this," and I take her torch. She fingers her way around the bolt and then the doorframe, then puts her crowbar in the gap between the door and the frame where the top bolt is. "I'm going to pull the latch down," she says, "and you push the door open at the same time. Ready?"

She pulls down, I push.

The cool air inside smells of damp. She lifts one arm to tug a switch above her; the whole garage illuminates. I'm almost expecting to see a body. There's just stuff stacked on shelves, thick with dust, except for a huge square block in the center of the garage covered from end to end with dustsheets. She walks past it.

"What's under there?" I say.

"My husband's," she says, and keeps walking toward the back of the garage. She takes a ring of keys from her pocket. I stop beside her husband's block.

Leticia comes back to me, and tugs a corner of the sheet, dragging it off in one piece. The black metal shines like it was just washed, brand new off the lot.

"1908," Leticia says. "One of the first—"

"Model T production cars," I say, and squat next to the back tire. Like bicycle wheels. Twelve spokes. Lean and mean. "I bet it's fast," I say. "Made to run on air and float. Can I open the door?"

She nods.

I climb inside and touch the smooth driver's seat, poke my fingers into the button wells of the upholstery.

"Vegetable oil," Leticia says. "Not air. Ford originally intended his cars to run off vegetable oils and hemp. To help farmers. Not just cars but tractors. There would be enough in one year's yield on an acre of land to power the machines necessary to cultivate that field for one hundred years."

"Marijuana?" I say. "Hemp?"

"Different seeds, plants. Ford wasn't the first. Rudolf Diesel designed his engine to run on seeds and vegetables. Had an exhibit in France in 1900 where his small diesel engine ran on peanut oil and nobody was the wiser."

"Must be a millionaire now," I say, placing my hands on the steering wheel.

"He was killed," Leticia says. I take my hands away. "Some say suicide, but he was on his way to a meeting about his engine when he died. He was traveling there by ship. The night before, he set a wakeup call for six in the morning, laid his nightclothes on his bed, then disappeared. His bed was not slept in that night and he was later found overboard."

"Must be horrible to drown," I say.

"Not for the gasoline industry," Leticia says. "Back then, the pressing billion-dollar question was what resource would power cars: gas, natural oil, or alcohol from potato farmers. With Diesel out the way and soon the push and prohibition of alcohol and hemp, gasoline—"

"You think they killed for it?"

"Well, we all use gasoline now."

Leticia takes my hand and pulls me along the car to a cabinet at the back. She unlocks it without any trouble; inside are rocks. Plain rocks. At least three dozen of them. "The whole earth is made of rock," she says. "To scientists they're solid crystals of different minerals that have been fused together into a solid lump."

"To you?" I say.

She slides out a drawer underneath the display. More rocks. I recognize flint and an arrowhead. Others are round like the counterfeit meteorite rocks street vendors sell to tourists. Leticia's been had.

"Take this one," she says, handing me one different than the others. "Found it in my yard about a year ago. I usually find these by a river." It's a round gray stone, the size of a half dollar. "The color of the minerals in the rock can turn it brown, red, green, or other colors." A single white band wraps all the way around it, a thick vein of sparkling white. "The ring is quartz," she says. "Essentially, an old crack in the rock was filled and glued back together by the quartz. Only happens if the rock's been broken."

"Broken?"

"Wind. Water. Ocean waves washing over them, banging them together, sometimes into smaller stones. The smallest rock is silt. Silt is smaller than sand and usually found at the bottom of rivers and streams. In any case, pressure over a long time."

"But some are mended?"

"For another purpose," she says. "Hold on to this one."

"I can't take your rock," I say, looking at the others. "I see they're important to you."

"Artifacts are important," she says. "Memorial stones. And I want you to have this one." She presses it into my palm like it's as valuable as an acre of vegetables before gasoline won.

I slide it into my dress pocket. Leticia grabs a red metal box from a shelf in the back. "Let's get these supplies back to Goldie," she says.

"There morphine in there?" Her eyebrow raises. "Not for me. I just thought it'd help Goldie heal faster."

"Faster," she says, nodding. "But not like us."

THIRTY-FOUR

—◄○►—

LOU, 1932

I feel as if I'm standing outside of my own body but I'm sitting here in the audience of this church. "Audience" is an overstatement as only seven of us have turned out for Metal Wally's funeral. Wally's the seventh head I count. It's an open casket.

The wooden legs of the pews are feeble here, as if they, too, caught polio and couldn't hold a large man without snapping.

The walls are beige. Everything is beige. No stained glass, no color, nothing, just the scent of gardenias wafting through the windows, covering the smell of mold that might be behind the walls or under the floorboards.

I keep my distance from myself. All this time writing about death and I still can't look her in the face. So it's not me sitting in the Church of Jehovah building in front of five other people, none of whom are under sixty years old, it's "Lou," the only Black person here, and she looks uncomfortable.

Wally's mother is the one crying next to the casket. His father and brother declined the invitation, as if there'd be another opportunity. It seems

"Lou" may be the only one who knows him both recently and personally because the others are saying he hadn't seen his mother or the rest of his family
in the last twelve years. "Lou" hadn't considered that Wally belonged to
anyone before his funeral anyway. Hadn't considered that he had a mother
or father or brother or sister. But Lou wants to start seeing people differently.

I want to.

I want to be able to honor people, sincerely. Be present in love and respect and kindness. I want to be whole and belong. So when Wally's mother
rang me and asked if I'd share a eulogy for her son, I said yes. Yes, because
Mr. Lawrence once told me we should honor people for who they *believe*
they are (or were). Or who they wanted to be to others.

Honor them for how, in their moments of blissful denial, they thought
other people saw them. "If you choose to do it, it's not about you honoring
your own beliefs or feelings. The only question for yourself is will you set
yourself aside?"

I had planned to tell the room that Wally was a hero for the people.
Then I decided on what felt truer. He did what made sense to him. What he
thought was right. I'd tell them he was a moral man against vice. Was for
the uneducated. For the hardworking man. In his story to himself, he had
integrity.

I begin my speech. "I first met Wallace in high school. He was opinion-
ated and sometimes funny—"

And now all six of us funeral-goers sit around a table eating berry cobbler, laughing about the awkward life of Wallace Stone, animal lover, magician, and reckless prankster. Because of the stories they share about him,
I know him better *because* he died. And as we leave, likely never to connect
again, it occurs to me that maybe it shouldn't be this way.

I collapse on my sofa, planted on the cushion closest to the door, the
front of my dress drifting up, leaving my stomach naked on the smooth
fabric, and I pray to God that when I die, whoever finds me won't find me
with my stomach out.

I reach down into my pocket and touch my pencil, glide a finger over Leticia's stone and prick it on the point of my razor. I don't need to look, it's healed. A bumping sound on the other side of my door makes me sit upright and wait for it to start again.

A knock comes instead.

"Hello," a man's voice says from behind the door, his "welcome" more like a whine. "Lou? You in there?"

I lean toward the door.

"It's me! It's JC!"

Jefferson's voice makes me feel loaded, like a heroine bender and I'm just getting started. I hurry to standing, hand-iron my dress, open my door directly. I'm lost now to his presence here.

He tips over into the side of my doorframe and I step back to give him room. His drooping eyes are red. "Hey," he says, raising his silver flask and his cheeks for a gay smile.

"I was just in the neighborhood," he says, too loudly from my landing. "Saw your . . . saw your. This your address?" he says. "You live here?" His knees buckle and I hold him, put my arms around him, help him inside. "Can I come in?" he says, already in.

"You've been drinking?" I say, and help him over to the living room, lower him to sitting. I slide off his light jacket and drape it over the arm of the sofa, put a pillow behind his head, and take off his shoes, one at a time, surprising myself. Like I've done these movements with him before, many times before. His flask tumbles from his hand and he reaches for it but kicks it instead. I lift him back to keep him falling, set his flask on the side table.

"Let me get you something to drink?" I say. "Water, considering your condition?"

"Why don't you sit with me?" he says, patting my cushion. "Tell me about your day?"

I go to the kitchen and fill a glass with water, bring it to him and sit down next to him. He takes the glass but pauses before he drinks. "I'm not

the man people think I am," he says, slurring his words. "Some hero." He
takes a swallow, then looks at me. "Lou, have a real drink with me? It'll help
me to not feel like a drunk."

I don't answer.

He closes his eyes and rests back in the sofa, shrinking in the cushion as
the caps of his shoulders press forward. Tears pool in the corners of his eyes.
"I couldn't even save my own dead son." He brings his hand to his face. "The
cemetery is moving, my boy'll be moved. He doesn't deserve any of this and
it's my fault. I couldn't save him, dead. My marriage."

"It's not your fault," I say.

He huffs. "Have a drink with me? Please," he says. "Just one drink?

I pick up his flask from the floor, untwist its cap, and let its insides burn
down mine.

He says, "Do you know what grieving is like when a loved one dies? It's
having strangers come up to you, ask you how you feel, and them not knowing what they're really asking is 'Tell me what your darkness feels like today.'
And the people who you wish would ask you about this darkness, don't."

I take another swallow.

"Grief," I say, "is to be numb. Is to not have anything left to give. Or
maybe it's not being able to take anything in. I can't remember not feeling
this way."

He nods. Shares a new swallow.

I resist my urge to fill this new silence with words.

He says, "When I woke up in the hospital after the accident all those
years ago, everything was so strange. I'd been in a coma for over a year.
The nurse was strange—a white woman I didn't recognize. And there was
such a heaviness inside me. A painful grieving. Not just because I didn't
know where or who I was. I felt I'd lost something important and couldn't
remember what.

"'Combative,' the nurse and doctor called me. It was like those injured
in the war.

"I'd come to recognize my mother and father from their visits to me. I had to learn to walk again. Talk. Read. My brother was sent to prison cause he'd killed that woman on the road. She was just walking. How innocent is that. He didn't see her.

"Our car flipped, my brother said he went for help. I couldn't. Waking up felt like waking in a new body, some body whose memories I had to learn again with stories my cousins would tell me, my mother would. And my father would tell me things that would have me laughing so hard.

"And he taught me. We fought the fires together." He looks at his hands. "This work is all I know. The fires. Those are the memories I remember making. With my father and in a uniform. My whole life until then was an inheritance. Even the tragedy. My son paid the price my brother owed."

"It's not your fault," I said. "Your son is not your brother's fault either."

"But isn't it?" he says, like a rhetorical question. "We inherit memories, why not tragedy? Our parents inherited slavery from their parents and grandparents, etcetera. Of the millions of Black people born in this country, most all didn't immigrate here. So why not this inheritance?"

I shake my head. I don't know how to disagree or comfort his question. He takes another drink.

"I don't know why God saved me," he says. "Let me wake up and start again just to punish me."

"You're not punished," I say, trying. "People die tragically all the time and there's no rhyme or reason. You know that. I've written about deaths and thought, this family didn't deserve this. Or this man. This woman. A child—never. I've asked myself, why take this person when there are people, evil people—*they* deserve it, but they're still here. But I don't ask that question anymore," I say. "Rain eventually falls on everybody and even with an umbrella, the wind will blow."

He's studies my face like he's searching for a particular freckle.

Fixated on my lips now.

He closes his eyes and lies back, the alcohol getting the best of him or him getting the best of it, surrendering to needed rest. I study his face as he drifts to sleep, this face I've drawn a million times.

Without opening his eyes, he takes my hand loosely. My fingers pour out of his grasp without any effort. It's when I notice his large hands, the hands that aren't supposed to hold me here. It's not the time for us. We don't belong to each other this time.

I sit beside him waiting for sleep to pull him under, then put a blanket over him, wrap my arms around one of his, defiantly holding on to my losses.

THIRTY-FIVE

Certain people in certain timelines are not meant to be together. Not in the way they've once been and maybe that's a relief, a necessary departure from the prison of people and patterns we've cemented into this life. Being born is clearing the deck.

Not all of us are born.

I haven't been for a long time.

For this, I'm grateful and believe it's the universe's mercy on those like me who don't have to inherit generations of trauma in our bodies like the born do. Theirs is historical trauma—severe emotional or mental distress and injury—passed down inside their blood from ancestors, or epigenetic trauma, where the physical expression of our DNA is transformed by our environment, not the code itself.

But I can still be hurt and taken advantage of because there is no cure to the ills of living with people—not wisdom, not old age—because most of us live in triage.

We spend most of our lives coping or distracted, taking care of the most egregious wounds and offenses. Or we wake up to make money. It's what immigrants come to America for, immigrants who believe the standard American is a white one. It's been said, "If you're going to succeed in America, do all things white and stay away from everything Black because white makes might, makes right," and forget Black is the main ingredient.

We fight among ourselves in this village of earth, wars to maintain elitism and its bounty, wars we should have never been fighting, where both winners and losers are traumatized and not just in war.

But in love.

Because somebody's love will betray you.

Eventually.

For me, it's never been his.

Before *him*, I'd never made love to a Chinese man. He was prettier than I was and his cheeks were always red from his soul blushing. He was also a healer, a doctor. His hands were the medicine—acupuncture and massage—along with the sweet herbs and bitter roots he'd prescribe.

It was 1871 then. My first year in Los Angeles, I thought. And in 1871, I woke for the last time near him. It was early morning at the inn; the sun had just reached into my window and painted the ceiling with a stroke of yellow. The empty sheets he'd left beside me smelled of sandalwood, his favorite incense to burn. *We were in this bed together.*

I felt the coolness of his silver coins sticking to my naked side. He always gave me money. Not because I charged for my affections but because he could never marry me. I was a "white woman"—or that was the understanding because of the pale shade of my skin—but I was in fact the child of a Black woman and Scottish man, which meant Black but I could pass as white if no one knew. And in either case, for me, a "white woman," and a Chinaman, there was nothing more to be done to solidify our relationship. "Buy you a dress," he told me. "Shoes to match," he said, and his English, with his southern cowboy drawl, was good, his Mandarin impeccable. He was the most popular doctor in Los Angeles because of his charm and because he knew how to heal bodies. Me and his wife's separately.

Most Chinese of our time were day laborers who'd come west for economic opportunity after the gold rush of 1949 and were building the first transcontinental railroad on the Central Pacific. For us, L.A. was the Wild West, and we lived in Negro Alley—not Negro because of its residents but Negro because of who owned the land—the Afro-Spaniards—but every kind of person lived here: quick draws and prostitutes, pastors and gamblers. Chinese and European, Mexican and Spanish. But it was known for its saloons and brothels and having only two sheriff deputies, men who had come to Los Angeles to escape their pasts, to find anonymity, and the State of California hadn't been ravaged by the Civil War. Ex-Confederate soldiers came in droves and left their losses behind, and many moved farther south of Los Angeles County to build lives in the County of Orange.

I was thinking of him when another coin slipped from the sweat on my pale hip, then another fell near my rib cage, tickling. When I rolled over, the last coin dropped from my navel, completing another dollar.

Even though he was in Los Angeles before I arrived, I told him he came here for me. There was no doubt in my mind because of the way he put his passion behind his patience, his control, his quiet ebbing, all in pace with mine. So when I woke that morning in the empty sheets among the cool coins, I wanted to kiss him behind his ear and tell him I loved him and that I wanted to go someplace where we could exist together.

I was on the stairwell later that morning when I first became afraid. Just outside our room, steps away from the door, there was a bloody handprint against the wall, pressed then smeared, the red fingertips a contour of war paint on the face of the inn's adobe. Too small to be *his* hand, wasn't it?

I searched for him. Asked around for him. "Dr. Yeh?" I asked a man in the courtyard. "Dr. Yeh?" I asked another. Everybody was on their way somewhere in a hurry, toward the commotion in the streets ahead, the loud noises in the distance. When I headed toward it too, I felt a hand on my forearm, squeezing my weak muscle. It was the young man who swept the church steps. He was my age, twenty-three, twenty-four. Blond and never married, without children, though white people were always promised more here. A better life. That usually means a family.

"What's the ruckus?" I said, pointing the way of the shouting.

"They've seen you two together," he said, holding me by my weakness. "I'd advise you to come in the church with me."

"I told you I'm not going in that church," I said. "And now's not the time for inviting." Gunfire erupted. Warning shots, not followed by gasps or screams.

"It ain't nice up there, Justine, so just come in here with me and I'll give you what I can so you can leave."

"Leave why? I haven't done anything wrong."

"If somebody pointed a finger at you, they'd remember you being too friendly with the Chinaman." And this was true. We'd been in love for three months by then, all out in the public and on display. He'd once kissed me in the barn behind the saloon. "If you weren't a pastor's daughter," he said, "I'd have it in my mind to let you go on up and chance your consequence, but as it is, you need to leave town."

I didn't leave.

I didn't sleep again in my dream either. I remember staying up through the night and learning the next morning that there had been a massacre that left seventeen Chinese men and boys dead. All were lynched on Commercial Street, swinging above upturned wagons. And that afternoon at his burial, I remember feeling robbed of my right to grieve for him with other people who loved him as much as I did.

A consequence.

Because I wasn't his wife.

I was just another stranger in the crowd paying my respects, and in my silence I honored what he deserved—a family left in peace. I had a funeral for him alone at home, holding the paper. A single black-and-white image of his body, their bodies, hanging from the gallows, reminded me of drying flowers in a lover's doorway. Precious roses, I had to tell myself, and one of them was my doctor.

Life changes so quickly in Los Angeles. You can sleep late one morning and wake up to a new and unexpected city.

THIRTY-SIX

LOU, 1932

The gym closed early today—noon—because they're packing up tomorrow, so I need answers today—better, I need the right questions to ask so Aaron can give me the right answers. I don't even know what to ask.

He's told me before, "When you're ready, come find me," so I'm here and ready for something. I let myself in.

The new boy, Little Fighter, was there cleaning so I asked him, "Is Aaron here?" The boy shrugged because even eight-year-olds understand loyalty.

"I'm here," Aaron says, his voice coming from somewhere near the bleachers. When he steps into the window's light, his hair is wet, his face drenched from sweating. White salt crystals have formed in the creases of his forehead.

The boy whispers to me, "He's leaving today."

"Not before I talk to him," I say, rushing toward him.

The glass globes of Aaron's eyes are shimmering and full of silver like someone poured it in as liquid, but I don't hesitate. "Do you know my family?" I say. "Know where I'm from? Why I was in the alley? The truth this time. Not a story."

"I don't have much time," he says, and reaches for my arm, then changes his mind and doesn't touch me. "Come with me."

I follow him through the gym and around to Mr. Lee's office out back, where he opens Mr. Lee's desk drawer and hands me a sheet of paper, a letter from the City after their vote. Fifteen days till they tear down this building for the Route. Mr. Lee can't refuse.

"What about the fighters who depend on him?" I say. "This community?"

Aaron is sweating profusely. I take a towel from Mr. Lee's desk.

"Tell me if you know me?" I say. I hold the towel out to him.

He backs away. "I know you."

He points to his canvas tool pouch. "There's an envelope inside. Can you take it out?"

I reach inside.

"Open it."

A locker key.

"At the La Grande train station, number nine," he says. "You'll find a bag. Take it to Leticia Thomas."

"How do you know Leticia?"

"Can you take it to her?"

"How do you know her?"

He walks out of the office without me, turning down the hallway, away from the fighting floors, down a corridor. I follow behind him, bothered by him. "Where are you going!"

He disappears into a tunnel on the left, under the building, part of the patchwork of tunnels that connect our neighborhoods, Downtown to Crown Hill. A plaque on the wall reads 1918.

The ceiling changes from plaster to plywood to concrete inside the mountain of workmen's tunnels, barely lit, its rock blasted out long ago and abandoned.

He's getting away from me. Swifter now. Sunlight pours through the mouth of the tunnel a ways ahead. He slides off his black cap and jacket, drops them on the ground.

"Where are you going?" I say. I pick up his jacket as I pass, bundle it under my arm. I look up and he's gone, the tunnel divided—a fork in the path—and I didn't see which way he went, left or right.

I call out to Aaron; no answer.

I listen for his footsteps. Nothing.

I go back to the start of the fork in the path, close my eyes and breathe. When I open them, I go left and find him stopped in front of a gray metal door not far ahead. He jimmies the door open just as I reach him. He rests back against the wall. "Don't touch me," he says, the gray of his eyes like mercury.

I hug his jacket into my chest.

A gust of wind sweeps our tunnel and rests on him, surrounds him, and I step back. "Lou?' he says, like he's sorry for me. A whirlwind now aglow like orange fire. His body seems to lose its depth in front of me and flatten like a white sheet, caught now in a gust of wind, flapping as it moves up and over the place he was, carrying him away in the wind fire. I stand unmoving, his jacket in my arms, the sound of city workers knocking their tools into pipes and metal somewhere in these tunnels.

"Aaron?" I say. "Aaron?"

No answer. He's just gone.

THIRTY-SEVEN

LOU, 1932

I knock on Leticia's front door weakly and hold myself upright in the door-frame, holding the duffle bag I got from the station locker with Aaron's key. When she opens the door, I shake Aaron's bag. "I think you know who I am."

She doesn't answer me, only walks away from the door. "Come. I've just made tea," she says.

"You said before there's a lot people you shouldn't know. How do you know Aaron?"

I follow her into the living room, where she points to her sofa. I sit in it, rest Aaron's bag on my lap. "Is Goldie here?"

Leticia lowers herself into her chair, moving slower, looking older than the last time I saw her a few days ago. "Goldie's with her mother."

She pours two cups of chamomile tea from her porcelain pot and it smells of bitter stems. She drops one lump of sugar in each and moves slowly again, placing my cup on the coffee table in front of me. I set Aaron's bag on the sofa and pick up the cup. I could use a drink.

She stirs her own cup slowly in counterclockwise strokes, watches the sweet lump come undone. She says, "When I heard you knocking, I thought it was the police coming back to speak with Goldie about the shooting," she says, and takes a sip. "The *Times* is reporting it as an assassination attempt on the mayor. How would Goldie know a thing about that? She certainly wouldn't have made herself a victim."

I slam my cup, and tea drops rocket out. "Who am I?"

She considers my spills on her table. "Would you like a pill to help with your nerves?"

I wipe the wetness with my sleeve and bring Aaron's bag back to my lap. I don't want a drink.

From the drawer of a table next to her chair, she pulls out a small box, shakes out a white knot, and gives me the pill. I bury it my mouth and chase it down my throat with her warm tea. "I lost a friend today," I say.

"Oh, Lou. I'm sorry."

"Aaron," I say, and watch for a change in her expression. "You knew him too."

"I can't say that I know any Aaron."

"You can't say or you won't say?"

Leticia rests back in her chair and reconsiders. "Aaron?" she says to herself, this time taking the time to remember. She shakes her head. "No, that's a unique enough name that I think I'd remember. Did this Aaron say he knew me?"

My body warms from the pill, already beginning. "He didn't say."

"But you're sure we were friends?"

"I don't know if you were friends."

"But he said we were friends?"

"I don't know. No . . ."

"How did the conversation go that you would think we were friends?"

"I don't know if you were friends. He knew you. I saw him and he said he knew you—"

"He said that?"

"Then he disappeared right in front of my eyes! Just gone!"

"You were there when he died?"

"Disappeared!" I clap my hands. "Gone!"

"Well . . ." she says, concerned for me, "when people transition from life to death, there can be a visible weight lifted. Losing someone is—"

"Not weight!" I say, my hands wild now. "I didn't lose him. He disappeared before my very eyes! Disappeared. Whoosh!"

Leticia watches me. "Loss can be confusing."

I close my eyes.

Take a deep breath.

I'm sure the pill has liquefied inside me. My cheeks are sliding down my face, but the stream of medicine is flowing upward from my gut, to my chest now—warm—my throat and now the top of my head, where it sits, throbbing, ready to escape. Instead it bubbles over like some outdoor water feature, percolating deep relaxation.

I breathe again. I'm ready now.

I tap the bag on my lap. "What's in this bag? Aaron wanted you to have it."

Her eyes widen; then she folds her hands on her lap.

I carry it over to her slowly and put it next to her, no heavier than a can of beans.

"What happened to your tattoo?" she says. "The heart on your hand?" I look at my clean hand. I forgot to draw it in. She says, "It's happened before, hasn't it? A burn that didn't leave a mark? A cut that healed too quickly?" Her voice is gentle. "Drink your tea, child."

I go back to my seat. Sip from my cup. "Who am I?" I say, my tiredness extreme. But I can't let sleep take me. Not until I get some answers.

"You'll rest here tonight," she says, and motions for me to stand. I do. She throws a blanket over the sofa and a throw pillow and makes it a bed. I lay my head there and she rests another blanket on top of me.

"Tell me what's wrong with me?" I say. "These dreams. Are they memories? Real memories?"

I sink into her cushions, cradled, and close my eyes. I hear her.

"Some call us immortal. I don't. Immortals are things of fantasy, world-weary and vain. But most of us don't know who we are. That we are. Thirty-six like us. *Were* thirty-six of us," she says. "We appear at a certain age every time. Vulnerable every time because people with no history are at risk. Children have it worse."

"What about Black immortals? Don't they have it worse than others?"

"You think Black people have always been in the state you see now?" She huffs. "The legacy of enslavement affects everything we see here. Even the relationship between the descendants of the enslaved and the descendants of enslavers. Brutalization passed down through generations. The transcontinental slave trade was the first time in history when slavery and sex slavery were relegated to skin color. Most people don't even remember the time before it. Tens upon thousands upon thousands of years back to the first man and woman in Africa. Nation builders, architects, peacemakers, lost in time.

"And, yes, we were sometimes slaves. Slaves alongside any person of any race who failed at life or became desperate for something. Today, it's just called debt. But never before the slave trade, that debt pass down through blood and make slavery an inheritance, attached to color. Undiluted evil," she says, shaking her head.

"So it got harder for people like me, like you, like anybody not white or a woman and not in their home country after the 1600s. America hasn't been our home country but we're the only people, besides Natives, who in large part didn't immigrate here. I arrived this time at about twelve years old. That's what happened to you."

"What do you mean 'happened'?"

"What happened to your friend, Aaron, is what happened to you and will happen again. Not just once. How old were you when you came?"

My eyes shoot open. "I was knocked on the head."

She nods, fingers the button on Aaron's bag.

"You said 'were.' There 'were thirty-six'? Is that what happened to Aaron? Somebody took him? Is that why he was running?"

"It's why you're in danger," she says. "It's why we have to look after one another. It's why I lost my husband." Her breath catches. "I wasn't looking."

"He died of natural causes."

"He did," she says, not disagreeing. My nose feels like it's sliding off my face.

"Most people are long lifers. Have a typical, statistical life. But not us. Not my husband, rest his soul, and not Aaron or you or I."

"Thirty-six?"

"Not anymore," she says.

"You're saying we are immortals?"

"Of a kind," she says. "Maybe we all are. Even those with short lives. They die young every time. Teenagers, the famous, babies—some have never even lived outside of the womb and still they teach strangers to love others. That they existed at all is enough."

"If it's true, what's happening to us?"

Without a word, she opens Aaron's bag. I watch her pull out its contents, palm it in her hand like she's weighing it—a thirteen-cent can of Campbell's pork and beans in tomato sauce. She turns it around and reads the lettering.

"What is it?" I say.

"A can of beans."

"I mean, what's inside it?"

"Beans, pork, tomato sauce, some spices, and—"

"Is there a trick compartment? A twist-off cap? Something else inside that Aaron left for you?"

She sits back in her chair like she's been defeated. "It's just beans," she says, and won't look at me.

"Beans?"

"It means you can't go back to your apartment. You'll stay here."

"Aaron told me I was in danger. Is that true?"

She looks at me with pity, wise beyond my years. "A lot of people want everlasting life," she says. "One way or the other."

THIRTY-EIGHT

LOU, 1932

I woke up on Leticia's sofa, drowsy and needing to pee. It was morning, dark, maybe four or five, and a strong smell of decaying rodent hit me on the way to the toilet. I didn't want to wake Leticia. Didn't have the mind or patience to have her restart her bedtime story from last night—our fiction of a forever life.

The odor was stronger when I went to lay back down, and I thought I'd find the poor bastard and throw him out if it was easy enough, if I could grab it with a wad of old newspaper.

I went in Leticia's kitchen and stepped on a discarded tile, careful not to make a ruckus, tip-toed toward the smell and found the source—a plate of forgotten food. It had been there at least a few days, and chitterlings don't keep. I thought I'd throw it out.

Slowly and deliberately, I opened her back door with the plate in my hand; a streetlight illuminated her yard and the rim of the trash can. I thought a dog would do well to run in this big open space and I thought of the story Jefferson told me about his dog, Hodges, when, two months ago, Jefferson was going into the kitchen to make coffee. He said Hodges followed behind him as always and went directly to his food bowl. Then Hodges simply looked up, stared at Jefferson for a moment, lay down, closed his eyes, and died.

The snap of a branch behind me turned me around. Pain to the side of my head is what I felt next. Thought I recognized the man holding the blunt instrument but it was so dark. I didn't expect him to be standing there. I should've been paying attention. It happened so fast.

THIRTY-NINE

SARAH, 2117

Sometimes I wish I could go back. Go back to that cold night in Los Angeles. Maybe I'd warn Lou to watch herself, stay closer to her friends, to be mindful of her exit. Aaron knew when it was his time to go. He had memories of leaving, and Lou had forgotten hers.

Maybe I'd tell her what to expect, that leaving is like death—a thief. When it's your time to go, you don't have a choice or a set date, unless you do it to yourself—I can't—but we all have the appointment. The only difference is the death rattle of those like me. Our silvering eyes and the unbearable heat that tells us the end is near. No, I wouldn't tell Lou that. Wouldn't tell her anything. What would you tell your younger self, if yourself would listen?

Maybe I'd just tell her I loved her.

Maybe I'd hug Lou, if she'd let me.

If she didn't think it strange.

And I'd be confident in the friends she had—ones who still represent the kind of friendship I wish I had with somebody, because hers weren't going to let her go so easily.

Leticia came looking for help that night. "I need to file a missing persons report," Leticia said to nobody from the front of the receptionist's desk. It was Sunday and every officer and clerk with the privilege of being off duty that day was off. It was just empty and cold. A police radio was on in the corner of the clerk's desk lying lazily like a black ball and chain. It chattered and squealed once an hour.

Leticia's finger triggered a bell over and over again. "A missing person's report," she said again. Over her shoulder, a thin, timid-looking, poorly white woman in a coat was sitting with her young son, her hat too big and pressed down over her eyebrows. She hooked her son with one arm and pulled him into her. "I need to file a missing persons report," Leticia said, and tapped the tip of the bell again.

"Hold your horses," an officer said, coming out from around a small office, tucking in his wrinkled shirt. Red lipstick was smeared to pink from the corner of his mouth to his cheek, making a brush stroke there.

"Now, what is it you're trying do, gal?"

"I need to file a missing persons report," Leticia said, composing herself.

"How long's your husband been missing?"

"My husband's dead, sir."

"Then how long's your boyfriend been missing?"

"She!" Goldie said, walking through the doors right after. She walked around Leticia, past the officer and his desk, right up the hallway, looking for somebody who might actually help.

"Ma'am!" the officer said. "You need to stay in the waiting room. I'll be with you shortly. Ma'am!" but Goldie kept going, checking office to office like she owned the place.

Leticia said, "Her name is Louise Willard. She goes by Lou."

"How long has she been missing?" the officer said.

"She left our house sometime this morning. Before eight."

"Was she walking?"

"What?"

"Did she walk away from home?"

"I don't know."

"Date of birth?" he said.

"I don't know."

"This is your daughter?" he said, leaning back. "Who is she to you?"

"Friend. She's maybe twenty, twenty-one."

He sighs. "Have you thought that maybe she found something better to do? May have just stopped by her boyfriend's."

"She's not involved with anyone," Leticia said.

"That you know. These young girls have different morals these days." He wiped the lipstick from his cheek. Pink got on his sleeve. "In either case," he said, "for a person to be reported missing, it has to be twenty-four hours since she was last seen. There's nothing—"

"Look, I know something's wrong," Leticia said. "She's missing."

"Did you check your house?"

"Of course I did."

"We did," Goldie said, coming back around. "Where's Officer Adams?"

LOU, 1932

I must have fallen. Or fallen asleep. This is dream paralysis. My foster father used to say that if you wake and can't move, it means a demon's lying on your chest, so swing your legs off the bed and slide under him.

I can't move my legs.

My neck is sore like an old injury has awakened. I breathe slowly, but the loud dryer noise against my head is an agitation, shuddering in my ears, like the dryer's got one damp shoe inside. *What is that noise? Why can't I move?*

My body rattles like it's being visited by a small earthquake, jittery as Leticia's tin of pork and beans on a shelf. I can move my head from side to side now and recognize the chair, a table, the clean walls. I can't remember where from.

I can't see my body.

"Hey, Little Sis," Vic says. His black and gray hair is pulled back into a rubber band and folded into a skinny and greasy braid to just below his neck. His dirty wife-beater covers his belly just above his shorts. "Foster Sis, Lil Sis? I prefer Little Sis. It's more pra-bah. That's prop-perrrr." He laughs and walks to the table across the room.

My arms are strapped down. I'm inside *his* lung machine. My brother's lung machine.

SARAH, 2117

How Goldie was able to find Officer Adams in the basement of the station, Leticia said she didn't know. She only followed her. Adams was there in Records, in plain clothes, poring over documents, files splayed across the desk next to four empty cups of coffee, a fifth mostly gone. "We need your help," Goldie said before she reached him.

He wasn't alarmed when he saw her, just tired despite the drinks. He held a single sheet of paper in his hand. "I've been thinking," he said. "Why would someone want to kill the mayor?" He holds his hand up as if to bless her. "Yes, I'm sorry you got hurt. But why the mayor? Sure, there are disagreeable things about him, the head and chief of L.A. is always a target, but why Mayor Shaw? Why now?"

"It's Lou," Goldie said.

He set his paper down.

"She's missing."

"We need the address of Victor O'Malley," Leticia said, rushing her words, the commotion in her voice a rattle shaking him from the solitude of Records.

"Calm down," Officer Adams said. He agreed to go upstairs with them.

"Victor O' Malley," Leticia said again, calmer this time.

"I can't just give you addresses. He's a private person."

Adams signaled for the officer with the lipstick to leave the desk. "Why Vic?" he said.

"He has her," Leticia said. "I'm sure of it."

"Vic is involved in a lot of criminal activity. Kidnapping a girl is not one."

"Look," Goldie said. "If she's there, you'll get credit for being the off-duty law enforcement officer whose gut instinct, quick thinking, and good police work saved the life of the young Black girl shown there on the poster on your wall. The poor youth you spent time with, played chess with. And if we're wrong, no one will know you gave us the address. We just knocked on a wrong door."

"She's in danger?" he said, suddenly troubled.

Within five minutes he was back with an address written on paper. "I'm going with you," he said.

"No, you don't," Leticia said, and stopped him. She reached out her hand for the sheet of paper, asking.

"She's like a daughter to me," Adams said.

Leticia took the sheet, unclasped her purse to put it in.

He grabbed Leticia's arm, stopping her. Goldie put her hand on his, waiting now for his next move.

He loosened his grip a little. He said, "You *do* know that I value Lou and my friendship with her?"

"No, sir," Leticia told him. "She's valuable to you but you do not value her. I have an old car, sir. One I keep covered in my garage. It's worth a lot because she's a beauty and one of the first. She's valuable. But you, sir, would take that valuable car and park her out on the street for a year, not driven and unwashed, exposed to the rain and the drying of the sun, rock chips, careless children, and bird shit. She's still valuable, but you, sir, have never valued her."

He let go of her arm.

"Come on," Goldie said. "I'll drive."

LOU, 1932

Vic is wearing open-toe sandals.

He unrolls a cloth pouch from the tabletop, and empty syringes roll out. He holds one up to the light—empty. The next—empty. A third and fourth, all empty. He turns to me. "Then I guess you'll just have to wake up," he says.

My mouth is too dry to speak.

"Can I get you water?" he says. "I'll get you water. You could use water. The skin on your lips are fish scales."

I have never seen him outside his metal lung. He leans forward out of my sight, but I can still see his feet. His toes have hairs that stand like black sprigs growing out of a cactus. I don't know how he gets his shoes on. If he ever wears shoes. His toenails reach out from each toe like petrified fingers. His heels are caked in layers of dead skin, yellow and crusty white, cracked like the Victorville high desert.

I open my mouth, my lips crack. "Why are you doing this?"

He brings me a glass of water with a straw. "You're the journalist. You've been investigating death all this time. You tell me."

He sits down on something next to me and presses the straw to my lips. I push it out with my tongue.

"What do you want with me?"

He snorts like the answer is obvious or he's not going to tell me. "Drink your water, girl," he says. "You'll need your strength."

My eyes adjust to the color swatches in front of me, his mother's painting of a castle at my sight line.

"It's all been a game of chess," he says. "And I'm good. The best. Best ever. I'm most proud of the shooting at City Hall. Was aiming for Goldie. She was always trying to protect you. That girl got me good at the market. Took me a month to heal and get my eyesight back. The limp hurt like the deuces. When y'all were arrested, I sent her a thank-you card. Did she tell you?" He leans forward into the light. The patches around his eye sockets are discolored from the rest of his skin, in the way a new tail grows back on a lizard.

"But nothing was like taking Leticia's husband. She thought she could outplay me. Beat me at this game I made. Aaron was quick. Sure. All these people watching out for you. I just had to be patient. Your father—"

"What about Mr. Lawrence?"

He adjusts his large body in the seat next to me, pushes one hand into each opening in the barrel where I lay. He runs one fat hand along my arm, down the sides of my clothes—I'm still dressed—and with the other hand raises my hem, touches my naked thigh. He says, "There are helpers in everybody's life. But yours failed. Leticia. Goldie. Aaron. They should've just been honest with you. Let you fight for yourself. But you were never a fighter." He closes his eyes and rubs his hand down my thigh and back up.

"Please don't touch me."

He squeezes my thigh. "And then there are those of us who . . . well . . . who aren't helping."

He inhales deeply with his eyes closed like he's smelling something good. I try to think of something to say to distract him, to get him to keep talking. "What's your intention?" I say.

His eyes open. "Baby doll, I'm going to live forever."

SARAH, 2117

I could not have known that Leticia and Goldie were searching for me that night or that they knew I was lost. Or that Officer Adams stood at the passenger side door of Leticia's car blocking her from leaving while Goldie was in the driver's seat with the car running.

"Adams, you gotta move," Leticia said. Goldie revved the engine.

"I'm rethinking," he said, holding the car door with one hand. He leaned in, peered around Leticia to Goldie. "I can't let you go if you have evidence. How long have you known about Vic?"

Moonlight struck an open bag in the back seat—screwdriver, lock picks—and drew Officer Adams's attention. "Those burglary tools?" he said.

"Work tools," Goldie said. "Construction at the church. Within my scope of employment."

Leticia put both feet in the car but he held the door. "Officer," she said. "We need to go."

"Tell me first if Vic's responsible for the shooting at the meeting."

"I believe so," she said.

"Why didn't you just report it before. Save me all this trouble."

Goldie pulled away from the curb, her speed closing Leticia's door.

LOU, 1932

Vic takes his hands out of the drum and rests back in his chair. I can't see him, don't know what he's doing. I say, "You. You're immortal?"

He huffs like he's offended, comes into view. "I prefer to call it *chosen*. I can choose myself. You act like all immortals deserve to be that way. Are better than me?" He pauses. "You think all immortals are good people? Is that what you think? Well, doll, even good people don't always like each other. I know plenty of 'em who can't stand to be around the other."

I don't know what he means.

He considers me. Studies my face. He says, "How do you like being around me?"

I only look at him.

"I'm like you," he says. "Just wasn't chosen by the universe . . . by God, whoever. But He would've chosen me if He had a real good look at creation and saw me there. If He'd compared me to who He *did* choose." He flicks his fat wrist. "Look at you, weak and 'chosen.' I'm strong and cunning and loyal to those who are weak and poor and lonely and—"

"Wicked," I say. "Poor, alone, and weak doesn't mean wicked."

"Lazy is. Complicit is. You do nothing. A waste of life." He eyes me, silent now, lowers his brutish and double-layered face close to mine.

I say, "Why kill Leticia's husband?"

"Bad information. I was told she and her husband were fostering you. Turns out it was Lawrence and Miriam. Lawrence of all people."

"He died of a heart attack."

"I know, I was there. I strangled him with my own two hands and yes, his heart stopped in the process. I'd call that a heart attack." He holds up his hands as if showcasing something in the sky. "Good Samaritan Walks by School and Tries (Though Unsuccessfully) to Resuscitate Local Man. Community Mourns Loss of a Beloved Teacher. That's a story even you could have written."

My whole body tenses. I reach down into my pocket for something I can use. Leticia's stone is still there. My yellow pencil. My razor's gone.

"And if I didn't get you from Leticia's," he says, "what would Esther have died of? Young starlet overdoses in the Hills? Takes her own life instead of facing the ravages of time? I'd go to her funeral too."

"That was you who touched my hand at Mr. Lawrence's service?"

"I could have done so much more to make you miserable," he says, laughing. "To make you suffer the way I suffer every day. Make you carry the losses I've carried. I don't have the luxury of forgetting. Not in a thousand years." He runs a plump finger across my cheek. "And I'll live a thousand more."

I push up from the inside. No use. "Look," I say. "Whatever you want. Whatever you think I have. I can't help you."

There are hinges inside the iron lung, ones with finger-sized pins that slip through. Together they allow the lid to swing open and shut. If I can get the pins out of the hinges, I can push to open it from the lid's wrong side.

I say, "How do you know that any of this is true. Who told you?"

"You really don't know?" he says. "Don't remember the woman who came to our town?"

I don't know what he means.

"A woman came to our town when I was eight. She had a story to tell. Was suicidal, I think, but said she had chosen my mother. Had a gift. She also said she didn't want to carry the burden of her life anymore and chose to die. Why would anyone want to die young? She was about seventeen.

"My mother had heard stories about immortals. Thirty-six chosen by God. The universe. But my mother wouldn't accept. She didn't deserve it, she said. There were others greater, she said, and I couldn't discern from her tone if she regretted it.

"'Have you considered my youngest daughter?' my mother said. She said it because I know she loved my sister more than she did me. But I have the woman's gift now.

"For weeks, my mother cared for this woman and the woman was kind to me. When she would smile at me, I'd see that mercury flowing in her eyes. A sign, my mother said, that she was breaking. A broken immortal can remember her pasts, and she can also give her gift to another. And when her eyes were full of that star shine—that mercury—all she'd need to do is touch someone. Make physical contact with another, as she's 'passing her anointing,' the woman said.

"When the woman gave it you, Little Sis, imagine my pain." He opens his arms wide and smiles like he's just walked onto stage, "Then imagine my joy thirty years later when, by destiny or fate, I walked into the Coliseum and found another patron there with a break in her eyes, that sweet mercury."

He straightens his back and cracks his neck.

"When my driver had to swerve to miss you that day on the street in Downtown the day you arrived. You looked different, for sure, but it was you."

"You stole it?"

"Won it," he says. "Fair and square. Do you know what I had to do to earn my way inside that woman's close court? Lose my dignity, is what. But when she was ready, I was going to be ready. Ambushed her, tied her up, and listened to her beg for her freedom and for me not to touch her. And as she began her ascension, I laid across her body like we were a pair. Took it and slit her throat. Slit. Her. Throat!"

He's going to kill me.

"Wasn't the last."

"You don't have to kill me," I say, my voice quivering. "You've already gotten what you needed. Eternal life."

"Were you listening to anything I said? I wasn't chosen for it. Talents that don't come naturally need work. Practice. And how does one practice immortality, huh? It goes away. And then I'm . . ." He makes a slicing motion across his throat. Smiles at me. "But I'm not giving up that easy."

I feel for the two hinges at the side of this coffin. Feel them on my left side—one below my tit, the other above my knee.

"I've paced myself, see. Living in this lung machine just in case I didn't find you in time. But there you were, dazzling in my living room, asking me about my dead mother. She wasn't my mother. I admit I took a chance asking the *Times* for you to interview me. What if you recognized me? What if you remembered?" He pauses. "My plan B took off."

"Aaron?"

"I didn't need him after all," he says. "Got you. I need just one life once every two or three lives, no matter whose, and guess what, sis? You're on fire."

I feel my body warming. Sweat runs from my forehead into the wells of my ears. "You've been stealing immortality from the thirty-six."

"Twelve," he says. "There'll be eleven soon. You're ripening in my lung as I speak."

I grip the head of my pencil. The lead is sharp. I try to pierce the pin in the hinge, push it out like a pool stick sliding through fingers. The lead snaps. *Damn.* "But why?" I say. "Why live forever?"

"Do-overs, second chances, failures—and who wouldn't? A better question is what happens when all of the thirty-six are gone?" He looks at me and waits.

He claps his hands. "*Boom!*" he says. "There's no reason for the universe not to start over. Rid itself of this mess. And let's face it. Coloreds especially should want a do-over. Look at who you are in this version of the world. Some lonely girl with a shitty job and an office in the basement. You used to be royalty."

The wood of my pencil is still sharp. I try again. Push the first pin out. Scoot down as best I can, close my eyes, and start the second. It's out.

Crashing, like metal pots falling in the tile kitchen, rings out from the front room. "Danny?" he calls. "Danny!"

No answer. My head is pounding.

Vic stands just as Goldie rushes in. A hammer is raised in her hand and she swings it once. Twice. To his neck, his collar. Misses his face.

I twist my shoulders and shake my body around to loosen the free hinges, hurl the cradle top off my chest.

A shot is fired in the other room. A second. Leticia's voice crying out draws Goldie's attention. Vic slams her jaw with his fist. Her hammer drops. Punches her again in her nose like she's a man. Slams her brow. He batters her middle like a bag with no person inside. She falls into the wall, swinging at nothing when she slams against it, cracking the mirror behind her; almost all of it crumbles down. In my reflection, my eyes are glass globes of liquid silver.

"Finally," Vic says, as he faces me. "It's beautiful," he says. "Stress can do stuff to a girl, can't it?"

My body trembles.

"What, her?" he says, motioning to Goldie. "I'd have done it to you if you were a fighter." His breath is labored. "I've been quite a gentleman, wouldn't you say?"

Danny appears in the doorway holding his side. It's bleeding. "Boss," he says, and collapses. I pick up Goldie's hammer. Vic charges me. Reaches for me and I bob and weave like the fighters do. Like Mr. Lee taught me to. I seat him on the floor with the flat edge of the hammer to his temple, thread the hammer like a needle that could go straighter though. The walls spray with a sudden red graffiti, his skin split like a block of white cheese with red inside.

The hammer hangs from his forehead like a doorknocker, holding him still as an unopened door. The hammer falls. His body follows. I feel sick. I go to Goldie. She's breathing hard against the wall, peering at me through swollen eyes.

Sirens blare from somewhere in the distance, getting closer. "You've gotta go," she says. "You don't want them touching you. I'm fine," she says. "I'll be fine."

I stumble through the hall into Vic's front room and find Leticia's on the floor, bleeding out of her chest. Her breath is labored, gurgling as blood escapes with air. I need her to tell me what to do.

I kneel down next to her. "Don't touch me," she whispers. "I'm healing already," she says. "I need you to find a place where no one can touch you. But don't go home."

I shake my head. I don't know any place.

"It'll take you tonight."

"The thing that took Aaron? What about my friends? What about Esther?"

The sirens are louder. I glimpse my reflection in a drinking glass tipped over on the floor next to Danny's half-finished dinner plate. Two halos of mercury. "Why didn't you tell me?" I say.

"You need to go," she says, her voice stronger now, the air escaping the hole in her lungs now silent.

Danny moans from the ground, and Leticia pushes herself up. She goes to him and straddles him. Takes a line of wire from her back pocket, wraps it around his neck, tightens it till he's quiet. "You need to go," she says.

I stand at the door, sirens closing in. I'm afraid. Tears roll down my cheeks. "What are we?" I say.

"Human," she says. "Fighters," she says. "And our survival depends on our collective abilities, not our individual might. That's what it means to be human."

FORTY

SARAH, 2117

That night I ran into the Los Angeles darkness, its heat engulfing me, the scent of that first murder still on me, soaking through my pores, my movements liberating what's true from the shadows. I trusted my steps forward, alone and unafraid. Every new step began to burn away the parts of me that weren't eternal, making room for the everlasting.

I began remembering First Granddaddy, First Husband, ones I've loved and those I've been before, time folding and running together in this timeless reunion.

Then, I stopped running.

I stood beside my selves, inside my selves. All of us an accumulation of our pasts, pasts that are always trying to hold on to us whether we want them to or not. I mourned my forgotten losses as if they were brand new, my dreams weighing me down. And I was sorry. Not just for Lou and her friends Esther and Jefferson—but for all my trains that have pulled away from the station. Countless times I've been onboard while those I loved were without ticket or carriage—yet.

Not every person or place I love is mine. All of this is borrowed. This voice.

Even this skin.

So I raised my hand again that night in a posture of goodbye, the only sign—universal—for "I hope to see you again."

FORTY-ONE

LOU, 1932

I walked to this place I don't belong—no niggers, no dogs, no Mexicans, no glass—and I stand here on the dock above the beach anyway, overlooking the cold dark of the Pacific Ocean. I think of the woman who drowned here on the night I was called. She didn't belong here either.

I think of her baby, unborn, thrown away in the pouch of her mother's skin but not thrown into nothing. There *is* something on the other side of this life, and your belief is not its validation. Is not the missing ingredient. And I have to believe for that woman, Betty Ann. For her child. For me. An existence beyond our ghosts. A life that begins after we've grayed from old age and death, after our skin and bones have crumbled, after we've snuggled down into the rainbow powder of stardust and deeply inhaled its perfumes. And then in that moment, our ghosts, with all of the impressions from this life, will thin to nonexistence and we will *become* ourselves again. Our best versions. Living the consequences of only our best choices, greatest experiences, with our greatest loves and friendships, even the animals and places we've loved. Perfect with our imperfections because they are, after all, only our personal bests and our own greatness.

But it's only a guess.

And because life is a balance of good and bad, I imagine bad things will again be a step away, lurking even in that happy place, waiting for the chance to whisper, "It's good but did you see so-and-so's best?" because self has always been our most persuasive adversary.

And at that moment of doubt, with the memory of our humanity re-awakening within us, we'll have to choose. Whether to give in to our old patterns and the past *this* time. Or be transformed.

I reach out my hand again toward the ocean and then up to the sky, frame the full moon with my gathered fingers, close one eye. A cluster of plush clouds are alight there like cotton balls dyed blue with a flashlight shining behind them. I follow the glow down to the water where it forms a triangle, one corner thinning and reaching from the water to the shore. I close my fist and feel my wrist pulsate inside the swirling orange glow around me. My mind stills in quiet anticipation of my coming absence and I imagine myself in different faces, different places. I imagine castles and moats and beasts and huts that don't exist anymore.

I won't exist anymore.

Here.

Passengers and beasts, it seems, we all are, on our way to some other destination. And here in Los Angeles is where invisible dragons skate over mountain ranges, deserts, streams, and salted waters, appearing only as wind welcomed home to the city where, at the ocean's edge, they collapse to their knees, tired and undone and dissolving to tiny bubbles where sea kisses sand. Even now as I am leaving, they are arriving again, waiting to be restored, to be hand-fed by angels because we are the City of Angels.

ACKNOWLEDGMENTS

There are no ordinary people. You have never talked to a mere mortal . . . It is with immortals whom we joke with, work with, marry, snub and exploit—immortal horrors or everlasting splendors.

—C. S. LEWIS

To my husband, Lee—an everlasting splendor—without whom this book would not be possible. To our superstar children, Ava and Ash Lee. To my loving, beautiful, larger-than-life Momma (or Ms. Mill), and my dad, John Jr., who died a hero. To my other loving parents in England—Mum and Dad, David and Dee—and to my brothers, John III, Jase and Bruce, Tony, Parker, and Michael. To my brilliant, brave, and beautiful sister, Katrina, and my youngest beautiful sister, Fuschia. To my nephews, Jayden and Kannon, and to my niece, Savannah. To all my Alabama family—the Hayeses, Harrises, Shaws, Jacksons, Lockharts, and Anchrums. To the brother I've never met.

To my ancestors.

To Los Angeles, where I was born and raised across the street from Dorsey High School, and to the extraordinary Los Angeles literary community where I was reborn. To writers who keep walking (or can't right now)—you're not forgotten. You are my tribe.

To the Santa Clarita Valley who also raised me—and now raises those I love.

To Rainham, Kent, England, where I started my family and built a lovely life I wasn't destined to keep.

To Jamie and David Wolf and the Rosenthal Family Foundation, whose support has given me moments of peace.

To my editor, Dan Smetanka—you are a gift to the world.

To Megan Fishmann, there is no greater teammate.

To Selihah White, my brilliant publicist; to Dana Li, my talented cover designer; to Jordan Koluch and Wah-Ming Chang, who both lovingly shepherded this book through copyediting and proofreading and gave me grace every time I needed to go back in and try better with a phrase, a sentence, a word or the way it appeared on the page. I'm grateful for this mighty team of women who joined me in wanting *The Perishing* to be the best version of itself for you, reader.

To Joshua Mensch, author of *Because*, who always seems to keep me alive . . . literally.

To Tom Stock-Hendel and Vivian. Thank you. To Douglas Wood and James Sie. Thank you.

To Coach Robby Robinson, a man with great heart and power: everything I learned about boxing, I learned from you. And to Devorah Robinson, who loves you most and is a powerhouse. To Mother Ellen.

To the Ming family, whose sacrifice, love, vulnerability, and leadership have been a light set on a hill for so many, and whose positive influence will be felt for generations. Thank you.

To my agents, Dara Hyde and Anya Backlund. You are among the smartest, most authentic, and biggest-hearted women I know.

To Dave Thomas, artist, friend, voice, and the spark for the character "Leticia," and to the late Anna May Wong, who inspires me still.

To bridgette bianca, author of *be/trouble*, Chiwan Choi, author of *The Yellow House* and *my name is wolf*, to Mike "The Poet" Sonksen, author of *Letters to My City*: for every poem on Los Angeles you've ever written and for the city tours that helped me reimagine our city, thank you!

To Sanura Williams, librarian and advocate for Black women; Minda Harts, author of *The Memo*; F. Douglas Brown, author of *Zero to Three* and *Icon* and *un::fade::able—The Requiem for Sandra Bland*. To champion Samantha Dunn, exceptional editor and the author of *Failing Paris*, and Kaitlyn Greenidge, author of *We Love You, Charlie Freeman* and *Libertie*.

To the NAACP, PEN America, Emerging Voices Fellowship, the African American Firefighters' Museum, Los Angeles, the American Library Association, Black Caucus, the American Indian Alaska Native Tourism Association and its project the American Indians & Route 66 Project.

To Cecilia Rasmussen, columnist and L.A. icon for capturing L.A. in so many interesting ways and in columns like "Then & Now" and "Curbside L.A.," and to Lynell George and Dana Johnson, masters of L.A. history and its storytelling.

To this team who fought with me for criminal justice: Shaun Jacobs, Meg Lodise, Mark Hart, Elizabeth Silver, Andrea Schoor, Farah Tabibkhoei, Andrea Guerva, Susan Janson, Noelle Natoli, Mary Serradas, and the National Lawyers Guild, San Francisco.

To independent bookstores and booksellers around the nation, especially Esowon Books and Skylight Books in Los Angeles, who first gave me a book home. To Los Angeles County libraries, Old Town Newhall Library in Santa Clarita and its Heritage Room Archives, including the help of librarian Morgan Lazo.

To the *Los Angeles Times*, the *New York Times,* and Jessica Grose. To the Pamela Krasney Moral Courage Fellowship and Marty Krasney. Thank you for the honor. And to the Mesa Refuge.

To the heart and brains of Charles W. Hamilton and these champions: Suzette Sommer, Stephanie Green-Smith, Peter Woods, Darrel Alejandro Holnes, Karina Luna, Natalie Obando, and Tod Goldberg and to the RE-DEEMED board of directors: Mike Weinstein, Michelle Franke, Dario Sarmiento, Katie Rogers, Jalysa Conway, Anthony and Karen Dorris, Jade Chang, Patrick O'Neil, Ashley Perez.

To Ike, my brainy law school study partner who completed suicide. The world and the legal profession are less bright without you. You would've been one of the greats.

To the Master's in Psychology Program (MSMFT) at Fuller Theological Seminary and my cohort, and to these mental health educators and champions: Dr. Cameron Lee, Kenichi Yoshida, Migum Gweon, Dr. Michael Hardin, Dr. Nanyamka Redmond, Kay Nahm, Melody Zhang, Dr. Alison Wong, Miyoung Yoon Hammer, and Dr. Terry Hargrave.

To the University of California, Riverside in Palm Desert MFA Program and to Antioch University, my UCLA Writer's Program family, including Robert Eversz and Charles Jansen.

To Glory Edim for all you've done for and with Black women writers through Well-Read Black Girl, and more.

To the Bread Loaf Writer's Program and the Iowa International Workshops, Lines & Spaces Program, specifically Cate Dicharry, Chris Merrill, and Kelly Bedeian.

To Novena Carmel, Jeff Eyres, Yennie Cheung, DJ Shai, Amanda Fletcher, and the Dirty Laundry Lit Family.

To Romus Simpson, the poet who first made me fall in love with words.

Thank you to every university, high school, and educational institution, book club, library, and space that's hosted me. I never took it for granted.

To this nation, the United States of America, that has shaped me.

And above all, thank you, Jesus.

NATASHIA DEÓN is an NAACP Image Award Nominee, practicing criminal attorney, and college professor. A Pamela Krasney Moral Courage Fellow, Deón is the author of the critically acclaimed debut novel *Grace*, which was named a Best Book by *The New York Times*. Deón has been awarded fellowships by PEN America, Prague Summer Program for Writers, Dickinson House in Belgium, the Bread Loaf Writers' Conference, and the Virginia Center for the Creative Arts. Find out more at natashiadeon.com.